Butterfly Storm

(The Butterfly Storm Book One)

by

KATE FROST

LEMON TREE PRESS

Paperback Edition 2016

ISBN 978-0-9954780-2-2

Copyright © Kate Frost 2016

Cover design by Jessica Bell.

The
Butterfly Storm

by

KATE FROST

LEMON
TREE
PRESS

Praise for *The Butterfly Storm*

"Any book that makes me stay up later than I intended because I'm desperate to know what happens next automatically gets five stars from me." Debbie Young, author.

"Beautifully written, carefully researched and expertly plotted – what more could you want from a book? That this is a debut novel is pretty amazing – I think Kate Frost is definitely someone to watch out for." Joanne Phillips, bestselling author of *Can't Live Without.*

"I do not believe I've ever read a book like this and do not believe I will again for a long time. I will most certainly recommend this to all my friends." Charlotte Lynn, A Novel Review.

"If you are looking for a thoroughly detailed story of relationship trials, family trials and decisions of the heart, then *The Butterfly Storm* would be the perfect book." Rhonda, Chick Lit Plus.

"I Loved this read with a capital L." Elaine G, Amazon Top 500 Reviewer.

"I thoroughly enjoyed the story, the setting, and the detailed and beautiful descriptions. The plot is absorbing with a cast of fascinating characters and a healthy dose of 'How is this all going to end…?'" Helen Hart, Publishing Director, SilverWood Books.

For Mum, Dad and Nik

Prologue

'Is it because you're pregnant?' Mum asked.

We were standing in her kitchen with two boxes filled with my old stuff between us: school books, paintings, boxing gloves, dungarees, a train-set and Anne Rice novels. It was three hours before my coach left for Heathrow and my goodbyes were not going well.

'Is that really the reason you think I'm going to live with him, because I'm pregnant?' I asked.

'Are you?'

'No.'

She poured herself a glass of white wine. 'Sophie, you did only meet him six weeks ago and have only actually spent one week together. What do you expect me to think?'

'Is it too alien a thing for you to comprehend that the reason I'm moving to Greece is because I want to be with him? I love him.'

She took a sip of her wine. 'Love is a strong word.'

'It's also the right one. Just because you don't believe in love at first sight doesn't mean I don't.'

'Oh, I believe in love at first sight alright, it's what happens after the initial honeymoon period that I'm wary of.'

'I really don't need your negativity right now.' I taped closed the flaps of the box nearest me.

'I thought I'd got rid of all this when you moved out,' she said, scuffing the box with her foot.

'Well, I can't take it with me.' I took a pen from my bag. 'Have you got some paper?'

She pointed to a used envelope wedged between the coffee and sugar jars.

'This is the address in Greece,' I said, writing it down.

'It doesn't exactly roll off your tongue.' She set her wine down on the black marbled worktop before pinning the address to the notice board next to the door. 'I'm going to make a stir-fry. Do you want some?'

I shook my head.

Her nostrils flared. 'The plane food will taste of plastic.'

I couldn't help but admire her attempt at mothering. 'Maybe a bit then.'

'The chicken is in the fridge.'

The huge American-style fridge was always full. I took out a cling-filmed plate of chicken breasts, and found bean sprouts, carrots, baby sweet corn and mange tout in the salad compartment. Arms loaded, I turned to see Mum bent over the worktop peeling an onion. Her hair was twisted and pinned in loose curls; the nape of her neck was tanned against the soft blonde of her dyed hair. Her vest top was burnt orange, bright against her white gypsy skirt. Despite everything, I wanted to hug her.

'Have you learnt any Greek yet?' she asked.

I slammed the fridge door closed with my foot. 'A little.' I dumped the food on the worktop and reached behind the bread bin for a chopping board. Mum chopped the onion as if it was a race.

I took the cling film off the chicken. 'Sliced or cubed?'

'Sliced, not too big.'

We stood in silence for a moment, our knives thumping wood.

'So,' Mum said, breaking our rhythm. 'How are you going to get a job out there?'

'Same way as here, apply.'

'Don't be smart. You know what I mean.' She broke off a

clove of garlic from the bulb and started peeling it.

'The best place to learn Greek is in Greece. I know I want to start drawing again… I can teach English if I need to. I was thinking of setting up an artist's retreat.'

'You've got high hopes.'

I stopped mid-slice. My fingers were sticky with chicken. 'What's wrong with that? I don't want to end up regretting my life.'

Her glossy lips pursed. 'I may still have a lot of hopes, Sophie, but I've no regrets.'

'Are you sure about that?'

She dropped the naked clove into the garlic press and squeezed. 'You've known this Alekos for less than two months.'

'So what? Because of your lies, I don't know my father at all.'

The garlic press clattered on to the worktop. She reached for her wine and gulped down half the glass. 'I'll be the first to admit I made a mistake,' she said.

'When have you ever admitted that?' I slapped the sliced chicken back on to the plate.

'What do you want me to say?' she asked.

'Nothing.' I turned away from her and washed my hands in the sink. Outside on the patio, the barbeque was filled with ash. Beer bottles looked out of place next to the trellis entwined with flowers.

When she finally spoke her voice was steady and controlled. 'I care about you Sophie, obviously too much.'

'It's not a case of you caring, it's you expecting too much from me – the serious job you've never had. Try sorting your own life out rather than mine.'

She topped up her wine and, marching over to the sink, slammed the empty bottle on to the draining board next to me. She used to smell of cigarettes and Oil of Olay, now she smelt of onions and the Dior Poison I gave her last Christmas.

'I'm not the one running away,' she said, almost spitting at me. I don't have her sapphire blue eyes. Mine are green, I presumed like my father's. I slowly wiped my hands on the towel. I couldn't even begin to guess the natural colour of Mum's hair she'd dyed it so many times. In photos of her when she first had me, all you had to do was take away the dodgy early eighties' haircut and clothes, and it was like looking in a mirror.

'I'm not hungry anymore,' I said, tucking the towel back on its rail.

'That's typical of you. Go on avoid the truth. You're throwing away a good job and life here, Sophie.'

'You're so full of shit.' I grabbed my bag off the worktop.

'What if you don't find the answers you want in Greece?' she asked. She sounded like a soap star, clutching at a cliché for something to say. She followed me down the hallway to the front door. My flip-flops went slap, slap, slap against the polished floorboards.

'I'm not going to find them here.' I unlocked the door. We'd stood like this so many times before – her standing her ground in her own house, while I escaped from her and her folded arms and her big, smothering personality. 'I'll make do with plastic plane food. Enjoy your stir-fry.'

I opened the door and a shaft of sunlight crept into the hallway. Outside cars glinted, even the dirty ones. The tree embedded in the pavement by the front gate had wilted in the heat.

From the shadows of the hallway Mum said, 'If Alekos doesn't work out, you know where I am.'

'Fuck you.' I slammed the front door of my childhood home for the last time.

I got back to an empty flat with no housemates to talk to. My old room had been stripped of me. Only faded curtains, a fitted wardrobe and a sheet-less bed remained. Only the red wine stain on the carpet showed I'd even been here. I used to love having the flat to myself on the rare occasions both my housemates were out at the same time but now I was desperate for their company as I wandered from room to room, at a loss of how to kill the two hours before my coach left.

I felt I should phone Mum and smooth things over but I got no further than thinking about it. I wanted to talk to my best friend Candy but after glancing at my watch I realised she'd still be working on set with her mobile switched off. We'd said goodbye over a bottle of wine and a curry the night before and had shed more tears together than Mum and I had in years.

I made myself a cup of tea, toasted a crumpet and sat by the window. I wanted to tidy, stay busy, but for once the flat was spotless, an ironic leaving present. I wedged the window open, rested my bare feet on the ledge and phoned Alekos.

He answered almost instantly. 'Hey Sophie, where are you?'

'At home. I'm ready, all packed, just waiting for the coach.'

His English was good but his words were caressed by his accent. His warm, deep voice tickled my ear. 'I can't wait to have you here, Sophie.'

Outside the traffic had snarled up with the beginnings of rush hour. The faintest breath of air filtered in through the open sash window. I didn't envy them in their cars below, those with their windows wound down, sweating. Different music escaped from car stereos, different tastes and beats clashing. Teenagers in school uniform hung about outside the newsagent opposite, some with ice creams in their hands, others with fags stuck between their lips, their bikes strewn carelessly across the pavement. 'I can't wait to leave,' I replied.

'We're going to meet you at the airport.'

'We?'

'The restaurant's open only in the evening... Mama is excited, she's been cooking all day.'

'I thought it was going to be just you. I don't want to cause any trouble.'

'No trouble,' he said. 'I told my sister and my uncles and aunts they have to wait until home to meet you. I thought everyone there too much.'

He couldn't see my smile but I hope he heard it. 'I'll see you tomorrow.'

The deep blue of the sea through the plane window made my stomach somersault. My legs tensed when the plane dipped into a descent and I saw the coastline spread out, glistening in the sun's glare. I was dressed for a Greek summer in a new cream-coloured short skirt, thin canvas shoes, a pale blue vest top and no make-up, only a brush of mascara on my eyelashes. I used my sunglasses, wedged on top of my head, to keep my hair out of my eyes.

My Greek phrase book was open in my lap; the words for hello, yes, no, how are you and I don't understand, tumbled around my head, becoming increasingly muddled the closer we got to land. I pulled my seatbelt tight and tucked my book and magazine away. Resting my head back against the seat I watched Thessaloniki fill the oval window. Hazy mountains were the backdrop, their muted colours blending with the city in the early morning sunshine. We dipped lower, tarmac and parched grass, bright buildings and signs accelerating into view until we screeched on to the runway with a jolt.

Emerging from the plane the heat hit me, like the blast of hot air you get in winter when walking into a shop. Heat steamed off the tarmac. I was grateful to leave the sunshine behind and enter the cool building. Luggage endlessly circled in front of me. I didn't want to move; I gripped the handle of my trolley tight.

Somewhere in here Alekos was waiting. Tucked inside my purse I had one photo of him taken just a couple of days after I'd met him on Cephalonia. His lips weren't smiling but his eyes were, shaded from the sun by his hand. His hair was damp and short, his chest tanned and beaded with seawater. In his other hand he held an octopus that we had later cooked over coals, before burning our fingers and tongues eating it.

Sandwiched between a striking woman and beaming bronzed man at the arrivals gate was Alekos, exactly as I remembered him. Butterfly wings fluttered against my ribcage. He grinned, dimples puncturing his rough cheeks. His hand shot up in a wave and the three of them stepped forward to greet me.

I was in Alekos' arms, head buried in his neck, my lips tasting the salt on his skin, his lips kissing my forehead, my cheeks. If I was aware of his parents watching, I didn't care.

Alekos pulled away from me. 'Sophie, this is my mother, Despina, and my father, Takis.'

Takis was a well-worn version of Alekos, as tall as him and lean. Despina was something else: vivid and memorable, her red top as loud as her. She grasped my hands and kissed me on both cheeks. 'Welcome!'

Takis stepped towards me and planted another two kisses on my cheeks. '*Ti kanis?*' he asked loudly. '*Kala?*'

I replied with a nod, hoping a nod was the right thing to do.

There was no respite from the heat outside. It was early July and the air smouldered. Alekos put his arm around my waist and I held on to him all the way to the car. I couldn't stop looking at him or smiling. His skin was darker in the sunshine and mine was like white chocolate against him. Despina led the way with Takis manoeuvring a trolley with my bags on it through the car park. He turned round and smiled at us at least five times between arrivals and the car, while Despina talked constantly at us. I didn't understand a word.

I stood with Despina as Takis and Alekos argued, I assumed good-naturedly, over how best to put my luggage in the boot. Despina kept clicking her tongue disapprovingly and commenting. She looked at me and flashed a red-lipstick smile. She reached forward, touched my hair and nodded. '*Parre poli oreo,*' she said.

I continued to smile.

'Very lovely. *Kokkino,*' she said, pointing to my hair, and then after realising I still didn't understand, pointed towards her lips.

'Red!' I said, nodding.

'Bravo, Sophie!'

The boot slammed shut and Alekos turned to us. 'Let's go.'

Expensive clothes shops lined Thessaloniki's pavements and amongst them I glimpsed familiar names of *Accessorize*, *Virgin* and to my disbelief good old *Marks and Spencer's* as we beeped and swerved through packed streets. Sweat pooled into the small of my back and I felt a trickle slide down the side of my face. The car's air conditioning was working flat out but that did nothing to combat the summer sun penetrating the back windscreen. Alekos held my hand, his thumb rhythmically rubbing up and down mine. The streets were a patchwork of shade with strips of sunlight fighting their way between the tall apartment blocks that made up the heart of the city.

Alekos leant towards me as I gazed out of the window. He pointed to cream buildings overlooking a square filled with people with a glimpse of sea beyond. 'The docks are over there,' he gestured somewhere in front of us. He wrinkled his nose. 'We're not going that way.' He squeezed my hand. 'You okay?'

My other hand clutched the back of Takis' seat. Every time we turned a corner, Alekos and I, belt-less in the back, fell against each other. I nodded.

'You can shower at home, sleep if you want,' he said. 'Before everyone comes over.'

'Everyone?'

'To eat. You'll love it, we have a feast prepared.'

The apartments thinned out the further we got away from the centre. The traffic didn't though and I gripped Takis' seat tighter as cars, including ours, veered erratically between lanes on the dual carriageway.

'*Thes nero*, Sophie?' Despina turned to me and asked. 'Want water?'

'Do you want a drink?' Alekos said. 'We can stop here.'

I shrugged. 'I don't mind.'

We screeched to a halt at the side of the road, double-parking alongside another car. Takis switched off the engine and the air conditioning stilled. The car rapidly became as effective as a night storage heater.

'*Psomi, kapoozi, nero ke Coca Cola*!' Despina shouted after Takis. He disappeared inside what looked like a grocer's and reappeared seconds later beckoning to Alekos. I took my phrase book from my bag as Alekos got out and used it to fan myself.

'*Ehi zeste*,' Despina said, imitating me flapping the pages of my book with her hand.

I felt sweat snaking down the centre of my back. I sat upright away from the seat and stayed very still. Takis appeared from the shadows of the shop with a blue carrier bag, while Alekos carried a watermelon in both arms.

'Like *kapoozi*?' Despina asked.

I took *kapoozi* to mean watermelon and nodded. 'Yes. *Ne*,' I answered, correcting myself.

She beamed at me as Takis started the engine and Alekos struggled on to the back seat.

For the rest of the journey I sat with my head resting on Alekos' shoulder, my hand on top of the *kapoozi* between us and let their rapid words wash over me. Maybe I would soak up the language like a sponge. I wanted to do more than just nod and smile but I was content for the time being to simply head to my new home.

Alekos nudged me awake from where I dozed, rocking against his shoulder, my arm still encircling the cool, green skin of the *kapoozi*.

'Home,' he whispered. His breath tickled my ear.

'I didn't mean to fall asleep,' I said, rubbing my eyes. The glare from the sun distorted my view. All I could see of my new home was a silhouette. The car slowed between open gates and crunched over gravel. Takis parked neatly in the shadow of the restaurant next to two other cars.

'What you think?' Alekos asked. I scrambled out of the car after him. I shaded my eyes with my hand and savoured the elegance of the building with its arched windows, red-tiled roof and pale, caramel-stained walls.

'I had no idea it was this beautiful,' I said.

Alekos grinned and hooked his arm around my waist, pulling me towards him until I was pressed against his chest. 'Are you happy?'

'Happy doesn't even come close,' I said. His eyebrows scrunched in confusion. I kissed him. 'I'm so happy I met you.'

He'd changed me. He'd made me question what I wanted, what life meant. He had dragged me out of the 9 to 5 rut. There was no normality about this place. *Estiatorio O Kipos* the sign above the restaurant entrance read. Alekos said it meant *The Garden Restaurant*. To me it meant a new life.

Takis dragged my luggage from the boot. Despina had disappeared inside and I heard her calling to someone. Alekos smiled and beckoned me towards the garden and sunshine.

Beyond the terrace there was a bar with the same red roof and warm-coloured walls as the restaurant. Olive trees lined the far edge of the garden, their intricately woven branches shading the seating below. I imagined couples getting cosy beneath the trees once darkness descended. The garden's centrepiece was a fountain encircled by a wooden bench. The place was so quiet I could hear the trickle of water.

I'd swapped housemates for Alekos and his family, a flat above an off-licence for a bedroom above a first-class restaurant, a kitchen windowsill of ailing spider plants for a garden the size of a football pitch, and noise and traffic for fields that merged with the sky.

'*Aleko, pes tin Sophie gia tin dulia,*' Despina called from the restaurant steps.

'*Ochi tora, Mama.*'

I looked at him. 'What is it?'

'*Tipota*. Nothing.'

'Go on, tell me.'

He shrugged and pointed. 'See the bar?'

I nodded.

'That's where you are going to work.'

'I'm going to what?'

'It's decided. You won't have to find a job. Mama thought it'd be easy for you.'

'I don't know enough Greek – any Greek yet.'

'Don't worry, you won't be alone.'

He caught my hand in his. I stared across the garden, trying to imagine myself behind the wooden bar, taking orders, pouring drinks, talking Greek and looking out on a patio of strange faces.

'Here is very different to England. We have waiter service, there won't be anyone at the bar,' he said softly. He turned my face towards his. 'I've said too much. I don't want to worry you.'

'I'm not. It's a lot to take in.' I pulled away from him. I could feel the nerves I'd been battling against building in my stomach. I took a deep breath. 'I was going to sort myself out.'

'I know. I told Mama…'

'Sophie!' Despina's voice pierced the air.

A shorter, darker and younger version of Despina appeared next to her on the steps with a baby clamped to her hip. She clattered towards us, her free hand held open. She planted kisses on my cheeks.

'I'm Lena, Alekos' sister,' she said. 'This is Yannis, my…' She turned to Alekos. '*Pos lene yios?*'

'Son.'

'My son.'

'He's gorgeous,' I said.

'Christo? Eleni?' Despina shouted into the shadowy restaurant. '*Ela edho!*'

I held on to Alekos tighter. 'My aunt and uncle,' he said. 'They came early to finish making food. Everyone wants to meet you.'

Takis' rough hand squeezed my shoulder. '*Endaksi, Sophia?*' he asked.

I nodded and realised I understood something. I was okay.

I lost count of how many times I was kissed before we got inside, and even then I was bombarded with questions, which were interpreted by Alekos, and made to try all sorts of food before Despina ushered me upstairs for a well-needed shower and a moment's quiet to adjust.

I washed away the grime of travel. Wrapped in a towel, I stuck my head out of the bathroom door before nipping across the empty hallway. The air conditioning was on in our bedroom. Our bedroom. It sounded so strange, yet the thought made me smile. I bounced across the room, my smile breaking into laughter I couldn't contain. My wet hair slapped against my shoulders and water trickled down my back. I dropped the towel on the floor where I stood and let the cool air caress my bare skin. The balcony windows were wide, the curtains open, but I didn't care. The sky was hazy and the bright white paintwork of the balcony shimmered. The bedroom door scraped open and then closed with a click. Alekos whistled under his breath. His warm hands on my skin replaced cool air, one hand on my stomach, the other sliding between my breasts. He nuzzled my neck, his stubble rubbing, scratching, his lips tickling, kissing.

'I like you living here very much,' he said. His hands smoothed across my skin. He pressed into me. His belt buckle dug into the small of my back.

'There are no neighbours,' I said.

'No. But they fruit pick. They see you.'

We made love on our bed, in our room. It was like the first time on Cephalonia again, discovering each other; the weight of his body on top, the tautness of his muscles and the warmth of him inside me as we moved slowly and silently together. He was my second skin and I wanted to know every part of him. He left me sleeping and I woke up alone. I heard him downstairs, confidently talking in Greek, an Alekos I would grow to know. I wasn't sure how long I'd slept for, but I felt refreshed, lying naked on top of the sheets. The sun had moved across the sky, stretching a block of sunshine further across the wall. Slowly, I pulled myself on to my elbows. The early haziness had dispersed and for the first time I saw Mount Olympus, clear and magnificent.

Chapter One

Three Years Later

Most couples celebrate the anniversary of when they actually got together. We don't have that. We could, I suppose, celebrate the day we first saw each other or the day we first said hello or the first time we kissed, even the first time we had sex. But for me, arriving in Greece was the start; a bigger decision than 'will you go out with me?'

It's early July and it's been over a hundred degrees in the shade all week. I've never felt heat like it. The cats lie spread-eagled beneath the vines, clinging to what shade they can. They look miserable, not even venturing towards the fields in search of mice, lizards or snakes. Even Takis, the calmest person I've ever met, curses the weather as much as Despina does. No one steps outside between midday and three. In the nearby village, roads are deserted and blinds and shutters are closed as if a hurricane is on its way rather than a heatwave. Only in the evening, after their siesta, do people reappear, to sit on their porches and fan themselves. Despina makes *frappes* and Takis drinks them outside the kitchen door as fast as they appear.

At least our room is bearable with the curtains drawn and the air conditioning on.

'It's freezing in here,' Alekos moans, but for me it's a respite from the unrelenting heat. I'm thankful for a day off. The kitchen is a sauna and Despina's temper is as hot as the weather. Customers cram into the air-conditioned restaurant to drink their *chipero* and eat, making more work for Despina. I'm glad to be spending the evening away from the claustrophobia of the kitchen, to be a customer and be waited on in someone else's restaurant. I tip my head upside down and rub my wet hair. Days like these are for sleeping or swimming in the sea, not working. Wherever we go tonight I'm going to wear as little as possible. I have a cream dress laid out on the bed. It is strapless, short and made of a delicate material that floats against my body. I know Alekos will like it. I throw my head back and feel the blood rush from my face. I think I hear something. I open the bedroom door and stick my head out. The hallway is stuffy and empty, and then Alekos calls, 'Sophie, come see this!'

'I'm drying my hair,' I shout back in Greek.

He pokes his head round the top of the stairs. 'Trust me, you don't want to miss this.'

I wind a towel round my head and pull on shorts, a vest top and slip my flip-flops on. I slap along the tiled hallway and down the stone steps. Alekos meets me in the kitchen wearing only shorts and sandals. His skin has deepened to the colour of coffee. My tan is like caffé latte against his but at least I'm not red any more. He grabs my hand and pulls me outside. The heat smacks us and is unforgiving, smothering us as we round the corner of the building. We skirt the patio with the comatose cats and Takis asleep holding a newspaper. We duck beneath the shriveled vines trailing from the archway and out on to the scorched grass beyond.

Olympus is shadowed by grey. Rain clouds move towards us, extinguishing the sun and blue sky and throwing the distant landscape into premature darkness. Thunder growls, but it is miles away.

On the other side of the patio wall, where a few flowers struggle for life, cream and red butterflies dance in the wake of the impending storm. But here the sun shines, hot on our shoulders and faces as we look towards the sky. Dozens of butterflies, caught by the strengthening wind, spiral into the air.

'Aren't they incredible?' Alekos says. He keeps hold of my hand and we both watch the butterflies' multi-coloured frenzy. 'I couldn't afford roses,' he says.

'You ordered them specially, did you?'

Towards the mountain the sky is misted with rain. But we remain in sunshine. Alekos' hand moves to the small of my back and he pulls me to him. He's hot and damp from cleaning the patio tables.

'Where are we going tonight?' I ask.

He leans towards me and kisses me. I wrap my arms round him and his back muscles clench. We are hidden behind the wall, so I let my hands wander the length of his back and down, fingering the edge of his shorts. His hands slide beneath my vest top and reach across my bare back.

'You're not even dressed,' he whispers.

'Neither are you.'

'I've been working.'

'You've not finished yet?'

Before he can answer, a shaft of silver lightning pierces the grey. We wait, watching the sky darken. Storm clouds slam together with a bang. The cats meow and one of them shoots for cover.

'I never thought I'd be so pleased to see rain,' I say. Storms in Greece are violent but brief, the lightning spectacular, clearing the air as effectively as if someone had waved a magic wand. The clouds creep forward, dark rolling giants in the sky, consuming everything in their path. Their shadow sweeps across the landscape, edging nearer until it reaches the apricot field. The sun disappears and I feel the temperature drop. The butterflies spiral higher. Alekos strokes my hand and our shoulders touch. I feel a cool drop of water on my forehead. With the onslaught of rain the butterflies disperse.

Takis has left the patio, the cats have fled and, rain-splattered, we head for cover. Despina has two of her cousins helping out for the night in the kitchen. One of them is seventy-three and looks on the verge of passing out. Despina is shouting orders, and we are met with a barrage of words. I've never heard her swear in the kitchen, but if ever there was a time, it is tonight.

'I don't understand why you want to go out for food. Eat here!' she says as we squeeze past her.

I catch the briefest of scowls between her and Alekos. 'Mama,' he scolds.

'Sophie, I miss you already,' Despina says. Although her face is beaded with sweat she looks pale.

'I've made all the salads and the sauces are done.'

'I know, I know.' She leans towards me and whispers, 'I'm working with amateurs.'

'It's stormy, Mama, it'll be cooler tonight,' Alekos says. He puts his arm around her shoulders.

She stands on tiptoes and kisses him on both cheeks. 'And busier.'

There is no winning when she's in this mood. We back up the stairs, leaving the steam, hot food and tempers behind. Alekos heads for the shower and I return to our bedroom. It is icy cold and dull. I pull the curtains open. Only a smudge of blue remains in the sky. Rain lashes the balcony and thunder continues to rumble overhead. I slip my dress on and glimpse movement. A red butterfly flutters and lands on the wall. Its wings are bright and still against the white, as if it has been painted on. I leave it there, safe from the storm. I gather my hair in a ponytail and quickly put mascara and lip gloss on. I turn the air con off for Alekos.

I knock on the bathroom door. 'I'm ready.'

Alekos emerges with only a towel wrapped round his middle. He looks me up and down. His eyes linger. 'That's quite a dress. Do you want to help me get ready?' he says, nodding towards our bedroom.

'I know you too well, Aleko,' I reply. I blow him a kiss and wiggle my retreat along the hallway. 'I'll be downstairs.'

I don't have to wait long. Alekos is down in minutes, wearing grey trousers and a short-sleeved shirt, his black hair combed and styled. He finds me with Takis, retrieving dusty bottles of ouzo from the store cupboard.

'Is the car ready to go, Baba?' Alekos asks.

Takis looks up from the crate of bottles and nods. 'Take me with you, eh?' He winks. 'Enjoy yourselves tonight.'

The windscreen wipers won't go fast enough. We drive in a half-light; the sky is so dark and heavy with rain. We head towards the dusky remains of the evening's sunshine and soon the storm is behind us, the rumbles distant and the flashes less intrusive. Alekos winds the windows down as the car heats up. We pick up speed on the national road and cool air rushes in.

'Are you going to tell me what we're doing?' I ask.

Alekos reaches for Takis' cigarettes on the dashboard and pulls one out. I tut.

'He doesn't mind,' he says with the cigarette between his lips.

'I do.'

He gropes for the matches and passes them to me.

'Only if you tell me where we're going,' I say.

He shrugs in defeat. I light it and watch him breathe in smoke before blowing it out through the open window.

'To the Olympus festival,' he says.

'To do what?'

'Wait and see.'

I don't have to wait long. We pull into a car park in the foothills of Olympus and fight our way into a parking space. The evening is cooler and the earth is damp underfoot. There's a fresh smell of soil mixed with the aroma of sweetcorn being grilled on a stall by the entrance. The sun has dipped behind the mountain, leaving a stain of red and pink spreading across the horizon. I look behind at the slate grey clouds gathering over the sea.

We round the corner and walk towards a ticket booth.

'We're seeing a play?' I ask.

I recognise where we are but I haven't been here since the first summer when Alekos showed me the sights. The sun, disguised by the breeze, had burnt me while I stood on the stage at the Ancient Theatre of Dion and bellowed the few lines I remembered from Shakespeare's *Romeo and Juliet*. It was an incredible setting nestled between the mountain and the sea.

Alekos buys the tickets. 'We would have come last year but I didn't think you knew enough Greek.'

'But now?'

'I think you'll enjoy it.'

He couldn't give me a greater compliment. He passes me the tickets.

'*Agamemnon*,' I say.

'I know. A tragedy. Not right for an anniversary.'

'I studied it at school.'

'We can do something else if you want.'

'No, no, this is great. I've always wanted to see a play here.' I reach for his hand and we follow the mass of people along the sloping path. At the top it opens out on a crowded and noisy amphitheatre. Far below is the stage I'd stood on three years before, but now it is shrouded in darkness and anticipation.

Hundreds of people are squashed on to rows of wooden benches and the amphitheatre buzzes with chatter. As floodlights light up the stage conversations turn to whispers. The appearance of a masked figure subdues the audience. They keep it traditional with a bare stage, but they are creative with their lighting, setting the mood with different colours. Sections of the stage are lit up to give the feeling of either intimacy or space. I glance at Alekos a few times to gauge if he is enjoying it or not. Each time he catches me looking, he asks if I'm okay. The figure of Queen Clytemnestra in dark purple and blue robes with braided hair commands the stage as her husband Agamemnon sacrifices their daughter. At times I struggle to keep up with the language, but I follow the story and understand more than expected.

After queuing to get out of the car park, we drive towards the coast, away from Olympus. The Greek entry from this year's Eurovision comes on the radio. Alekos hums along.

'You like this?' I ask.

'It's catchy.'

'Do you know the words?'

'No.'

'Are you sure?'

'Okay, maybe a few.'

It is a clear night away from the lights of the Ancient Theatre of Dion. Hundreds of stars speckle the sky and the moon is just a pale slither. The landscape spreads out as we drive, with clusters of lights finishing in a line along the coast. Lightning still flashes on the horizon. I have an idea of where we're going, especially when we turn on to the coast road towards Platamonas with its fish restaurants by the beach.

But Alekos isn't predictable for once. We leave the dark glint of the sea behind as the coast road curves inland. We climb a winding road, thundering past another car struggling with the ascent. Then, from behind a shroud of trees, I see Platamonas castle. Perched at the summit of the hill, it overlooks the Aegean Sea. The castle's turrets and stone walls are the colour of honey, floodlit by the lighting skirting its base. We pull sharply on to a steep dirt track that zigzags up the hillside to the castle.

'It's spectacular,' I say, as we rumble up the track. 'It looks so different at night.'

We pull up on the grass in front of the castle walls and Alekos switches off the engine. The air stills and all I can hear is the sound of crickets surrounding us. We get out of the car and I look around at the weather-beaten castle walls looming above us.

'Open the boot,' Alekos says with a smile.

I click it open and find a picnic hamper and cool box inside.

'You romantic,' I say.

'I didn't want to take you to a restaurant. I thought it would remind us of work.'

I kiss him. 'This is perfect.'

We take everything out and find a flat spot a little way from the car. We lay a rug out on the grass by the edge of the hill and sit with our backs to the castle.

'Did I make that?' I ask as he brings out a bowl of salad.

He nods.

We eat hot feta, roasted red peppers and *spanakopita* in the dark. Alekos rests a torch on the rug to shine on the salami and cheeses, bread and olives. A moth flutters between us, drawn to the light. We drink straight from a bottle of sweet red wine, taking long gulps and passing it to each other.

'It's so good to be out,' I say. There is more food but I'm full. Alekos manoeuvres himself towards me and I snuggle back into his arms.

'I've never felt this happy before,' he says. He holds me close. 'Have you?'

'I've been happy before but this is different. I want to pinch myself to make sure this is really happening.' I wriggle my toes in the long, scratchy grass. 'There are probably snakes and things in here, aren't there?'

'And lizards.'

'I don't mind lizards.'

'You will when one bites you.'

'It can't be as bad as the bloody mosquitoes.'

'At least I can't see your bites in the dark.'

'I only have two bites.' I elbow him and he squeezes me tighter.

'I love you, even with ugly, red marks,' he says.

'I'll take that as a compliment. Anyway it only means they find me tasty.'

'Me too.'

There is something about night time that leaves me with the feeling of being cut off from the rest of the world. High on the hill the darkness is threaded with lights that reflect off the sea.

'We were somewhere over there earlier.' Alekos points to a far off cluster of lights. It is different at night and peaceful, away from the summer crowds – the beach is filled by mid-morning, not with so many people that you feel your space is invaded, but close enough to hear each other's conversations. Up on the castle hilltop it feels timeless, empty, as if we are the only people for miles, surveying our land. I'm getting carried away – but why not. My contentment is more than just an evening of theatre, or the food and wine filling my stomach, more than Alekos' arms around me, or his lips tickling my neck. It is the feeling of belonging, of finally being satisfied, of hope for the future without any fear of what it might hold. It may feel unreal but I realise this is normality – the lights piercing the darkness below belong to a country I have embraced. I wouldn't change it for anything.

We leave the car parked on the grass outside the restaurant and avoid the gravel in an attempt to not wake Despina and Takis. We tiptoe through the dark kitchen and up the stairs.

'That was the best evening,' I say as we reach our bedroom door.

'Shush,' Alekos says, putting his middle finger against my lips. 'They'll hear.'

'I'm only talking.'

'Whisper.'

I sigh. Loudly.

He takes my hand and says, 'Follow me.'

We creep back along the dark hallway past Despina and Takis' bedroom and pad down the stone steps and out through the kitchen door.

'What did I do?' I ask. I follow him across the garden.

'You wanted to talk. I could tell.'

'I always want to talk at night you know that. I'm past being sleepy.'

'We can always have sex if you're not tired.'

'We've plenty of time for that.'

He tickles my sides and I wriggle away from him and run towards the far end of the garden. We slump together on one of the seats beneath the olive trees. Takis calls them the love seats after more and more couples end up locking lips on them at the end of the night.

'We should sleep outside, under the stars,' I say.

'With all the insects?'

'Maybe not. But I'm so awake.'

I untangle myself from him and walk across the garden and past the patio. A velvety darkness stretches endlessly in every direction. I go through the archway and out on to the grassy area behind the restaurant. The security light from the patio clicks on and shines through the gaps in the wall making diamond shapes on the grass. The ground is so dry puddles have formed after the storm. I see a fleck of white in one and bend down. I pick up a cream butterfly, drowned by the rain. I can barely feel it in the palm of my hand; its wings are like tissue paper.

Alekos slides his arms round my waist from behind. He kisses my neck and rests his head on my shoulder. 'What have you got there?'

'A butterfly.'

He reaches over and picks it up by one of its wings and places it in the arch of the patio wall. He turns me around so we face each other.

'You're beautiful, Sophie.' He brushes the loose strands of hair off my face and kisses me, his tongue lingering, teasing. My hands entwine with his behind my back.

'Marry me,' he says.

I can barely see his face but I hear the sincerity in his voice. I can't speak. The silence between us grows. The muscles in his legs tense and his grip on my hands loosens.

'Yes,' I finally say and laugh. 'You're serious aren't you?'

He relaxes. 'I'm serious. I have no ring though; I have nothing to give you.' He pauses. I think he's grinning at me. 'I didn't plan this.'

'I know.'

We wrap our arms around each other and cling on. I want to cry, I want to laugh. I don't know what to do. Words are pouring out of him so fast it's hard to keep up. 'And children,' Alekos says with his head still buried in my neck. 'I want you to have my children.'

'I want that too,' I reply.

'I wasn't sure you did.' He pulls away from me.

I reach out and stroke the stubble on his chin. He watches me, gauging my reactions, needing to know if I'm serious.

'Really, Aleko, I want children.'

'How many?'

'More than one. I don't want them to grow up an only child like I did,' I say. 'But I want you to promise, Aleko, that we get a place of our own. Soon. Before we commit to anything. I don't want to be married and living with your parents. Promise me.'

'I've been thinking about that for ages too,' he replies. 'I promise.'

So much has changed in such a short space of time. I feel like those butterflies, lost to the breeze, allowing myself to be taken on a journey, not caring if I'm ready or if there's a way back.

Chapter Two

'The last customers have just left,' Alekos says, entering the kitchen through the swing doors. He glances at his watch. '03.40am. A new record.'

I spread the final layer of spinach and feta between filo pastry, ready to be baked in the morning. 'I'm almost done here.'

'Where's Mama?'

'In the office cashing up.'

He slides his arm round my waist and kisses me. 'I hate working Friday nights, I don't get a chance to see you.'

I wiggle my sticky fingers at him. 'Give me five more minutes and we can go to bed.'

His lips brush my cheek before nibbling my neck. 'That's five minutes too long.'

The swing doors swoosh open and one of the waiters appears. 'Sorry Aleko,' he says, hovering in the doorway. 'I was just going to ask if there was anything else you needed doing? All the tables are clean, the floor's swept...'

'That's all for tonight, thanks Luka, have a drink if you want before going home.'

'Thanks boss,' Luka says and winks.

Alekos pulls away from me and takes a handful of euros from his pocket. 'I better give these to Mama.' He disappears down the corridor past the storeroom to Despina's office at the back of the building.

03.40 in the morning and it has been a long and busy August night with the weekend still to go. I finish with the spinach mixture and put the last layer of filo pastry on top and fold the edges in neatly. Takis, with a cigarette stuck between his lips, walks beneath the light outside the kitchen window and waves. I wave back. I wash my hands, take off my apron and walk down to the office. Alekos and Despina are talking; I knock and push open the door.

'But I need to start later tomorrow evening, Mama,' Alekos says.

'Since when?' Despina takes her glasses off and looks up from the bundle of euros on her desk.

'I told you last week, I've been asked to play the volleyball match in Paralia at five tomorrow evening.'

'Well I need you here.'

'Mama, I'm asking for a couple of hours off just this once.'

'And you should get preferential treatment over the other waiters because you're my son?'

'But they all know I'm playing in the match. And anyway, the other waiters have asked you for time off before. I wouldn't ask unless it was important to me. I never play volleyball any more.'

Despina looks at me. 'I suppose you want time off too?'

'You've already given me the time off,' I say, glancing between her and Alekos. 'That's why I've prepared extra tonight because I'm not starting until eight tomorrow evening. I asked the same time Alekos did last week.'

Despina clicks her tongue and scrapes a load of one-euro coins off the desk and into a money-bag. 'I'm too busy to be thinking about your social life. I suppose I have no choice then.'

'Don't be like that, Mama,' Alekos says. 'I'll make it up to you, I promise.'

Alekos holds my hand as we traipse across the sand away

from the bars and restaurants in Paralia. After five minutes of walking the beach is deserted and I'm sweating and longing for some shade from the August sun. There are only a few people lying on the sun loungers beneath the permanent thatched umbrellas and the volleyball net's not even been put up yet.

'I hope more people turn up,' Alekos says.

'They will, it's early yet.' I wave at Demetrius and Katrina already camped out beneath the umbrellas. 'Anyway, I prefer it like this, empty.'

'I know, but I want a crowd.'

'Show off.'

'*Yasas*!' Katrina calls. We join them by the sun loungers and she kisses both of my cheeks.

'Where is everyone?' Alekos hugs Demetrius.

'Don't worry, they'll be here,' Demetrius says as he greets me. 'It's early yet.'

'See, Aleko, I told you. Listen to Demetri.'

I lay my towel on the sun lounger next to Katrina, strip down to my red bikini and sit down.

Katrina grabs my hand. 'That engagement ring is so beautiful.'

I lift my hand up so the small square diamond sparkles in the sunshine.

Katrina turns on her side and props herself up on her elbow. 'So, have you set a date yet?'

'Seriously Kat, we've been working so hard we've not had a chance to think about it. There's no rush, it's not going to be until next year at least, and anyway I kind of fancy a winter wedding.'

'Are you serious? Despina will freak out. She'll be like "it's too cold… what if it rains…" You know what she's like.'

'I certainly do.'

Alekos needn't have worried about no one turning up. By the time the volleyball net is put up and the other team arrives there's a crowd of people sat on the seating stand behind the umpire's chair and the sun loungers have begun to feel crowded. Alekos and Demetrius in matching blue shorts warm up, tapping the ball between each other while their opponents get ready.

Katrina and I lie on our fronts facing the volleyball court with our sunglasses pushing our hair back.

'Alekos is the star player.' Katrina says. 'Demetrius thinks he's the best player but everyone knows Alekos is. But shush don't tell Demetrius I said that. It's a shame Alekos doesn't play that often.'

'He would if he could.'

The umpire blows a whistle and a cheer goes up from the crowd of people watching from the stand. Alekos serves, grounding the ball into the sand on the other side of the net and gaining the first point. I wolf-whistle and Demetrius and Alekos high-five each other. I take a bottle of water out of my bag and sit up cross-legged on the sun lounger. 'How do you and Demetrius find it living with your parents?'

Katrina shrugs. 'It's fine. It doesn't bother me, it's my home, I've always lived there.'

'You don't ever wish it was just the two of you?'

Katrina rolls on her side to face me and rests her head on her hand. 'Are you worried about keeping the noise down when you and Alekos are... you know...' She makes a suggestive motion with her hips.

'God no, I didn't mean that... Although I'd prefer it if Alekos' parents weren't sleeping in the room next to ours. No, I mean don't you ever want some space of your own? Your independence? To do what you want and eat what you want when you want?'

'I'm lazy, Sophie. I like Mama cooking and looking after us. But we will move out sometime. When we've saved enough money we'll get an apartment of our own. Definitely once we have children. Are you finding it difficult living with Alekos' parents?'

'It's because I've lived away from home since I went to

university at eighteen and even when I moved back to Bristol I lived with friends instead of with my Mum.'

'Apart from the two summers him and Demetrius worked on Cephalonia, Alekos has always lived at home.'

'And now that we're engaged I feel there's even more reason to move out.'

'Sophie, it's normal to live with your parents or your husband's family, even when married like us.'

'I know; it's a Greek thing.'

Another cheer goes up from the crowd; Demetrius has just smashed the ball into the sand on their opponent's side. Alekos can't stop smiling. Him and Demetrius work faultlessly together communicating via the hand signals they give to each other behind their backs. Alekos is quick on his feet, darting across the sand to reach the ball, jumping high into the air, his arm stretching out, his chest muscles tightening as his fingers connect with the volleyball and flick it across the net.

'You're late,' Despina says the moment we enter the kitchen.

'We won, Mama.'

'Winning's not helping all those people out there get served.' Despina throws olive oil into a pan and the sound of sizzling engulfs the kitchen.

'Well done, son,' Takis says from the corner of the kitchen where he's uncorking a bottle of wine. He pats Alekos on the shoulder as he heads towards the restaurant. 'You can tell me all about it later.'

'Thanks Baba.'

'Sophie, don't just stand there looking pretty, it's eight-thirty already,' Despina says. 'Take over from Kostas, I need grilled octopus and sardines for table seven.'

I drop my bag on the floor and kick it into the corner out of the way. I take an apron from off the back of the door.

'I'd better go and get changed,' Alekos says.

I grab his hand. 'Aleko, you were great out there today. I'm really proud of you.'

He squeezes my hand and the smile he had on the volleyball court briefly returns. 'And now it's back to reality.'

Chapter Three

It's the day of the yearly Kakavetsis family summer outing when the restaurant isn't open until the evening. Despina has allowed me to finish early after doing most of the food prep for later and it's just gone ten, eight o'clock in England and I'm debating whether it's too early to phone Candy. I dial her number before I change my mind. It rings and rings. I open the balcony door and a warm breeze wafts in. The phone rings once more and goes to answer phone. I don't leave a message. She's probably already up and out or dealing with her six month-old son Jake. For Candy at least so much has changed in the last three years. I put suntan lotion, a hat and sunglasses in a bag and I'm about to go downstairs when the phone rings.

'Sorry Sophie,' Candy says when I answer. 'I was changing Jake's nappy and couldn't get to the phone.'

'How is he?'

'Teething. He's so grumpy but still adorable,' she says with a laugh. 'I've not heard from you for a while. How are you?'

'I'm okay, just busy. I've been working six days a week since the beginning of June so I can't actually wait for the summer to be over. Despina's closed the restaurant for lunch and given us all the day off to go to the beach together.'

'You don't sound happy,' Candy says.

'I guess I'm not really. I feel stuck in a rut. Don't get me wrong, I love being a chef and I'm good at it, it's just I keep thinking about the plans I had when I first came over here and becoming a chef wasn't part of the plan. And as for going to the beach today it's a big family outing when all I want to do is spend some quality time alone with Alekos.' I lower my voice. 'It's driving me mad living here. Despina's so controlling. And now that we're engaged all she bangs on about is when are me and Alekos going to set a date for the wedding.'

'And when is it going to be?'

'Don't you start.'

'I'm only teasing.'

'She'd love you, having a baby all within eighteen months of meeting Lee.'

'Yeah, but we did go about it the wrong way round, getting pregnant and having Jake before even getting engaged and I'm still waiting to get hitched.'

'I so want to meet them. It's just plain wrong that I've not met my best friend's partner and son yet.'

'Have you heard from your Mum recently?' Candy asks.

'Not since Christmas,' I say. 'Why, has your Mum talked to her?'

'A couple of weeks ago. She's loving Norfolk and already has two clients who want her to organise their weddings for next year. It's the perfect job for her.'

'Seriously, a wedding planner is the perfect job for my Mum? The woman who has never been married and has never even managed a long-term relationship.'

'She's creative, like you, she's outgoing, got the gift of the gab, an eye for detail, doesn't take any bullshit and is a true romantic at heart. She's perfect for it,' Candy says and then pauses. 'She'd love you to visit. I've seen photos of her new house and it's totally gorgeous. She says she doesn't regret moving away from Bristol.'

'Why are you telling me this, Candy?'

'Because she misses you and I know deep down you miss her too.'

'I miss how our relationship used to be, not what it's

turned into.'

'If you invited her to Greece, she'd come.'

'I'd rather you came to Greece first. You do realise it's more than three years since I last saw you.'

'We'll come to Greece, I promise, providing I'm not pregnant again.'

'You're trying?'

'Maybe…'

'Sophie!' Despina yells from the hallway. 'Are you ready?'

'One minute!' I call back in Greek. 'Sorry Candy, I've got to go, the Kakavetsis big day out remember.'

'Have fun.'

'Give Jake a big kiss from me and I'll speak to you soon.'

I grab my bag and a couple of beach towels from the cupboard and close the bedroom door behind me.

'Aleko! Sophie! Takis! Where are you?' Despina's shouts bulldoze through *O Kipos*. 'Lena's here!'

I collide with Alekos coming out of the bathroom. 'It's like a military operation,' I say as we head downstairs.

Despina stands outside the kitchen door surrounded by bags, deflated lilos, a picnic hamper and three beach umbrellas.

'Where's Takis?' she asks as we squeeze past her, stepping over the bags into sunshine.

'I'm here,' he says with a sigh from the shadowy kitchen.

Lena sits on the patio with her husband, Spiros, shaded by the grapes, her hands resting on her seven-month bump. Yannis is running round in circles on the grass, seemingly chasing an invisible something.

'Let's go!' Despina yells. Yannis whoops and runs to the car as fast as his legs can go.

Platamonas Castle overlooks one end of the beach. Pale yellow sand stretches endlessly in the other direction. It *is* a military operation setting up camp. After lugging our bags and umbrellas as far as Lena is prepared to walk in the heat we find a spot a few metres from the sea and Despina sets about organising us.

'Get the mats out, Takis. Start blowing the lilos up, Aleko…'

I open one of the umbrellas and wedge it in the sand for Lena.

'I love this,' she whispers. 'Mama won't let me do anything. It's almost worth the uncomfortable nights and swollen ankles. Yanni, no!'

Yannis watches the sea lapping at his toes.

'Wait until we're settled, Yanni, and then everyone can go for a swim.'

I'm as eager as Yannis. It's unbearably hot even in the shade. We discard our clothes and fling them over the umbrellas. Tanned flesh is on show in swimming costumes, bikinis and shorts. Alekos and Spiros sit in the sun blowing up the lilos, their faces turning beetroot. Takis takes his mat and spreads it out on the edge of our camp, and without a word, lies down and closes his eyes. Despina props herself up on a lilo next to the food.

'Swim first, eat after,' she says.

'Can I go swimming now, Mama!' Yannis cries, jumping about in front of Lena and kicking sand everywhere.

'Let Uncle Aleko put your wings on first, Yanni,' she says.

Alekos catches hold of Yannis, lifting him effortlessly as if he's a ragdoll rather than a wriggling four-year-old. Alekos tickles his stomach and he giggles. His laughter is infectious. With his water wings on and his feet back on the beach, Yannis grabs Alekos' hand and drags him into the shallows.

Spiros finishes blowing up the lilo and sits down on it next to Lena and curls his arm round her shoulders. 'Aleko can entertain Yannis for a while,' he says.

I wade into the warm water.

'Look at me!' Yannis says. He knocks a blow-up ball to Alekos.

'Well done, Yanni.' The sand sinks between my toes and

the water gets cooler the deeper I go. I launch myself on to my lilo and lie stomach down, bobbing up and down on the gentle movement of the sea, my fingers trailing in the water. Alekos is only wet up to his thighs, while Yannis is shoulder deep. They tap the ball between them. Yannis charges through the water to retrieve it when he misses.

'Yanni,' Alekos says. 'Put your hands like this.' He straightens his fingers and taps them together. 'Hit the ball with the tips of your fingers.'

I rest my head on my hands and drift, moving away from them with the current and watch tiny fish dart beneath the clear plastic of the lilo.

'Yanni wants a baby brother,' Lena says as I sit down next to her and rub myself dry with a towel. She rests her magazine on her bump.

'What do you want?'

'Truthfully, a girl. Maybe you could supply Yanni with a cousin to play with.' She smiles knowingly at me. 'One day, before he gets too old to play. I'm sorry, I sound just like Mama.'

Despina is delving into the picnic hamper in-between Takis and Spiros who are both snoring.

Lena leans towards me. 'Mama went on at me from the age of eighteen, when was I going to make her a grandmother? Even when I wasn't with anyone – especially when I wasn't with anyone. Alekos was expected to work in the restaurant; I was expected to get married.'

'And she expects the same of me now.'

'You'd better set the date sooner rather than later. You've been together three years, that's two years too long in Mama's mind without a wedding or a pregnancy, or both preferably.'

'I was saying exactly that to my friend Candy this morning.'

She gasps and her hands fly to her bump. 'Baby's on the move.'

She places my hand on her perfectly rounded and hard stomach. I feel a kick. Shivers wriggle up my arm.

'Alekos is good with Yanni,' she says.

'That's because he's a big kid too.' I watch him scoop Yannis up in his arms and carry him from the sea to the beach.

'More!' Yannis shouts.

'I have to rest,' Alekos says. 'I'm not as young as you.'

Yannis' bottom lip juts out in a sulk. Alekos puts him down and he sinks on to the sand.

'Yanni, you'll be covered,' Lena says. Yannis falls sideways and rolls, giggling, until his skin is covered with grains of sand and the only clean bit left is his face.

'I have to go back in now,' he says.

'My Mum never wanted to be a grandmother,' I say, watching Despina brush down a giggling Yannis. 'She thinks she's too young.'

'But you're not.'

'Despite being only twenty-eight? My biological clock is counting down fast. At least Despina thinks so.'

'Lena, Sophie, Aleko,' Despina says. 'Food!'

Chapter Four

I'm writing today's specials on the chalkboard above the restaurant bar. It's ironic that I'm the only foreigner in the place and yet I have the neatest Greek handwriting. The swing door to the kitchen slams open and Despina marches into the restaurant followed by Alekos.

'But Mama,' he says. 'If the band are in the corner next to the bar we gain two tables seating an extra eight people.'

Despina halts and surveys the restaurant. 'But then the band will be obscured by the pillar and squashed in the corner between the bar and the fireplace. I don't like it. We put them where they've always been.'

I finish writing the main course specials on the board and start on the sweets.

'Mama, it doesn't make sense putting the band where they've always gone. It's November, we should have as many tables available inside as we can. We're always fully booked. And having the band next to the bar is the answer.'

Eleni, one of the waitresses, is on the other side of the room laying the tables. She glances at Alekos and then me before swiftly polishing the cutlery again.

'Alekos does have a point,' I say, putting the chalk down.

'Sophie, it's okay, it's Mama's restaurant, it's her decision.'

'I know it's her restaurant but that doesn't mean she should completely disregard a good idea.'

Despina folds her arms. 'I've been running this restaurant

for over twenty years. I know what works. It's the success it is for a reason.'

'It doesn't mean that change is a bad thing.'

'Sophie, leave it,' Alekos says. His fists are clenched and he stands rigid in front of Despina with his back to me.

'You should listen to Alekos more,' I say, challenging Despina. Eleni slips from the restaurant down the stairs to the toilets. 'He's suggesting moving the band from one side of the room to the other to gain two extra tables. That's simply good business sense. He's not suggesting you paint the walls pink.'

Despina's foot taps the tiled floor. She smoothes down her apron. She might be about to give in when I say, 'You may have been running this place for twenty years but Alekos has been working his arse off as a waiter for you for over ten years with very little thanks. You could at least give him some credit and stop treating him and his suggestions like he's ten.'

'Don't you dare lecture me about my son.'

'How can you expect me not to defend my fiancé when you put him down all the time? You'd be the first to defend him if it was the other way around.'

'Mama,' Alekos says quietly. 'I'll put the band where they've always been.' He turns and looks at me. 'Come with me.'

He storms into the kitchen and I follow. He stops at the bottom of the apartment stairs. 'Why can't you keep quiet?'

'Aleko, I'm sorry, but can you not see the way she treats you?'

He looks over my shoulder and doesn't say anything.

'Why are you so ungrateful?' Despina says from behind me. She goes over to the oven, heaves a tray out and a rich aroma of roasting lamb is released into the kitchen.

'I'm not ungrateful,' I say, looking between her and Alekos. 'I never said that. I'm frustrated at being here twenty-four hours a day and having very little time to myself or alone with Alekos. I'm annoyed by the way you sometimes treat Alekos and the way he reacts to you. But I'm not ungrateful.'

'You have a job and a home here. We've treated you from the moment you arrived like one of the family, but you make it clear you can't wait to leave and I don't understand why?'

'Why? How can you not understand us wanting some independence? I love working here and I appreciate all you've done for me, but I thought *living* here at least was temporary.' Alekos remains quiet and it doesn't seem like he's about to back me up. I figure now's as good a time as any to release everything that's been on my mind for the last few months. 'I've been working here so much I've not had time to concentrate on what I really want to be doing.'

'And what about Alekos? Are you going to drag him away from his work, his family and his home?'

'I'm not dragging him. We both want this. To have a place of our own.' My voice trails off as Despina huffs. 'What happened out there,' I point to the restaurant, 'just proves it. He's got great ideas and passion for what he does and is fantastic with people but you stifle him. He's only still here because you put pressure on him to stay. He doesn't want to be a waiter forever. Let him lead his own life.'

The spoon she's using to baste the lamb clatters on to the work surface. She swings around, her cheeks flushed. 'You little…' She doesn't finish the sentence and instead unties her apron and chucks it on the side before pushing past Alekos and clattering up the stairs to the apartment.

'Why did you say that?' Alekos asks.

'I'm only stating the truth. Something's needed to be said for a long time. She's holding you back, Aleko.' I reach for him but he shrugs me away.

'Is it really me she's holding back or you?'

'It's us Aleko. We're going to get married, start a family. Surely we're not going to be living here when we have children?'

'Of course not.'

'You've got to break away at some point, however hard it is.'

He takes my hand. 'Come on, let's try and make peace with her.' We go together up the stairs and open the door to the apartment.

Despina is pacing the living room and talking at Takis who is sat on the sofa in front of the TV, looking bemused. As soon as the door closes behind us Despina looks directly at Alekos. 'I wish you'd fallen in love with a good Greek girl!'

'Mama!' Alekos says.

'Well, it's the truth.'

Forget about keeping the peace. 'So you want a good Greek girl for a daughter-in-law. Someone who will happily live here, no questions asked, and do everything you want her to do. What do you want, Aleko?'

Despina and I turn to Alekos.

'I want you both to be happy,' he says quietly.

'And how are you going to make that happen?' I ask.

'I don't think I can.' He takes hold of my hands. 'Why did you move to Greece, Sophie?'

'To be with you.'

'Then why's that not enough?'

'Because I know you're not happy here. I know you've got ambitions. What about your music? What about everything we talked about on Cephalonia? Do you not want that anymore?'

'Mama needs us here.'

'No she needs *you* here.'

Despina tuts. 'You're the chef, Sophie, I need you.'

Alekos' cheeks flush red and his eyes flicker away from his mother's. I hate her for that comment. Alekos is so desperate to please her and prove himself at *O Kipos* and I know me being in the kitchen makes him want to impress her even more, because I'm the one getting the praise, from Despina and the customers. She's proved that again today.

Alekos steps forward and holds my face in his hands and rests his forehead against mine. 'The thing I want most is to marry you. Let's concentrate on planning our wedding. The most important thing right now is you.'

'Your problem, Sophie,' Despina says. 'Is that you don't speak to your mother. So how can you possibly understand what it means to be a close family?'

'Despina!' Takis suddenly stands and joins his wife in the middle of the room. 'That's enough.'

She waves him away with her hand. 'All I mean is our culture is not like yours in England. Families stick together. Grown-up children live with their parents. All Alekos' friends still do.'

'That's not exactly true Mama. Nikos doesn't, neither does Demetrius.'

'Nikos works in Athens, that's different. Demetrius and Katrina live with her parents in their small apartment, which makes life difficult but they still manage. We have a large apartment.'

'Lena doesn't live here,' I say.

'No but they lived with his parents until they had children. It's expected.' She looks at Alekos. 'You don't like living here?'

'Of course I do Mama, it's just...' he shrugs and glances at me. 'I can't please you both.'

'Then I'll make it easy for you, Aleko, carry on doing what you've always done, pleasing your mother.' I turn to Despina. 'You have no idea about my history with my mother. You also have no idea how all my life I've longed to be part of a family. But I just need some space, Alekos needs space, Takis needs space, my God you need space even if you don't realise it. I'm not asking you to give up your son and never speak to him again, I'm just asking for a little piece of him. We're talking about my future husband. Me wanting us to live on our own is simply natural, not selfish.'

'I didn't say you were selfish,' Despina says. 'I said ungrateful.'

'You have to have the last word, don't you?'

'Everyone!' Takis shouts. 'Silence!'

I don't think I've ever heard Takis sound so angry. Maybe Alekos can learn something from his father.

'Alekos, Sophie, you need time together.' Takis takes his wife's arm. 'Give them a few minutes to talk *alone*. We've got a restaurant to open.' He steers her out of the apartment and the door closes shut behind them.

'Well done, Sophie.'

'It's about time someone stood up to her.'

Chapter Five

It is rare to be on my own despite the restaurant being built within an empty landscape of farmland and mountains. Since *that* argument six weeks ago I'm spending more and more time at my spot by the fence. I retreat here daily for a bit of 'me' time but I always feel watched. There are plenty of places for people to spy on me from. I catch Despina peering down at me from her bedroom window, a folded sheet in her hands. Our eyes meet and she busies herself. I know Alekos and Takis, even customers, can see me from between the arches in the wall that shelters the patio. It's like I'm a housemate on Big Brother. But there is seemingly no release from this house, no Davina to guide me out the other end.

If Despina is unaware of my mood she's certainly concerned why I'm outside in 'bitter conditions'. Her words. It is cold but it's hardly a damp creeping cold that chills not only your skin but also right to your core – that's my memory of freezing, miserable winter days in England. The fence looks as if it's been dusted with icing sugar. The ground is hard and decorated with frost patterns. With the haze of summer gone, Mount Olympus is clear, its rocky crags revealed, dark against the snow; a jagged white outline against the darkening sky. I have a scarf slung round my neck, for comfort more than warmth, and I've shed the thick winter coat Despina makes me wear the moment I step outside.

Soon people will arrive for the New Year's Eve

celebrations, not just customers (mostly regulars who know Despina and Takis well) but friends and family, basically anyone, however loosely connected to the Kakavetsis family, will be here. It isn't a normal night. Despina refuses to slave in the kitchen, so we've prepared a massive buffet all laid out on tables that stretch the length of the restaurant. There will be live music and dancing – and I mean a lot of dancing, until our heads spin and feet ache.

The frost has melted where I've gripped the fence so hard. My fingers are frozen and red. I hear a car crunch its arrival. I lean back against the fence and face the restaurant. It's decorated with tiny lights that can be seen all the way down the road. On this side of the patio wall was where Alekos proposed to me in the summer. I remember waking up early the next morning, creeping from our bedroom, past Despina and Takis' room, and outside into the warmth of dawn. The puddles from the storm had nearly evaporated; the garden, grass, flowers, trees and fields looked drained of colour, dry and weighed down by the intense summer heat. I'd crossed the patio and lawn to this fence and looked towards the clear outline of Olympus with its varying shades of purple and grey against the blue sky. I found the drowned butterfly, its wings flattened and pale against the red bricks of the arch. I buried it in the ground where Alekos had proposed.

'Sophie, you will freeze!' Despina suddenly shouts from the archway. She's wearing a fur coat with the collar turned up and matching hat and gloves.

I slowly walk back across the grass.

'Our guests are arriving,' she says, hooking her arm in mine before marching me to the front of the restaurant. 'Alekos is serving drinks, Takis is laying out the food, and I need you to make your delicious mulled wine.'

Mulled wine is my little piece of England that Despina has actually taken a liking to, unlike Yorkshire puddings, bread sauce and horseradish, each of which she'd tasted and turned her nose up at.

Alone in the kitchen I pour countless bottles of red wine into a cauldron-sized pan and add cloves, star anise, cinnamon sticks and slices of lemon and orange and stir it gently over a low heat.

'I thought I could smell something good,' Lena says, slipping into the kitchen. 'Any chance of a sneaky drink before anyone else?'

I ladle some of the wine into a glass and hand it to her. 'You like it as much as your Mum does.'

'I can't believe we were missing out on this for so many years before you came here.'

'This is my Mum's recipe,' I say. 'Although she always used to add a very generous helping of Cointreau or any other spirit we had in the house at the time. She liked it strong.'

'Do you miss her?' With her hands cupped round the glass she blows on the hot wine.

'I'm beginning to. My memory of her and home is outdated since she moved away from Bristol. Do you think I'm terrible never having invited her here?'

'I think you have your reasons.'

'She's infuriated me, made me angry, made me sad but I miss the way she could always make me smile. I miss the way I used to be able to talk to her about anything, and I mean anything.'

'You're lucky; Mama's wonderful but I was always embarrassed to talk to her about personal stuff, you know, my feelings.' Lena takes a sip of the mulled wine. 'That is so good.'

'It reminds me of Christmas parties at home with Mum, my friends loved it. We'd get pretty pissed on the mulled wine Mum made.' I ladle myself a glassful and take a sip. 'Not bad.'

'What did you use to do for New Year in England?'

'Go out with Candy and our friends in Bristol or go to a party at someone's house.'

'Do they still do that?'

'Not Candy so much now she has Jake and is pregnant

again, but my friends who are still in Bristol will be getting together tonight.'

'Are you going out later?'

'With Alekos and his friends? I think so.'

Lena knocks her glass against mine. 'To the New Year and more of this wine! I'd better check if Callia needs feeding, plus Mama will be wondering why I'm not serving drinks and being a good host to our guests. Alekos is far better at being sociable than me; he has a natural way with people, but what Mama wants...' she raises an eyebrow and we both smile.

The band is playing by the time I emerge from the kitchen with a tray of glasses filled with mulled wine. A few guests, led by Despina, have already made a circle on the dance floor. The first time I'd been made to dance at Alekos' cousin's wedding, I'd surprised myself at how much I had enjoyed it. I was rubbish though, particularly at the fast dances, where my feet would get muddled and I'd crash into the person next to me.

My tray of wine is soon emptied and I stand at the edge of the dance floor and tap my foot to the music.

'Sophie!' Takis calls as he sidesteps past me. He puts his free arm across my shoulders and pulls me into the dance. My feet follow Takis', stepping forward, forward, back and across, along with everyone else circling in time with the beat of the music. This is what I love about Greece, the spontaneity, the passion and zest for life. Alekos is on the opposite side of the circle sandwiched between Despina and Demetrius. His face is hot from dancing and his shirt buttons are undone halfway down his chest. He catches my eye and winks.

The dancing continues until nearly midnight when the band stops playing, although I barely notice with the amount of shouting, laughter and singing going on. Everyone holds hands. The TV above the bar is on. Alekos holds me, and a stranger's sweaty hand grips my free one. We drown the Athens crowd out with our countdown: '*Dheka, enea, okto, epta, eksi, pende, tesera, tria, dhio, ena! Kali xrhonia!*'

Alekos kisses me, his arms encircling me as he whispers. 'This is our year, Sophie.' Then he's dragged away by Despina and I'm left with strangers kissing me on my cheeks and wishing me a good New Year. That is the least I'm hoping for. I want more than a good New Year. I want a perfect one. The New Year is supposed to bring us our independence. It doesn't matter if it's an apartment the size of a garden shed, as long as it's the two of us on our own. Then there's our wedding the following year and after that the possibility is there, to start a family.

I slip out of the restaurant and into the dark kitchen. It's cold without the ovens on or the lights blazing. I sit halfway up the stone steps that lead to the apartment. The live music has started again and vibrates through the place, along with the stamping of feet and clapping of hands. I hug my knees to my chest and can't stop myself from crying.

'I'll be here for you if it doesn't work out.' Those were Mum's last words to me. There was no truth in them. Why wouldn't it work out? I love Alekos. End of story.

He finds me sitting on the shadowy stairs. I have no idea how long I've been here but I feel numb with cold and my cheeks are tight from tears I can't be bothered to wipe away.

'It's snowing,' he says. Standing a couple of steps below me our faces are level. His brown eyes bore into me but I can barely look at him. 'What's the matter, Sophie?' He lifts my chin up. 'You've been crying.'

'We need to sort our lives out.'

'Right this minute?' he asks. 'We're going to Katerini soon.'

'I'm not going.'

He kneels on the step below me. 'You're joking, right?'

'I know it's New Year's Eve but I feel sad.'

He takes my face in his hands. 'Actually it's New Year's Day and you should be happy.'

'Well, I'm not.'

His hands drop and he moves next to me, so we're

shoulder to shoulder on the stairs.

'We can talk if you want,' he says and sighs.

'You won't want to hear it.'

'Try me.'

'This year's going to be different, isn't it?'

'I promise.'

No,' I say, turning to look at him. 'Don't just promise. Let's do it – move out.'

He's silent for a moment. The coldness of the stone steps has seeped through my trousers. I twist the engagement ring on my finger.

'We're getting married in less than eighteen months time, Sophie. If we wait until after our wedding we can sort ourselves out a bit more,' he says slowly. He looks ahead and not at me. Our shadows are huge against the white wall, we look like shadow puppets. Our conversations are a performance, each of us saying the same things over and over again, night after night, month after month. It's getting tiring. The fact he can't look me in the eye tells me he's breaking last summer's promise. I stand up and head down the stairs.

'Where are you going?' he asks.

'To see the snow.'

He scrambles after me.

Outside the kitchen door white flakes glow in the light as they fall thickly to the ground. I hear voices from the other side of the restaurant and Yannis' unmistakable giggle. I go as far as the patio and switch on one of the heaters. Alekos joins me at the table. Through the arch in the wall, Christmas lights cast red and green light on to the nearly white field. All the children, Yannis included, are running about, trying to catch the snow. The music rumbles inside, the tempo faster than the falling snow. Darkness spreads away from *O Kipos*.

Alekos' teeth are chattering. I know what Despina will say if she catches us sitting outside, in the snow, with no coats on.

'How much more sorted do we need to be?' I ask.

'What?' Alekos frowns.

'We've got enough money. We've got jobs. We work for your parents for God's sake. You said if we left it until after we're married…'

'There's no rush.'

'Aleko, you're thirty this year. I'm twenty-nine. How can you possibly think there's no urgency? I was living away from home when I was eighteen. I miss that freedom.'

'So do I. I've spent two summers away from here too.'

'Then what's stopping us?'

He doesn't answer. The snow's falling thickly now, settling on the table between us. The heater glows with warmth and the snowflakes landing on it melt instantly. Alekos moves to the edge of the bench to be as close to the heat as possible. I watch him. His year-long tan looks washed out.

'It's your mother. I know she wants you to stay here,' I say. 'But you can't do what she wants all your life.'

'You don't understand. It's just the way family life is here.'

'What about having a life of our own, Aleko? Time together, a place where we don't have to abide by your mother's rules. That's what I want. That's what we talked about. I thought we both wanted the same thing.'

'We do.'

'Really?'

'We both want to start a family.'

'Not like this I don't.'

He looks at me, open mouthed, as if I'd just punched him in the gut.

I shrug. 'Promises don't mean anything unless you act on them.'

'I've been trying.'

'For over three years?'

'That's not fair,' he says.

I know it isn't but I need to take my frustration out on someone and who else do I have to talk to. I reach across the patio table and hold his hand. 'I'm sorry. I've just been thinking about how good it would be to start again. Maybe go back to Cephalonia. Just have a break. Spend some time together. Wouldn't it be great to have our own restaurant?'

'You were the one who happily moved over here. The only promise I made to you in the beginning was wanting to be with you. And I still do.' He stands up. He's shivering. 'I'm going inside. Nikos and Demetrius are waiting to go to Katerini.'

I watch him trudge back across the patio. He leaves footprints in the snow. Yannis' laughter rings in my ears, as he screeches in delight with the other children. On the few occasions it snowed when I was a child, Mum would wrap us both up in hats, scarves and gloves and we'd go out into the back garden and make the biggest snowman we could. We'd raid the vegetable box for a carrot for the nose and we even had coal for the snowman's eyes because of the open fire in the living room. Mum used to be as excited as I was the moment the first flake of snow fell, until the cursing began because the car wouldn't start and the key snapped in the lock.

'Sophie! You're going to make yourself ill!' Despina calls across from the corner of the restaurant. Despite the Christmas lights and glow coming from the kitchen, I can barely see her she's wrapped up that much. She has my coat folded neatly in her arms. 'Come inside before you freeze to death!'

Chapter Six

It takes another eight months until we manage to both get a long weekend off from the restaurant but we go to Santorini instead of Cephalonia. The view from our bedroom at *O Kipos* towards Mount Olympus is difficult to beat but this spot on Santorini is something else. From our apartment's balcony I can see across the blue sea of the caldera to Oia and its cluster of whitewashed buildings clinging to the end of the island. Blue ocean stretches to Crete and then North Africa beyond. It's so peaceful. No voices, no music, nothing to disturb the early morning.

I go back into our holiday apartment. We have a kitchenette and seating area with white flowers in a vase on the table. Beyond, through an arch is a four-poster bed shrouded in white chiffon. Alekos is still asleep. I perch on the edge of the bed and stroke the back of his neck. 'Breakfast is on the table outside,' I say. He moans and buries his head further into the pillow.

I'm up early because I want to walk the caldera path to Oia and it takes two hours and is best not to be attempted in the midday sun.

'There's omelette, bread, fruit, coffee and *bougatsa*, your favourite.'

He rolls over. 'We could just hire a car and drive,' he says.

'Where's the fun in that? It's a gorgeous morning. Come on, Aleko, think about lunch at the fish restaurant.'

'Five more minutes and I'll get up.'

Even at eight in the morning I can feel the sun beating down on my shoulders. We leave the hotel apartment, walk past the inviting infinity pool and set off along the stony path on the rim of the caldera. Far below, a ferry sails across the deep blue water towards the port at Thira. Oia is a long way off, nearly halfway round the island from our hotel. I trudge along the path feeling only the faintest hint of a breeze.

'You've got to admit, Aleko, that this is spectacular?'

'I agree,' he says, catching my hand in his. 'I just resent getting up early when we're on holiday.'

'It'll be worth it.' I swing our arms as we walk. 'I feel so free here, spending time outside, instead of being holed up in the restaurant everyday. We work too much.'

'But working hard is paying for this holiday and our wedding.'

The path follows an incline and we puff our way up as what breeze there was disappears. We round a corner and reach the summit and suddenly the other side of the island is revealed. The island slopes down to a flat expanse of patchworked fields and whitewashed buildings ending at the southern side of the island with beaches and the sea. It's a dramatic contrast to turn back to the caldera on our left and the steep drop to the sea crashing against the black rocks below. We start down the winding path that still clings to the edge of the caldera. Basking lizards scuttle from their sunbathing spots on rocks as we walk past.

'Do you remember the evening at the beach on Cephalonia when we cooked the octopus we'd caught on the fire,' Alekos says.

'Do I remember? Are you crazy? Of course I do. It was the best night ever.'

'I knew that night I wanted to spend my life with you.'

'Me too.' These last three days on Santorini have been what we both desperately needed for months now, time away from *O Kipos*, work and Despina. 'I'm not looking forward to leaving tomorrow.'

With Alekos leading we walk on and concentrate on our footing when the path gets steep and rocky. The soil changes from a rusty red colour to ash white and charcoal black and clings to our trainers. We've been walking for over an hour and have lost sight of Oia but I can see across to where I think our hotel is. The ferry we'd seen crossing the caldera earlier is in the port. The whitewashed buildings of Thira are stacked one on top of each other spreading from the sea to the top of the cliffs. We walk to the top of the next hill and reach a whitewashed church with a domed roof and blue bell tower. We sit on a low wall next to the church and share a bottle of water.

'I'm not looking forward to going home tomorrow either,' Alekos says.

'You're not?' I look across the sparkling water to the rim of the volcano in the centre of the caldera.

He shakes his head. 'I've enjoyed seeing you happy these last few days and I know that's going to change as soon as we get home.'

'Don't make this all about me. It's not just me who's unhappy at home. These last couple of days I've seen a glimpse of how you were on Cephalonia. You need to get back the optimism you had, that we both had. Were you writing music last night when I was getting ready to go out?'

'It was nothing, just some ideas I had.'

'Going home tomorrow is going to affect both of us.' I take the suntan lotion out of my bag and spray it on my arms and shoulders and rub it in. It's so quiet here with just the sound of insects and the gentle rush of the waves breaking against the rocks below. 'I'm fed up pretending to your Mum and Dad that everything's okay. Aren't you?'

'I'm fed up of trying to keep the peace between you and my mother.'

I bite my tongue. I wish he wouldn't try and keep the peace. He's like a faulty firework. I can see the frustration building and building inside him but he never explodes. If only he would. 'Come on let's get to Oia before it gets any hotter.'

The path leading into Oia overlooks pretty whitewashed houses, terraces and swimming pools cut into the edge of the caldera. Houses built on top of houses – a stunning expanse of brilliant white, with touches of deep blue, and pots filled with vivid pink and red flowers. The narrow lanes are packed with tourists and lined with cafés, restaurants and souvenir shops.

'We should get something from here for Mama's birthday,' Alekos says, as we stop in front of a shop selling Santorini wine. I shrug. 'On the way back,' he says.

We head away from the packed lanes, past the castle on the furthest tip of the island and make our way down the steps to the harbour. Clinging to the rocks is a derelict house with a for sale sign stuck on its broken door. I look at Alekos but he's striding ahead to the harbour. Fishing boats bob in the clearest and most stunning turquoise water I've ever seen. The fish restaurant we go to is run by an old school friend of Takis' who greets us with a hug and kiss on both cheeks before returning to the red hot coals he's grilling fish over. We choose a table on the wooden jetty overlooking the harbour and order. From where we're sitting I can see shoals of tiny fish darting through the water.

The waitress brings us a cold beer each quickly followed by grilled octopus and sardines, fried mussels with lemon, aubergine salad and the local dish of fried Santorini tomatoes.

I take a sip of my cold beer and stick my fork into a fried mussel. 'Did you see that house for sale on the hillside?'

'What the one with broken windows and no roof?'

I nod. 'Just think what could be done with it.'

'With a fortune spent on it maybe.'

'I'm only making conversation; I'm not suggesting we actually buy it.' I savour the smokiness of the aubergine salad and take a bite-sized piece of grilled octopus. 'Anyway, it's too small. There's nowhere for a restaurant plus we'd need rooms for artists to stay and plenty of space outside.'

'We've been talking about buying a one- or two-bedroom apartment near to *O Kipos*... The wedding's costing too much for us to be investing in any more than that.'

'Then we should elope. Get married in Vegas, just the two of us. I've never wanted a big white wedding with four hundred Greeks gawping at us, half of whom even you won't know the names of.'

Alekos puts his fork down on his plate and wipes his mouth with a napkin. 'I thought you were happy with the wedding plans.'

'I want our wedding to be simple and intimate. I gave into having our wedding in May instead of December and I said yes to getting married in church because I know that means a lot to you, but your mother is getting carried away with the reception afterwards. Just think what we could do with the money we'd save if we kept the wedding small.'

'You know Mama and Baba want to pay for the reception.'

'And if they pay it means we have the kind of wedding your mother wants.'

He takes his wallet from the back pocket of his shorts and puts twenty-five Euros on the table. 'Let's go, shall we?'

We walk in the opposite direction to Oia and the harbour, along the wooden jetty until we reach a dusty path curving around the base of the rock with the castle perched on top. The water looks clear and cool, an inviting turquoise merging into dark blue where it gets deeper.

'I think we should have the church wedding with a small gathering of close family and friends at *O Kipos* afterwards,' I say. 'And we should move out before our wedding.'

Alekos shoves his hands in his pockets and strides away from me around a rocky outcrop.

'Why are you all so scared of upsetting her?' I call after him.

He turns back to me. 'And why are you so intent on

fighting her all the time?'

'Because I hate the way she uses you and that upsets me. Someone needs to stand up to her.'

'That's enough. We're staying at *O Kipos* until after our wedding. It'll break Mama's heart if we leave now.'

'What about breaking my heart?'

'Sophie I'm not making this decision to hurt you, I'm just doing what I feel is best for all of us.'

The sun's heat is oppressive, burning my shoulders. 'How are we going to make a marriage work if we both want such different things?' I try and twist my engagement ring but my finger is too hot and swollen. I yank at it until it comes off. I hold it out in front of me and the diamond sparkles in the sunlight. Alekos is open mouthed; perhaps he thinks I'm going to chuck it into the sea. I grab his hand and push the ring into his palm and close his fingers around it. 'I can't do this anymore, Aleko. So maybe we should put our wedding plans on hold until we both figure out what we really want.'

Chapter Seven

I'm at my spot by the fence. The whole of Alekos' family and their friends are in the restaurant garden behind me, talking, laughing, shouting, drinking, dancing and celebrating Despina's 60th birthday. I've just watched the sun disappear behind the dark outline of Mount Olympus. I can see the moon, pale and uneven like a chunk of feta. Mum used to tell me it was made of cheese when I was little. And I believed her.

'Sophie, *ti kanis*?' Alekos' voice carries across the empty field. I turn and see his tall silhouette in the arched entrance of the garden bar.

'Watching the sunset,' I call back.

He raises his hands. 'We've got guests.'

'I'll be there in a minute.'

He shrugs his broad shoulders and disappears through the arch. I turn my back on the mountain of the Gods, and head towards the flickering light. I walk through the arch and I'm lost in a world of music and laughter, of patchwork stone and vibrant reds. Grapes shade the terrace on the other side of the arch. In daylight their deep purple is misted with the breath of dawn. Takis' infamous homebrewed *chipero* is made from the skins, boiled and distilled until a clear liquid remains, ready to be flavoured and bottled. I catch sight of him, with a glass in his hand, by the glowing coals of the *psistaria*. A whole lamb turns on a motorised spit. Liquid fat drips from the flesh and sizzles on the embers in tiny flames. After seven hours of slow cooking the lamb overpowers the smell of wood smoke. I watched Takis and Despina prepare the lamb in the morning and decided I'd be better off making the salads after witnessing Despina ram a skewer in one end of the lamb and out again through its mouth.

'Sophia, Sophia, Sophia, beautiful Sophia,' Takis says. He pours me a shot of *chipero* and taps his glass against mine, '*Yamas*!' He pokes the embers and the fat spits in retaliation. He turns to me. A frown creases his leathery forehead. 'Did Alekos find you?'

I nod and take a sip of *chipero*. Aniseed ignites my taste buds. 'Does he want help with the food?'

'I think Despina was asking after you.' Takis gestures towards the field. 'You seem very thoughtful tonight. Is everything okay?'

I shrug. 'I just wanted a bit of time to myself.'

He takes hold of my hand and motions at the pale mark on my finger. 'Losing the ring. Is that what really happened?'

I pull my hand away from his. 'Despina will need me in the kitchen.' I down the rest of my *chipero*, put the glass on the brick shelf next to the spit and walk towards the restaurant.

The music quickens. A cry goes up from the terrace as a local *Pontiako* song fills the air. Alekos is in the middle of the group, showing Yannis the steps to the dance. I creep between them and the patio table – filled with bowls of Greek salad, *tzatziki* and mincemeat-stuffed cabbage leaves – to the restaurant. I poke my head round the kitchen door. Despina, sparkling in a jewelled pink top over black trousers, pulls a dish of *kokoretsi* from the oven. The stomach-churning smell of liver-filled intestines sticks in my throat. I wrinkle my nose at the delicacy.

'Ah, Sophie, there you are!' Despina's smile is fuchsia pink, her face immaculately made up. She places the *kokoretsi* on the side to be carved and hands me two bowls of mussels steaming in tomato and feta. 'I find you, Alekos disappears.'

'He's teaching Yannis to dance.'

Her pink lips tense. 'There's food to take out, wine to open.' She unsheathes a gleaming knife. It slices through the *kokoretsi* effortlessly. 'The lamb?'

I hover in the doorway with the bowls. 'Ready.'

She nods and waves me away. 'Go, go. Tell Alekos, wine!'

Emerging from the warmth of the kitchen I feel the refreshing lick of cooler air. I'm longing for the hot summer nights to give way to autumn. There seems such finality when the leaves begin to curl and crisp, their vivid green fading to the colour of worn leather. The last holidaymakers of the season will clutch at the waning sunshine, spending every waking moment prostrate on a beach before the warm sea is cooled by rain.

The terrace is filled with family and friends dancing in a circle. I can just make out Yiannis' curly hair amongst a forest of tanned legs. I place the bowls of mussels next to the salads and pop an olive in my mouth. Its saltiness makes my cheeks clench.

Fingers pinch my waist. 'I saw that,' Alekos says.

I spit the olive stone on to the dusty soil. 'I'm starving.'

'You've been drinking too much.'

'What's that got to do with me being hungry?' I look at him. His cream T-shirt glows against his deep tan. His fingers play with the experimental beard he's growing. 'You should shave.'

'You don't like it?'

'Do you?'

He shrugs. 'Mama doesn't like it.'

'Then keep it.'

He breathes in sharply. 'I was showing Yannis a *Pontiako* dance.'

'I saw.'

'You should have joined us.'

'I'm not feeling too sociable.'

'I noticed.'

'Anyway, your mother wants our help,' I say and begin to walk away. 'You teaching Yannis to dance is, in your mother's opinion, you disappearing.'

I walk back into the heat of the kitchen, Alekos follows. Bread is piled in a wicker basket and *kokoretsi* layered on a large plate. Despina reapplies lipstick, squinting at her reflection in a silver platter that leans against the wall.

'Aleko, I need the wine open,' she says without even looking at him. She smoothes down her already straight hair and switches the oven off.

'I forgot to say earlier, we're fully booked tomorrow night,' Alekos says. He starts to open the first bottle on the worktop.

Despina smacks her lips together and turns to me with a smile. 'We must make *baklava* in the morning, Sophie.'

I nod, pick up the bread and a tray of hot feta in earthenware pots and retreat outside.

Takis keeps topping up my glass with *chipero*. And I've mixed drinks: the aniseed kick of *chipero* with sweet red wine. Sixteen of us squeeze round two tables joined together on the patio. Spoons dip in and out of salads; forks stab roasted red peppers and juicy chunks of pork *suvlaki*. The lamb is carried over from the coals, de-skewered and placed on a massive plate in front of Despina to be carved. The meat falls off the bone in great chunks and is passed along the table. Its rich meaty scent disperses into the night air.

Our voices are carried into the starless sky. Sandwiched between Spiros and little Yannis I'm hot, my belly full of too much drink and not enough food. Despina, at the head of the table, stands and raises her glass. We all follow. Yannis grabs hold of my hand and Lena's and we pull him to his feet. His sticky fingers curl into my palm.

'I want to thank all of you for a wonderful day,' Despina says, looking around the table at each of us. Yannis fidgets next to me. 'It's lovely to see all my friends and family together, celebrating with me. *Yamas*!' Everyone leans in and clinks glasses. 'To health, happiness and more grandchildren!'

Alekos leans across the table and catches my eye. He has a sleepy smile plastered across his face. Wine sloshes in our glasses when we knock them together. '*Yamas*,' Alekos says to me.

In the distance the sky growls. Despina gazes up to where clouds blanket the stars. 'The sound of the end of summer,' she says. The flames from the torches make the jewels on her top sparkle, and she smiles as she looks over at Takis quietly sipping his wine. 'Everyone eat, eat!'

Thunder rumbles closer and then cold droplets of rain splash into drinks and the remains of food. The effect is immediate; a stampede towards the warmth of the restaurant, everyone under orders from Despina to grab a bowl of food on their way.

I head in the opposite direction and duck beneath the umbrella of grapes. I don't want to go into the heat and brightness inside; I don't want to be bullied into being sociable by Alekos. Outside, rain pummels the ground like a fist against a punch bag. The restaurant is an oasis, a pinprick of light within a shroud of black. Only occasional headlights break the darkness, flashing by on the road that passes in front.

I lean on the rough stone of the arched wall and peer into the night. Fat drops of rain splash on to my hands but the rest of me stays dry beneath the vine. After each rumble of thunder I count... one, two, three, four, five, six, seven... and wide-eyed I watch the darkness flicker to life. Jagged silver light splits the horizon open, a strobe-like flash backlighting the outline of Olympus.

I don't hear Alekos shout for me. Mesmerised by the electric storm I'm unaware anything has happened until Alekos grasps my shoulders.

'What are you doing out here?' His voice is strained. 'I've been calling you.' His black hair glistens with water; droplets cling to dark eyelashes. The rain has soaked his T-shirt and splattered his jeans.

'Sorry, I didn't hear you,' I say. I wipe rain off the bridge of his nose. 'It's too stuffy inside... the storm's incredible. What's up?'

'You've got a phone call from England,' he says.

'From who?'

'I'm not sure but it's about your mother.'

I turn my back on the Gods of Olympus for the second time that day and follow Alekos inside. A rush of hot air, cigarette smoke and laughter greets us. I catch sight of my hair in the glass panel of the door: it looks like dark-red fronds of seaweed plastered to my neck. I leave a trail of water across the marbled floor. The middle dining tables are laid out with the left over food and music blasts from the speakers on the wall. Everyone claps Christos and Takis who are energetically dancing.

I retreat into the darkness of the kitchen. 'Hello?'

'Hello, is that Sophie Keech?' It's a woman's voice.

'Yes.'

'My name's Lorraine, I'm a staff nurse at Norwich University Hospital. We've got your Mum here.'

'In hospital?'

'I'm afraid so,' she pauses. 'Is there someone with you, Sophie?'

'Yes.' I look over at Alekos in the doorway. He mouths something. I wave him away and look at the floor.

'I'm afraid your Mum was admitted after a motorbike accident earlier today. She's been taken good care of and is now in a stable condition but she has suffered serious injuries.'

'She doesn't have a motorbike.'

A flash of lightning lights the kitchen with an electric blue glow.

The woman pauses. 'It was her partner's bike.'

The plum-coloured varnish on my toenails is flaking off.

I didn't know Mum had a new boyfriend. 'But she's okay? She's going to be okay?'

'She's stable, but she's got a broken leg, is suffering with bruised ribs, concussion and has had stitches to a cut on her right arm.'

Thunder rumbles overhead.

There's a pause in the music. Despina shouts something to Takis.

'Does your Mum live alone?' the nurse asks.

'Yes.' Music starts up again, faster and louder.

'Any relatives or friends close by?'

'Only her parents in Sheffield, but they don't get on. I wouldn't know about any friends. She's moved since I lived with her.'

'She'll be in hospital for a few days but she's going to need looking after once she's discharged. Will you be able to make arrangements?'

'Yes. Yes of course.'

I scribble the hospital's phone number and Mum's ward on a notebook tucked next to the menus. I say goodbye and put the phone down. The rhythmic drum of rain on the kitchen windows is nearly drowned by the noise from the restaurant. Alekos walks over.

'I have to go to England,' I say, gazing at the piece of paper in my hands.

'Why?'

'Mum's been in an accident.'

He opens his mouth to say something and then closes it again. He pulls me close and wraps his arms around me. He smells of wood smoke. 'Is she okay?'

'I think so... I don't know.'

'Come upstairs.'

His hand is hot in mine. We climb the stairs and head for our bedroom. Alekos switches on the bedside lamp and I sit on the wicker chair next to the balcony window. He faces me with his arms folded, legs tense, rooted to the spot.

'Sit down, for God's sake,' I say. He does, on the white sheet folded on our bed. Our whole room is white walls and white furnishings. My hair is the most colourful thing in the room. Despina likes everything fresh and clean.

'You're seriously going to go?' Alekos asks.

'The nurse said she needs looking after.'

Perched on the end of our bed he leans towards me. 'You haven't seen her in over four years.'

'I know.'

'Will she even want you there?' Our knees almost touch.

'She doesn't have much choice, Aleko.' I don't care. It's been three weeks since we returned home from Santorini and already I want to escape again even if it means facing Mum. Our room lights up with another flash of lightning. My hand finds his. 'Come with me, Aleko.'

His silence is all too familiar and the way his eyes shift away from mine so predictable. I know the answer before he says a word.

'You know I can't,' he says. 'Mama will need me here.'

'And I don't need you? Have you forgotten everything I said on Santorini?' I pull away from him and slump back into the wicker chair and hug my knees to my chest. My head is blurred with wine and ouzo. Behind the rhythmic drum of rain on the window, the music from the party continues in the restaurant below. Alekos wipes sweat from his forehead and rolls his t-shirt sleeves to his shoulders revealing tense muscles. He still looks like the man I first met but he behaves like an obedient mummy's boy. 'I'm sorry Aleko, it's just I could do with your support. I haven't seen her in a long time. We've had our troubles but she's the only family I've got.'

'I'm your family, Sophie.'

'Then get on the plane with me tomorrow.'

His fingers reach for his cross and he pulls it from side to side on its chain.

'Do you realise how difficult it was to get Mama to allow us four days off to go to Santorini? You know I would go with you if I could. But she won't be able to cope with us both gone.'

'For fuck's sake, Aleko, stand up to her for once. You

haven't even been able to tell your parents the real reason why I'm not wearing my engagement ring. Stop making excuses for everything.'

He jumps up. 'They're not excuses. I respect my mother…'

'Unlike me? Is that what you were going to say? I'd respect both our mothers if I knew mine respected me to begin with, or if yours understood that you… that we need some space. Can you not make a decision without having to think "but what will Mama say"?' I scramble to my feet, turn my back on him and watch the rain splatter the window and streak down the glass. 'More time away from here would do us good. Time together.'

'I thought you were going to England to help your Mum, not another holiday for us?'

I turn and face him. 'You're not listening. I'm talking about going for a couple of weeks to help out.'

'I'm sorry.' He takes my hands in his and rests his forehead against mine. He smells of aniseed and wood smoke. His cross lies against his skin in the dip of his throat. His familiarity is reassuring. I knew the moment I met him that he was everything I'd ever wanted, yet his predictability and unwillingness to move on is wearing me down. I don't want to lose him. I don't want the situation here to force us apart. I want to kiss him. I want him to hold me close and tell me he'll be there for me.

'I'm scared, Aleko.' I squeeze his hands.

'Don't be. Your Mum's going to be all right.'

'I'm not talking about Mum.' He pulls far enough away from me so I can see his frown. 'I'm scared about what's happening to us.'

'There's nothing to be scared about.' A smile forms on his lips and I know he doesn't understand me.

Footsteps falter outside our bedroom and then someone knocks. The door scrapes open. Alekos releases my hands and I look over his shoulder and see Despina standing in the doorway, her pink-jewelled top glinting in the light from the hallway. Her cheeks are flushed and match her lipstick. She holds two glasses of wine up. 'Aleko, Sophie! *Taga, taga*! I'm about to cut my cake. Everyone was asking after you.' She bustles into the room. 'I said you were probably making babies.'

I can't believe she's just said that. Actually, I take that back. I can believe it, that's the trouble. This is everything I'm trying so hard to fight against. She glances in the dressing table mirror before handing us the glasses of wine. Her dyed blonde hair is sprayed so rigidly that a hair wouldn't move out of place even if she went and stood in the rain.

'Takis said to cut the cake without you. I said, no, I want all my family with me.' Her eyes rest on me. 'Sophie, what's wrong?'

'Mama, not now,' Alekos says. 'Sophie had a phone call from England...'

'Aleko, leave it.'

He glances at me then back to Despina. 'We'll only be a minute.'

'You've been crying,' she says, ignoring Alekos and peering at me.

'I'm fine.'

She clicks her tongue and shakes her head. 'Sophie, I know you're not...'

'I'm fine, really,' I say. Alekos tenses next to me. Let him. It's pathetic. Why can't he just face up to her and say 'get the hell out of our room.' I could scream. Despina opens her mouth to speak again and then closes it. With a nod she backs out of the room and shuts the door with a click. I put the wine glass down on the dressing table. There's a lengthy pause before her footsteps clip clop down the hall.

'This is exactly what I'm talking about. No space!' I fling my hands into the air. 'Your Mum walks in here, thinking we're having sex and doesn't see anything wrong in that.'

'It's only because...'

'I know, she wants more grandchildren. There might as well be no walls in this place.'

'I can't change my family,' he says.

'I'm not asking you to.'

Still grasping the glass of wine, he steps towards me. 'It's going to be okay. I promise.'

'Go join the party. I need to find a flight for tomorrow.'

'I'll talk to her. About coming with you.' He kisses my forehead before retreating from the room.

All I can see through the window are rain clouds smothering the moon and stars like a blanket. Everything I want from life feels as if it's escaping through my fingers. I want to look to the future but once I get on that plane tomorrow, I'll have to revisit my past.

Chapter Eight

It's no fun being hungover at 35,000 feet in the air. I'm sure the lady next to me can smell the alcohol on my breath; she probably thinks I'm a typical drunken English-woman. I sense her disgust when we hit turbulence and I reach for the sick bag. I know she's surprised when she asks if I'm okay and I reply in Greek: 'I've been better, thank you.'

'You speak Greek very well,' she says in perfect English.

I breathe deeply for a moment before tucking the sick bag back in the pocket next to the in-flight magazine. 'I've lived in Greece for four years,' I say.

It's difficult to tell her age. Her hair is black and short and her cheeks round. A smart trouser suit disguises her plumpness. She smells expensive. A rich fragrance lingers on her skin. I'm cheap in comparison, my cardigan stale with last night's smoke. I rub my eyes and gaze out of the window.

'It was a late night for you?' the woman asks.

'A birthday party. Too much homemade *chipero*. I was meant to be working not travelling today.' My hair sticks to my neck. I lean against the headrest and close my eyes. If I'd known last night that I'd be flying within twenty-four hours, I'd have eaten more and drunk less. Someone behind me sneezes. I shuffle in my seat, unable to get comfortable.

'Are you staying long in England?'

It takes a moment to work out that the Greek lady is talking to me again. I open my eyes. 'For a week or two.' I lean forward and twist my tangled hair into a ponytail. 'I have a lot to sort out.' The muscles in my thighs are tense; squashed in the window seat I feel trapped. I fiddle with the air conditioning above until a trickle of air filters out. Far below, through the oval window, is an endless patchwork of fields and forest.

'My name's Rula,' she says.

'Sophie.'

'Ah, a Greek name.' She has smiling brown eyes. 'Your parents chose a good, strong name.'

'Luckily my Mum decided to choose the sensible name on her list.'

'There were other names?'

'Blossom... Cher...'

Rula raises a plucked eyebrow. 'The singer Cher?'

'Oh yeah, Mum was a huge fan.'

'But your father liked Sophie?'

'I've never met my father.'

'I'm sorry.' She looks at me differently now, a soft, motherly look. Her black eyebrows arch and fine lines crease between them. Her hand reaches for the butterfly brooch studded with emerald and turquoise stones pinned on her blouse.

'Don't be,' I say. I stretch my legs. 'Who are you visiting?'

'My daughter and her family in Oxford.' Her accent is faint and I realise how good it is to have a conversation in English with someone besides Alekos. I imagine she'd make a good mother-in-law. She leans towards me. 'Are you visiting your mother?'

I nod. 'I haven't seen her since I moved to Greece.'

'She must miss you.'

I shrug. 'I've missed her.'

Rula has perfectly manicured nails. She plays with her diamond wedding ring. I tuck my ring-less hand beneath my cardigan.

'Ah finally, dinner,' Rula says.

A smiling airhostess passes trays to us. 'Tea? *Kafe?*' she asks with a thick Greek accent.

'*Kafe*,' I say. A strong cup of coffee is just what I need. My brain pounds against my skull. The dryness of the cabin makes my eyes ache. Even after four years immersed in Greek life I haven't mastered the art of sophistication. Rula looks as if she was born sophisticated: her hair neatly sculpted, red lipstick lip-lined into place. Mum always called me her redheaded wild child. I had no hope.

'You have a husband in Greece?'

'Boyfriend,' I say.

'He didn't want to come with you?'

'His mother wouldn't let him.'

'Oh.'

I release the steam from the foil-lidded tray and poke my plastic fork into what looks like chicken in a cream sauce with over-cooked potatoes and green beans.

Rula places her hand on my arm. 'I'm sure your boyfriend will be longing for you to come home.'

'He'll be too busy to miss me.'

I enjoy Rula's company, her ability to listen and the comforting familiarity of her accent during our no-man's land conversation across Europe.

Standing in the middle of Heathrow arrivals, we're strangers again. Rula's happiness to be here only magnifies my uncertainty. After collecting her luggage she kisses me on both cheeks.

'I hope things work out for you,' she says.

I lean on my empty luggage trolley and watch her retreat, eager to find her daughter and family. Four years ago I couldn't wait to leave, to get on a plane and fly to the excitement of a new life in Greece. Now I feel lost in a country I used to call home.

I find my mobile at the bottom of my bag and phone Alekos. It rings and rings. Suitcases pass by in front of me. I glance at my watch. Just gone 7pm; 9pm in Greece. Alekos will be taking orders in the restaurant, serving drinks – even cooking if Despina lets him.

The ringing stops. There's fumbling, then Alekos' voice '*Ela.*'

'It's me.'

'Hey you,' he says. 'Good journey?'

'Long.'

'How are you feeling?'

'Better than first thing this morning.'

I hear him stifle a yawn.

'You okay?' I ask.

'Busy night.' He pauses. I can hear the clatter of knives and forks in the background and a muddle of loud voices.

'You know what's really strange,' I say, looking at the mass of strangers' faces surrounding me. 'This is where I phoned you the first time, as soon as I got off the plane from Cephalonia. I remember the minute I landed I couldn't stand being here.'

'And now?'

'I don't know, it's different.'

In the background Despina shouts and Alekos says, 'I've got to go. Phone me when you get to the hotel.'

'It'll be late. I've got to change coaches in London.'

'Phone me, whatever time.'

After retrieving my suitcase I find myself in an organised queue for the first time in four years. No elbows dig into my ribs, no weather-beaten old lady in widow's black viciously steps on my toes. Instead, I wait patiently for my coach ticket amongst an impatient queue. I bite my tongue when the couple in front give the lad serving them grief over the booking fee. After weeks had turned into months and months into years I've forgotten what annoyed me about this country to begin with.

It's cold on the coach and it doesn't help that I'm tired. I'm used to buses that resemble airless coffins with windows. Public transport that cooks you alive. No fifty-seated twelve-standing rule. In Greece everyone's squashed together like paperbacks on a shelf. And it's wonderfully noisy. School kids shout to the driver to let their friends on, and when you think there's really no more room, another kid is squeezed in, accompanied by the tut tut of old ladies' tongues.

The man next to me snores. His stomach spills over his trousers. One leg sticks out into the aisle, the other edges into my space. His head droops to one side, mouth open, worryingly close to my shoulder. He wakes himself up with a snort. I want to be home, snuggled up in bed with Alekos, not making patterns with my breath on the smeared glass of a coach window.

An orange glow stains the horizon. The motorway narrows and the glow becomes streetlights, then a flashing billboard plugging the latest album from a band I've never heard of. I realise we're driving on the wrong side of the road, crawling towards the heart of London. I'm wide-eyed, like a child, my nose pressed against the cold glass taking it all in. I should try and sleep but I can't yet, not until darkness descends once more, after the hectic blur of the city.

It is late by the time I reach the hotel in Norwich. I feel sick from dozing with my head knocking against the coach window. Gone midnight and the city sleeps. Only lone travellers, taxi-drivers and drunks are awake. The taxi journey from the coach station to the Travelodge wakes me up, cobwebs of sleep dispersed by the driver's chatter.

In a daze I check-in, find my room, unpack my suitcase and clean my teeth. In the bathroom mirror I notice rings of mascara round my eyes. My tanned face looks diluted from the journey, my freckles pale. I don't bother removing what's left of my make-up.

I lie beneath the duvet, in the middle of the double bed, and wake Alekos up. His phone rings for a long time before he answers. 'It's gone three,' he says.

'I told you it'd be late.'

'I'm glad you rang.' I hear him shuffle about in bed. 'Is it raining there?'

'No, it's muggy, it's horrible.' I play with the edge of the duvet cover. 'I'm thousands of miles away and the first thing you ask about is the weather? How about what I'm wearing?'

'What are you wearing?'

'Shorts and a vest top… that's not exactly sexy, is it?'

'You make anything sexy.'

Silence. I yawn. 'I'm so tired, but I'm not sleepy. Does that make sense?'

'It's the middle of the night, Sophie, nothing makes sense.'

'It's been a long day.'

'I ended up cooking tonight.'

'How did it go?'

'No one complained.'

It's hot beneath the duvet. I throw it off but feel exposed with only Alekos' voice for company and not his arms around me.

'What time are you going to the hospital tomorrow?' he asks.

'About eleven.'

A gap in the curtains throws an orange glow from a streetlight on to the bare wall opposite.

'What did you eat tonight?'

'Nothing since the plane.'

In our bedroom Alekos can see dark sky through curtainless windows. At night moonlight paints the walls.

'You should have eaten something.'

'You sound like your mother,' I say, wriggling my head deeper into the pillow. 'Actually, you sound like mine.'

'Don't all mothers sound the same?'

'No, Leila Keech is one of a kind.'

'So what are you going to say when you see her tomorrow?'

'I don't know, I've got a feeling she's going to tell me to piss off back to Greece.'

'I'll be here if she does.'

'That's the trouble; you're there and not here with me. Tomorrow's when I need you.' My words are met with silence. Seconds tick away. My eyelids feel heavy. 'I'm worried she's not going to want me here at all.' I yawn again. My eyes water, the room's a blur. My head wants sleep.

'Then make her change her mind,' he says. 'You're good at changing your own mind.'

'About what?' I frown, then realise where he's steering the conversation. 'I'm not talking about that now.'

'When then?'

'Aleko, it's late, I've been travelling all day...'

'Now who's the one making excuses.'

It's easier to stop an unwanted conversation when there's no one looking you in the eye. All I have to do is press end call.

'Whatever happens I'm going to stay for a while. Can we say goodnight now?'

'Fine. Goodnight.'

'I miss you,' I say too late.

Chapter Nine

'Take the lift to the third floor,' the hospital receptionist says while holding a phone to her ear. 'Bear right, take the second corridor on your left, go right down to the end, turn left and the ward's the last one on the left. If you reach Paediatrics you've gone the wrong way.'

Gathered next to the lifts is a lady in a wheelchair with a nurse, and parents with a gaggle of kids. I take the stairs instead. I reach the third floor and the receptionist's directions become meaningless. At least the Paediatric ward is cheerful; the bare walls reserved for the rest of the hospital are splashed with colour from children's drawings and the curtains framing the ward windows are filled with smiling yellow bears.

I backtrack past nurses in pink uniforms and blue scrubs, bashing through doors. Serious faces rush past me and I nearly collide with a trolley. My nostrils tickle from the sting of antiseptic. My trainers join a chorus of other shoes in a rhythmic squeak down a corridor, shiny and identical to the last one. Grey polished floors and stark white walls are only punctuated with occasional swing doors.

There are no cheerful curtains framing the window of the end ward. I push open the heavy doors and they wheeze shut. Ten beds line the walls. The room's too bright because of the large window at the end. A woman in the first bed sits upright, coughing repeatedly like a machine gun. There are other visitors besides me, their laughter sounding false as I walk down the middle of the ward trying not to stare at each patient.

Lying in one of the beds is the woman who made rum punch for my fifteenth birthday and encouraged me and my friends to down it. Her skin looks fragile like tissue paper and just as pale. Fine lines form creases around her eyes and lips. The only time I've seen her without make-up was at breakfast, before I went to school. She looked good then, her skin flawless, almond-shaped eyes and plump lips refreshingly devoid of colour.

Time passes, I'm aware of that. I'm closer to my thirties than my teens, Mum in her late forties. She wasn't middle-aged like the other mums. Candy said she was more like an older sister — someone you could swap clothes and talk about boyfriends with. We've lost time together; seeing her like this makes me realise how close we came to losing time forever.

I sit in the plastic chair next to the bed and stare at her. Her breath is soft and the rise and fall of her chest faint beneath the sheet. Eyes flutter under closed lids. Her arms are flat against her sides with a thick bandage covering her right arm. One leg is plastered. Blue veins snake across her slender hands. Her hair is darker than when I last saw her, lying in tangles against her hospital-gowned shoulders.

Sunshine streams into the ward. Dust dances in the light. An elderly woman, attached to a drip, sits in a chair next to the window, book clasped in her hands, her mouth open spluttering snores. Footsteps patter across lino; I hear the scrape of a curtain being pulled back. I sit still, unsure what to do, unsure how Mum will react when she wakes.

I struggle out of my cardigan and let it fall over the back of the chair. The heat here is different to Greece, a humidity that leaves me sticky, rather than a dry heat smouldering on my skin. Tomorrow is the start of September and already I long for the cooler touch of autumn.

There's a bunch of lavender in a vase on the bedside cabinet. I reach up and read the note attached:

All our best wishes, Leila
With love,
Robert & Co at The Globe.

I don't know anything about her life or who Robert & Co are. I don't know how Mum will feel about me being here. What am I doing? I grab my bag from the floor.

'You must be Sophie.'

I turn to see a young nurse smiling at me. She's pretty with shiny black bobbed hair.

'We spoke on the phone,' she says. When she talks I can see a tongue piercing. She pulls one of the curtains closed. 'You got here quick.'

'I got a flight yesterday.'

'I've never been to Greece.'

'You should go, it's a beautiful place.' I get to my feet.

She squeezes behind me and pulls the other half of the curtains shut.

'I'm in the way,' I say. 'I should leave you to it.'

'There's really no need,' she says. She writes on the chart clasped in her hands. 'We moved your Mum here from intensive care yesterday afternoon. She gained consciousness during the night and has been sleeping peacefully ever since.'

'I'll come back later when she's awake.'

'Stay, she might need you.'

'I doubt it.'

Her eyes flicker across my face before she hooks the chart on the bed and tucks the pen in her pocket. I hang on to my bag and cardigan, and watch her check the dressing on Mum's arm. Her actions are business-like. This is what she does every day. She reminds me of Mum when I was ill, the no-nonsense approach. I could never wait to go back to school.

She places a hand on Mum's arm. 'Morning Leila.'

I'm cocooned within these curtains, like a moth desperate to free its wings. There's a gap; I can see a square patch of sunshine on the cream wall opposite, can hear the old lady's rhythmic snores. Maybe I can slip away unnoticed.

'Sophie?' Mum's voice, barely more than a whisper, startles me.

'Hi.'

Her bloodshot eyes stare across at me from sockets so dark they look bruised.

The nurse wedges another pillow behind Mum's head. She gestures towards me and says, 'She flew in yesterday to see you.'

'Really? The accident must have been worse than I thought.'

Maybe I deserve that. I bite my lip. The nurse glances at me, her smile now a little subdued. The three of us are silent within our curtained room: Mum half sitting, half lying in bed, forehead creased while the nurse busies herself with medicines. I stand in the corner like an awkward teenager.

Mum's frown deepens. 'Where's Darren?'

'Dr Mantel is on his way to talk to you and see how you're doing,' the nurse says. Her tone is unchanging, assured in her disregard for the question.

Mum glances towards me. 'Why are you here, Sophie?'

My mouth's dry. It's as if I've backtracked to my childhood and whatever I say will sound childish and false. I'm saved by heavy footsteps that pause just outside. Our curtain is whipped back and a tall man with rolled up shirtsleeves and a stethoscope walks in.

'Good morning, Ms Keech,' the doctor says, picking up her chart.

'It's Leila,' Mum replies.

'I'm Dr Mantel.' His face is subdued. His frown is so deep, his dark eyebrows nearly meet. He's the kind of man that Mum used to go for when I was in my teens: dark haired, clean-cut, thirty-something, with a plain gold band on his wedding ring finger. He holds the chart tight against his chest. 'How are you feeling?'

Mum shrugs. 'Sore.'

'I treated you when you and your partner were brought in after the accident,' he says brushing past me. The nurse stops what she's doing. I hug my bag and watch him place his hand on Mum's good arm. He leans towards her and almost whispers, 'I'm so sorry... there was nothing we could do...' The patch of sunshine on the wall through the curtains looks inviting. I could be sitting in a bar on Olympic Beach right now, sipping a frappe, wriggling my toes in the sand. Alekos would be there, his hand resting on my knee beneath the table, Demetrius and Katrina laughing with us...

I don't want to watch but it's as if I'm a passer-by at a road accident, unable to tear my eyes away. Well-rehearsed words slip from the doctor's mouth in a hushed tone. He's a pro, said it a hundred times: 'I'm sorry there was nothing we could do, he was pronounced dead on arrival.' I'm witness to the split second between the words leaving the doctor's lips and reaching Mum's consciousness. The words punch her in the gut. Her hands reach for her stomach, eyes and mouth wide open in a silent scream.

The doctor's hands on her arm are little comfort. I want to hug her. I can't stand to see her damp face screwed up with pain but I'm rigid in my corner unable to move. I hardly dare look at her. My knuckles are white from gripping my bag. I swallow back tears.

With wide damp eyes Mum looks up at Dr Mantel. 'I was wearing his crash helmet,' she says. Her face is flushed and puffy. 'Stupid bastard...'

The nurse hands her a tissue.

'He didn't suffer...' Dr Mantel says quietly. His words trail off leaving the curtained cubicle filled with Mum's short, sharp breaths.

'Does his wife know?'

I nearly drop my bag at her words. The nurse and doctor glance at each other. Mum scrunches the tissue in her hand.

Dr Mantel nods. 'We informed his family yesterday.'

'He's got two children,' Mum says between sobs.

'I'm so sorry for your loss,' Dr Mantel says. He removes his hand from her arm. 'I'll be back to see you later today.' He nods at me before disappearing through the curtains.

Mum lies still and stares unblinking at the ceiling.

The nurse leans towards her. 'Is there anything I can get you?'

Mum shakes her head. 'I'd just like to be left alone.'

I find my voice. 'Mum…'

'You too,' she says, turning away from me.

It's noisy outside Mum's cubicle. The daily grind continues. Not even the death of a patient's loved one causes a ripple in the routine. I walk down the ward, my trainers squeaking my retreat on the lino.

'Sophie!'

I turn and wait for the nurse to catch up with me.

'I'm sorry, I thought she might want a familiar face around,' she says, moving me out of the way as a trolley slams through the doors. 'People deal with grief in different ways.'

'I didn't know him,' I say. 'I don't know how long they were together…'

'I'll keep an eye on her, make sure she's okay.'

I nod and the smile she greeted me with returns.

'Let her get some sleep and come back and see her later.'

Chapter Ten

I leave the ward and go in search of the restaurant. It smells of chips and fried food. The choice of pizza, macaroni cheese or steak and kidney pie turns my stomach, even the well-stocked salad bar doesn't entice. I take my tray and pot of coffee and find a table by the window, away from the few people dotted around the large seating area. Like the ward, the restaurant's annoyingly bright. I can feel the sun on my back. The plastic blue tablecloth is sticky with heat. There are a few flowers stuck in a glass vase next to the salt and pepper and packets of English mustard and salad cream. I pour myself a cup of strong, black coffee. It takes two cups before I feel human again. The window's open but I sweat, despite wearing only a vest top and cropped trousers. Outside the sky is a dirty blue streaked with fine clouds. The sun is watery and makes the city below sparkle.

The only person I know in the whole of this city doesn't want to talk to me. Giving her time to sleep off her anger and sadness won't change her feelings. All I want is to hear words of comfort from Alekos. I pick up my mobile and almost call him. Instead I scroll through the names in my address book until I reach Candy's number. I press call without meaning to but let it ring.

'Hello?' The voice on the other end sounds out of breath.

'Candy, it's Sophie.'

'Sophie, I'm so sorry I haven't spoken to you for ages.'

'How are you?' I pour the last dregs of coffee into my cup and tip in two sugars.

'I'm good,' she says. 'Busy as always. It's great to hear from you. When was the last time I spoke to you? Just after Holly was born?'

'Something like that. I've been meaning to phone you for weeks.' I stir the steaming coffee and wish it was an ice-cold coke instead.

'Me too. How rubbish are we?' There's a pause. 'How are the wedding plans coming along?'

I glance at my bare ring finger. 'Okay, there's still another nine months to go.'

The restaurant is getting busier. My quiet spot by the window is sabotaged by a worryingly pregnant woman and her partner. He helps her sit down. She's got her hands on her belly and breathes deeply.

'How are Lee and the kids?' I ask.

'Fine. Jake's just started nursery and Holly's being uncharacteristically quiet at the moment.'

'Thanks for emailing the photos of them.'

'Aren't they adorable?'

'Gorgeous. I can't believe how grown up you are.' I take another sip of coffee. 'By the way I'm in the UK.'

'You're kidding me?'

'I'm in Norwich with Mum.'

'Is Alekos with you?'

'No.'

'No?'

'I'm visiting Mum on my own.'

'You left him alone in Greece?' She sucks in breath as if she's about to tell me off.

'He's got his family.'

'I wasn't thinking he'd be lonely.'

'Don't be so cynical,' I say with a smile. 'It's good to hear you haven't changed.'

'So you finally decided to visit your Mum. I'm really glad,

Sophie.'

'It's not quite like that…'

A baby's wail interrupts our conversation.

'As always, I spoke too soon,' Candy says. 'She's an angel really.'

'I'd better let you go.'

'How long are you staying for?'

'I'm not sure, for a while, I hope.'

'You absolutely have to come and visit us. I've missed you.' Baby Holly's wail turns into a scream. 'I've got two more weeks' maternity leave before I start back at work, come and stay for a couple of days.'

'It might be a bit difficult, Mum's actually in…'

'Jake! Leave your sister alone!' Candy cuts in. Jake starts to cry too. 'I'm so sorry. What were you saying?'

'About visiting.'

'You must. Sophie we've not seen each other in more than four years. Plus I want to see your tan.'

'It's not that impressive.'

'Tan or not, I'm not taking no for an answer. I've got to go.' Her tone is more urgent now. Holly is screaming the house down. 'But call me when you're free.'

'I will. It's so good to talk to you.'

'You too. Bye.'

I down the rest of my sweet coffee.

There was a time when I knew every detail about Candy's life and she knew everything about mine. It's always been easy talking to her, despite four years of only chatting over the phone or via email. The last time I saw her, the night before I left for Greece, she was a single career girl and now she's a mother-of-two.

I take a pen from my bag and draw on my coffee-splashed napkin: Candy, with a kid slung under one arm, a mobile clamped to her ear and a cigarette drooping from her mouth. My cartoon is the only way I can imagine her: a woman of conflicting realities and the least maternal person I've ever known.

They are distributing the next day's lunch menu round the ward by the time I go back. The curtains are open and Mum's propped up against pillows.

'What's the choice?' I sit on the plastic chair.

She doesn't look up from the piece of paper clutched in her hands. 'Cottage pie, baked cod or cheese and tomato quiche.' She lets the menu drop on to the sheet. 'Let's forget the small talk, shall we?'

'You want us to talk about it right now, do you? Dredge up the past and my father and all the shit that happened, right after you've had an accident?'

'You didn't care about leaving me four years ago, so why bother coming back now?'

I shrug. 'I am beginning to wonder.'

'Did you know about Darren?' Her voice is strained, yet there's a calm authority to her question.

I shake my head. 'No. I knew you were both in the accident, but... I had no idea what they were going to tell you.'

There's constant movement up and down the ward; the gentle thud, thud, thud of a trolley and dull ring of the ward phone. The drone of subdued talk between patients and relatives is mixed with the welcome antidote of nurses' lively chatter.

'So it took an accident for you to visit,' she says.

I could be ten years old again, getting told off for trailing my bike through the hallway. But I'm not her little girl any longer. I grab my bag and stand up. The chair scrapes along the floor.

'I came because it was the right thing to do and yes it might be too little, too late but I'm here,' I say. Mum is rigid and so pale. She raises her hand to stop me walking off and I falter. 'Are you going to say something to make me want to stay or are you going to start spouting lies again?'

She wipes her eyes with the back of her good hand. I tug a tissue from out of the box on her bedside cabinet and pass it to her.

'You should go now,' she says.

Back in my hotel room, I long for the familiarity of my bedroom in Greece. I have comfort food: a bucket of KFC and a bar of fruit and nut. I open the window but outside it's airless. The room reeks of fried chicken. It seemed like a good idea at the time but now I feel queasy. Emerging from the shadows of the hospital into sunshine, I didn't know what to do with myself. Passing KFC reminded me I hadn't eaten anything since a piece of cold toast earlier that morning. Biting into crunchy coated chicken took me back to Monday lunchtimes as a junior designer at an advertising company in Bristol. Our 'sticky finger' lunch we called it – not at all sophisticated but it helped us get through Monday mornings. It wasn't the same eating it on my own.

The heat from outside suffocates. I wash my hands in my very own steam room, the en-suite is like a sauna. I fill an empty bottle with water and drink half of it. Fried chicken lies heavy on my stomach. The can of coke I downed makes me feel bloated.

Leaving the window wide open, I close the curtains on the growling traffic bumper to bumper on the road below. No air comes in but I want to rid the room of the fried chicken smell clinging to my nostrils. It's a characterless room with plain cream walls, tidy blue and yellow bedspread, obligatory tea and coffee making facilities and TV all crammed in. The bed's comfy enough. I plump up the pillows and settle myself on top of the covers.

I think of Mum, crying herself to sleep. I've never seen her look so weak, as if somewhere inside her a light has been switched off. For the moment at least, until she's better, I can steer our relationship in the direction I want it to go in. Until now, it had always been the other way round, her moulding me into what she thought I wanted to be.

I was always known as Leila's daughter, never Sophie Keech in my own right. I grew up in her slender shadow, dwarfed by her larger than life personality. She made friends with complete strangers. She was as confident as I was awkward, as flirty and feminine as I was tomboyish. I wonder how much we've really changed. I snuggle into the pillows. Tomorrow, after sleeping away her emotions, she might find my unannounced presence a little easier.

The next thing I know my mobile's ringing. I open my eyes and blink a couple of times. I'm half-sitting, half-lying on the bed, propped up against pillows. My neck aches. My fingers find the answer button.

'Hello.'

'What took you so long?' Alekos asks.

'I must have fallen asleep.'

'What time is it there – nine?'

I glance at my watch. 'Near enough. I've been asleep for hours.'

'How's your Mum?'

'Out of intensive care…' I pause, not sure what else to say.

'But?'

'Her boyfriend died in the accident.'

'Shit, Sophie, why didn't you tell me?'

'I didn't know until today. I was there when they told her. I was expecting to see her pissed off, not upset. I had no idea.'

All I can hear is his breath in my ear. 'I should be there with you,' he eventually says.

I bite my tongue as I find the TV remote, switch the telly on and mute the sound. There is a re-run of *Only Fools and Horses* on.

'What did she make of you turning up?'

'She's not happy, as expected,' I say, flicking through MTV, Living and E4. I get glimpses of programmes I haven't seen for ages. 'Where are you anyway? It sounds quiet.'

'Outside, waiting for Demetrius to pick me up,' he says.

'We might go to Olympic Beach, get a pizza.'

'Your Mum can spare you, can she?'

'We both had tonight off, remember.'

'Sorry, I forgot. I'm a bit wound up, that's all.' I switch the TV off. The room goes dark. At night, its compactness makes it seem quite cosy.

'Baba wants help putting some lights up above the sign tomorrow. Like this place isn't lit up enough as it is. I swear you can see it from over a kilometre away. What are you going to do this evening?'

'Nothing much. Going to watch a bit of telly. Read my book. Sleep.'

'Are you seeing your Mum tomorrow?'

'In the morning.'

'I've been asked to play in the volleyball match at Paralia on Friday.'

'That's great.'

'It's one of the last matches of the season,' he says. He tries to stifle a yawn. 'Mama and Baba send kisses and hope your Mum gets better soon so you can come home.'

'I'll speak to you tomorrow,' I say.

'Okay. Love you.'

'Night.'

When the light on the mobile dies the darkness is only broken by car headlights flashing past. Alekos' words tumble around my head as I tuck my hand beneath a pillow and hug it.

Chapter Eleven

After more than twelve hours' sleep, I should feel refreshed, but I don't. I fumble across the room in my pajamas and pull the curtains open to a sunless day. The sky's the colour of a ripe bruise. The traffic's snarled up, heading in the opposite direction from last night. I close the curtains and switch on the bedroom light. Having a bathroom to myself is a luxury and I take a leisurely shower. In Greece the four of us share one bathroom plus the outside shower in summer and taking more than ten minutes results in Alekos or Takis impatiently knocking on the door. They moan about Despina the most.

Enclosed in the en-suite's plastic curtains, I let the warm water pummel my skin. I long to step from the shower on to grass thirsty for rain and feel morning sun on my bare shoulders. Instead, I step on to a bath mat and rub myself down with a thin towel that fails to soak up any water. I wipe the steamy mirror with a handful of toilet paper until I can see my reflection. There never used to be any arguments over the bathroom when I lived at home with Mum. She took long, scented baths in the evening, while I preferred a quick shower in the morning. The few times I brought a boyfriend home, Mum, forgetting we had company, wandered round the house with only a towel wrapped round her. She even held serious conversations with my boyfriends, undressed like that.

By the time I finish drying my hair, rain is drumming against the window. This is the England I remember:

temperamental and unpredictable.

At the hospital I take the stairs despite a lift pinging open as I pass. It feels better this morning, knowing what to expect, knowing Mum will be, at least physically, okay. I think I've gone into the wrong ward because there's a man sitting at what I thought was Mum's bed. I carry on walking when I recognise the woman in the bed next to the door. All I can see of Mum is her plastered leg sticking out and her good hand playing with the edge of the sheet. The man's broad shoulders hide the rest of her.

I stop at the end of her bed and say, 'Morning.'

Mum doesn't smile but her friend does. He has perfect white teeth and laughter lines.

'Sophie, this is Robert.'

Robert is already on his feet. He grips my hand firmly. 'It's so good to finally meet you.'

'Hi. I presume you're the Robert who sent the flowers.'

'Yes,' he replies. 'Lovely, aren't they?' The three of us gratefully turn our attention from each other to the lavender. We stare in silence for just a little too long.

Robert breaks our trance and gestures to the chair. 'Please, sit down.'

'No, no, I'm fine really,' I say, glancing between him and Mum. 'I've spent the last couple of days sitting on a plane or coach or in a hotel room. It makes a change to stand.'

The plastic chair remains empty between us. Mum makes no effort to talk, wanting certainly me, if not both of us, to leave her in peace.

'So how do you know each other?' I ask, deciding polite chit-chat is better than silence.

'We're friends, and neighbours of course,' Robert says, looking at Mum. She rubs the sheet between her fingers and seems to stare straight through him. 'I'm the pub landlord.'

'Are you just visiting today?'

'No, I'm staying in Norwich until the end of the week. My daughter gave birth to a son last month, my third grandchild, so I'm spending some time with them.'

He looks too young to be a grandfather. I suppose he must be well into his fifties but he wears it well, his middle age appearing as handsome ruggedness.

'My son's down for the day too, he's parking the car.' He glances at his watch. 'In fact he's been ages.'

'Who's running the pub?' Mum asks.

'Marcy today, then Ben's in charge.'

Mum's eyes widen.

'The responsibility will do him good, Leila. It's not for long and it's not like it's weekend business. Anyway, Marcy's around to keep an eye on him.' Robert pauses. 'Do you need me to let anyone know business-wise?'

Mum shakes her head. 'I was on holiday. Everything can wait. Maybe check my emails when you go back home.' She stops talking and rests her head against the pillow.

Robert turns to me. 'What do you do, Sophie?'

'I'm a chef.'

'Really.' He sounds interested and surprised. 'I've got a restaurant at *The Globe.*'

'Robert,' Mum's voice is weak. 'I feel sick.' Her ashen face whitens as the blood drains from her cheeks. She leans forward and closes her eyes. Robert looks anxiously along the ward.

'Here Mum, have a drink.' I pour water from the jug on the bedside cabinet into a plastic cup. Robert leaves us; his shoes squeak up the ward. Mum takes the cup from my hand. Her wrists look as if they will snap with the effort. She brings the cup slowly up to her lips and takes a sip. Soft lines cling to the corners of her eyes. Her eyelashes are long even without mascara. She takes another sip of water. Robert returns with the reassuring footsteps of a nurse.

'I hear you're not feeling too good,' the nurse says, slipping a container on Mum's lap. 'How does a sleep sound, Leila?'

Mum nods and lies down.

The nurse turns to us. 'I think she might be getting a little ahead of herself. Too much talking for one day.'

'We'll go get a coffee,' Robert says, 'and let her rest a while.'

It's impolite to say no, so without meaning to, I find myself sitting in the middle of the packed hospital restaurant with Robert. When I talk he pays full attention and when he talks he doesn't lose eye contact. It's an intensity that's quite appealing at first. I'm intrigued and a little puzzled by him and his relationship with Mum.

'How long are you here for?' Robert asks. He takes his coffee black, one sugar. He stirs it while looking at me.

I shrug. 'For as long as she needs me or allows me to stay. I want to help. Catch up. You know.'

'She's going to need looking after for quite a while and she's not going to like it.'

'You know her well then.'

'She's going to be driven mad not being able to do much.'

I have a cappuccino sprinkled with chocolate. I melt the chocolate top into the coffee. In Greece, when we go out in Katerini there's a bar that always serves cappuccinos with smiley faces etched into the froth. I always order one, even in the middle of August.

'Excuse me, I must just let Ben know where we are.' He reaches into his jacket pocket, pulls out his mobile and sends a text.

'You work together at the pub?'

'For the time being, yes. Ben's finding his feet.' He doesn't explain further, instead he asks, 'Where are you staying?'

'The Travelodge.'

'You realise it's going to be a little while before Leila is discharged.'

'Yes, I know. I didn't really think about that at the time. I just wanted to be here.'

Robert takes a sip of his coffee. It's the first time since we sat down that he hasn't looked directly at me. His forehead creases. He leans forward and catches my eye. 'Why don't you stay at Leila's? It's crazy you paying for a hotel room.'

'No, it's fine, really. It's close to the hospital. I've got everything I need.'

He shakes his head. 'I'll talk to Leila. Her house needs looking after anyway. You can get it ready for when she comes home.'

'There's really no need,' I say.

'Leave it with me.'

'Thanks, but I don't want you to ask her.'

I can see by his firm look that he means business. I presume he's got a certain amount of influence over Mum but I've no idea why. She's always hated being controlled by anyone. I speak without thinking it through just so I can make a decision of my own. 'Anyway, now you're here I'm going to take the opportunity to visit my best friend in Bristol. I've not seen her for four years. I thought I might go tomorrow, so I won't be at the hotel for a couple of days at least.'

Robert nods and doesn't push the issue any further.

'You're coming in each day to see her?' I ask.

'Of course. Vicky, my daughter, lives close by. I was planning on coming down later this month, but after what happened I thought Leila could use the company. I didn't think... I didn't know you'd be over.'

'It's about time I came,' I say.

'Ah, here he is,' Robert says. My eyes follow his towards the restaurant entrance. A man walks towards us with shoulders as broad as his father's, hugged by a worn T-shirt. We both stand when he reaches our table.

'Ben, this is Leila's daughter, Sophie.'

He's taller than Robert, his handshake firmer and damp.

'Sorry,' he says, releasing my hand and wiping it on his thighs. 'It's a bit wet out.' He pulls up a chair and sits down. He has deep blue eyes. A scar carves a pale line through the stubble on his chin like a teacher's tick on homework. My eyes drop back to my cup.

'Do you want a coffee, Ben?' Robert asks.

'No thanks.'

I sip my cappuccino.

'Are you sure I can't get you anything to eat?' Robert asks me.

'No, I'm fine. I pigged out last night,' I say. Ben looks at me as intently as his father does. He leans forward in his chair, arms folded on the table. I glance between father and son. A black tattoo nudges from beneath one of Ben's short sleeves. I stir my drink. 'We tend to eat late afternoon back home in Greece – have a good breakfast and save ourselves for a big dinner.'

'There's a great place in Athens I used to go to for breakfast, they make the best *bougatsa*.' Ben says.

I'm caught off guard. 'Did you go there on holiday?'

He smiles but there's sadness in his voice. 'No, business.'

'It's my boyfriend's favourite thing *bougatsa* for breakfast,' I say.

'I usually skip breakfast but make up for it at lunch and dinner,' Robert says.

'Isn't it just the worst and best thing about working with food,' I say. 'Putting up with gorgeous smells all day and eating the leftovers at the end of the night.'

'I'd eat steak every day if I could,' Robert says.

'You can't?'

Robert sits back and pats his lean stomach. 'Watching what I eat.'

'He's been worrying about his weight since he started noticing middle-aged spread.' Ben picks up a sachet of sugar and folds it between nicotine-stained fingers.

'Your Mum's a good cook,' Robert says. 'Better than she'll admit.'

'Candy, the friend I'm going to visit, used to love coming for tea at our house. Mum used to experiment all the time and not everything worked. If she ever suggests spinach pancakes for dinner, say you're busy.'

'I'll keep that in mind.' Robert looks at me intently. 'Leila's never visited you in Greece?'

'I never gave her the chance.'

'Oh?'

'This is the first time I've been back.'

'Why so long?' He leans forward and clasps his hands together on the plastic tablecloth. The backs of his hands are hairy, his fingernails short but neat and he has a plain gold band on his wedding ring finger.

'Dad, what's with all the questions?'

'I'm interested that's all.'

'That's fine,' I say. 'But it's between me and Mum. I'd appreciate it if you let me sort things out with her.' I take the last couple of gulps of my cappuccino and unhook my bag off the back of the chair. 'I'm going to make a move, thanks for the coffee.'

Ben tucks the sugar packet back in its holder. 'I should go say hello to Leila if you want me back at the pub by five.'

Robert nods a reply but looks at me. 'She misses you.'

'Can you tell her I'll be back in a couple of days.' I stand up. 'I don't think I'm doing her any good at the moment.'

'Give her time.'

'It's good to meet you both.'

'Likewise.' Robert pushes his chair back. His hand is big and warm in mine and he squeezes it tight before releasing it. 'We'll see you in a couple of days.'

I weave my way through the bustling restaurant. I look back before leaving. Ben's in my chair, his elbows resting on his knees, his legs spread round the table leg. He's older than Alekos, his face looks worn like his T-shirt, comfy, inviting. Robert rests his chin on folded hands. He hadn't wasted time in sending those flowers to Mum or in getting himself down to Norwich and close to her. I imagine him playing with his wedding ring. But he is just a friend. Darren was her lover. I can't wait to get out of the hospital and into drizzle.

A short taxi journey later and I'm back in my uniform white and blue room. The curtains are open but I switch on one of the bedside lights because the incessant rain dulls everything. Despina would approve of the room: plain, tidy and, I suddenly realise, the colour of the Greek flag. I phone Candy and at the beep leave a message.

'Hi, it's Sophie. I know this is a crazy suggestion and short notice, but I was thinking of coming to Bristol tomorrow. What do you think?'

I make a cup of tea and flick through the TV channels while it brews. Fed up with the weather and bored, I resign myself to children's afternoon television and wait for Candy to call.

Chapter Twelve

Heading down the M32, I want it to feel like coming home. Through the coach window I can see Bristol spread out in front, masked by hazy sunshine and, despite its familiarity, there's no pang of regret or missed heartbeat of longing. My childhood was spent in the city, being handed across the fence to play in our next-door neighbour's garden. I used to bounce along the uneven pavement on my tricycle, tearing up our terraced street to the park. Ice cream vans would announce their arrival at the top of our road with a squeaky tune, which would send me running from our house with a fifty-pence piece clutched in my palm to exchange for a Fab lolly or one of those ice creams with bubblegum at the bottom. My memories of Bristol were Andy's newsagents at the bottom of our road selling two sweets for a penny, cars parked bumper to bumper, the smell from the Indian takeaway, and terraced gardens filled with barbeque smoke on summer days.

Candy opens the front door of her Victorian terraced house in Redland, lets out a squeal and hugs me. Her face is immaculately made up as always and she looks relaxed in loose cotton trousers and a close fitting T-shirt, her boobs even bigger than I remember.

At thirteen, Candy went from being flat-chested and spotty, to being 34C and spotty. The spots didn't seem to matter anymore. Mum said I was blessed with freckles instead of spots. I wasn't blessed with 34C overnight though. I was a tomboy, happy in jeans and baggy T-shirts, while Candy was a girlie girl. Not only did she have a bust girls envied and boys lusted after, a face that wouldn't have looked out of place on the cover of *Just Seventeen* but she had the brains to match. I should have hated her.

'Shouldn't we kiss on both cheeks?' she says, pulling away from me. 'God, you look healthy. What do you mean no tan!'

'It's just brought out my freckles.'

'Are you kidding me? You look great!'

She ushers me into the hallway and I drop my bag on the polished floorboards and follow her into the open-plan kitchen-diner. Holly, wide-eyed and open-mouthed sits in a high chair dribbling into her bib.

'Do you want a drink?' Candy asks. She takes a bottle of red from the wine rack on the work surface next to the six-ringed stainless steel oven. Garlic bulbs and a sprig of bay leaves hang from a hook on the ceiling.

Holly watches me. 'Yes, please,' I say, raising my eyebrows and wiggling both hands at Holly.

'Red or white?'

'Water for now, please.'

'Water?' Candy says, taking a glass and filling it with water from the fridge. 'That's not the Sophie Keech I used to know.'

'I've mellowed.'

'Bollocks.'

'Okay, I live above a restaurant and our garden has its own well-stocked bar. I just don't tend to drink before six.'

This is what I've missed. I've watched Alekos with his friends talking like I used to with Candy – the familiarity, the freedom and intimacy of talking to a best friend. I tell her about Mum and it feels good to be hugged.

It only takes until Lee gets back from work at six for us to start on the wine. He shakes my hand and chucks his tie over the back of the sofa. I can't believe this is the first time I've met the father of my best friend's children. With Lee looking after the kids, it's like old times up in Candy's bedroom, both of us raiding her wardrobe for a suitable top for me to wear out. It feels as if I've backtracked ten years. We could be teenagers again about to down a £1.99 bottle of wine or a few cans of Scrumpy Jack before blagging our way into a club. But back downstairs, seeing Candy bend down and kiss three-year-old Jake's forehead, erases that feeling. I'm watching the perfect nuclear family: Mum, Dad, son, daughter. It's how Candy grew up, and Alekos. Lee has Holly in his arms. He rocks her from side to side and she gurgles with laughter.

Candy tops our glasses up with wine from the open bottle of white in the fridge. It's crisp and ice cold. Jake is ready for bed in stripy blue pajamas that are too big for him. He scrunches up his face when Candy says it's bedtime. He folds his arms across his chest.

'Come on, be a good boy. Say goodnight to Sophie.'

He shakes his head hard. I place my wine on the table and crouch in front of him. 'Love your PJs,' I say, trying to catch a glimpse of his face beneath his sandy coloured hair. He curls himself into Candy's black trousers. I ruffle his hair and say, 'Goodnight.'

'Let me put them to bed and we can go out.'

Candy has booked a table in a Moroccan restaurant just round the corner from where I used to live with Mum. This is the territory of my teens, but the pub opposite which I remember being grungy, dark and serving cheap pints is now an Australian themed bar.

'I thought you might like it here,' Candy says, pushing the door open. The compact restaurant is full of conversation and incense. It's dusky and exotic. The tables are candlelit and the benches and chairs are padded and thick with gold, red and green embroidered cushions. A waitress with blonde dreadlocks greets us. She leads us to a table near the door.

'Can I get you something to drink?' the waitress asks. She has a hint of an accent but I can't quite work out where from. Her face is striking; she has cheekbones even Candy would kill for and a sparkling silver stud in her nose.

Candy looks at me. 'Red?'

'Just for a change, eh? Bottle of Cabinet Sauvignon, please.'

The waitress leaves us with menus.

'It's so good to see you,' Candy says. She reaches across the knives and forks to squeeze my hands. 'Where's your engagement ring?'

I pull my hands away conscious of my bare finger alongside the sparkling diamond on hers. 'It's a long story.'

'That sounds ominous.'

'We're working through some things.'

'The wedding's still on though? It'd better be as I've got the 2nd May in my diary. We're all flying out for it.'

I nod. 'Me being here and Alekos being in Greece isn't helping the situation though.'

'Maybe a break from each other is a good thing.'

'A break from Despina is certainly good. Anyway enough about all that. I'm here now with you after four long years.'

Candy laughs. 'I shouldn't be surprised about you turning up like this you always were impulsive. What does your Mum think of you being here?'

'Not a lot,' I say. 'Unfortunately for me her memory's unaffected.'

'You walked out of her life and pissed her off, so what? That's no worse than what she did to you.'

'I wanted to come and see her. I wanted to comfort her but couldn't. I feel so stupid.'

'You're not being stupid. To be honest, I didn't think you were ever going to come back.'

The waitress returns with an uncorked bottle. 'Would you like to try it?'

Candy shakes her head. 'No need, just keep on pouring.'

The waitress obliges and I open my menu. The table opposite has all kinds of dishes laid out; I can see steam rising from a tagine and peppers sizzling on a platter.

'Are you okay?' Candy asks.

I reassure her with a nod. 'I can't choose. I could eat everything,' I say, running my eyes over the menu. 'I'm used to the Greek way of eating with all the food laid out in the middle of the table and no deliberating over just one dish.'

'How about sharing the *Mezze* for a starter – lamb parcels, fried aubergine salad...' Candy orders and we clink our glasses of wine together.

'I can be critical of restaurants now, working in one,' I say. 'But I'm impressed.' There's an infectious atmosphere, everyone looks relaxed and I can pick out laughter from up and down the room.

Candy folds her bare arms on the table. 'I can't believe you're a chef. What happened to art?'

'Life.'

'Life?' She laughs. 'At least cooking is artistic.'

I nod. 'I've surprised myself by how much I love it. If it wasn't for Despina forcing me into it in the first place, I'd never have contemplated it as a career.'

I relax and listen to Candy talk about how torn she is going back to her job as a make-up artist on *Casualty*. She makes me laugh when she says she's looking forward to Halloween when Holly and Jake are older and they can go trick-or-treating in costumes smeared with the fake blood she's nicked from work. It doesn't take long for the *Mezze* to arrive on a large platter with two empty plates. I dip my fork into what I think is the pumpkin relish and enjoy its smoothness and kick of garlic on my tongue.

'So things are no better with your Mum?' Candy asks.

'It's only been two days. We started to argue.'

'About what?'

'The same old stuff; she had a dig about why I left in the first place.' I stab a falafel with my fork. 'In fact it's never about why I left here; it's about why I left her.'

The windows have steamed up and the spices warm my throat when I swallow. My bare arms look bronze in the candlelight. The restaurant reminds me of Mum's old house: the defiant dark blue walls splashed with ruby red hangings and seating strewn with cushions.

'So, you left your Mum in hospital and decided to go out with me.' Candy presses her wine glass to her lips but her eyes give away her smile.

'I don't think I was doing her blood pressure any good.'

'Has she ever admitted she was wrong?'

I shake my head. 'She had a friend there. Two friends in fact. Father and son. I didn't know them.'

'Father and son, eh? Good-looking?'

'Candy!' I say, shaking my head at her. 'The father, Robert, talked to me like I was his best friend, started organising me. Mum behaves like I'm a stranger, which is fair enough. It felt really wrong being there.'

'It gives her time to do some serious thinking.'

I lean back on the cushions and tell her about Darren.

'Do you think she'll ever get married?' Candy asks after a while.

'I can't see it happening.'

'Not even having a serious, long-term relationship with someone?'

'What if this poor guy was that?'

Candy shakes her head. 'She wants someone with no strings. The elusive Mr Right.'

'Elusive? You've already bagged yourself one.'

'How do you really know if the one is *the* one?'

'Candy? Are you and Lee...?'

'God yeah, we're fine, really.' She takes a gulp of wine. 'We've had our moments but things are good.'

'So why the concern?'

'Oh, you know, things happened so quickly.'

'Like what?'

'Life, same as you. I left university and got a make-up job straight away, a great job. Then I met Lee, it was a whirlwind romance, totally crazy. I wasn't grounded and suddenly we're in a serious relationship with a mortgage, an incredible house… Then oops I'm pregnant, with one kid then two. Then bang, life's one big responsibility.'

'My life is like yours was five years ago: no house, no mortgage and no kids, my only real responsibility is to myself.'

'You should make the most of the freedom while it lasts,' Candy says, taking the last lamb parcel.

'But Candy, that's the problem, there is no freedom. We live with Alekos' parents, going to work only means walking downstairs and my culinary skills are Desina's discovery and she treats me like she owns me.'

'Do you know how jealous I was of you falling in love with Alekos and deciding just like that to go and live with him? Greece is somewhere people save up all year to go on a fortnight's holiday and you get to live there. I've seen the photos Sophie, you can see Mount Olympus from your bedroom window.'

'I know, I should feel lucky and I do…except…'

'Except what?'

'My concerns are for the things I've not got, the independence from Alekos' family I crave. I want more.'

Our main courses arrive with another bottle of wine. I'm envious of Candy's sizzling platter of chicken, peppers and onions, until my plate of olive and lemon chicken arrives with a bowl of steamed saffron rice.

Candy re-fills our glasses. 'Remember at school,' she says, 'this is all our friends ever talked about, being grown-up, having a career, a husband, a family. Having it all.'

I shake my head and take a mouthful of spiced lemon chicken. 'That's not what I wanted.'

'Me neither.'

'Until Lee.'

'And now you have Alekos.'

I nod. 'Now I have Alekos.'

She clinks her glass against mine. 'To Alekos and Lee.'

'And Jake and Holly,' I say. 'I still can't believe you've got kids. You,' I point my finger at her. 'You were the one who vowed to be an eternal career girl, never get married and never, ever have kids because they'd ruin your body. You're not looking too bad for it.'

'I like not being perfect.' I can hear the two bottles of wine we've shared coating her voice. She half rises from her seat and pulls her top up at the side to reveal hip-hugging trousers. 'See, stretch marks.'

The couple on the table next to us glance over and we all get an eyeful of pale stretch-marks scarring Candy's non-existent love-handles.

'I've had two kids, Sophie Keech. Two.' She sits back down. 'What does Lee expect?'

'Alekos wants children,' I say, mixing a spoonful of rice with the sauce.

'Do you?'

'Yes. And no.'

'Yes and no, what kind of indecision is that?'

'We talked about it, a while back... His mother's desperate for us to have children, in fact his whole family are. It's like they think I'm some fertility time bomb. I'm twenty-eight. I've plenty of time. Years.'

'What's wrong with now?'

'What's right?'

Candy looks at me carefully before putting her knife and fork side by side on the plate. 'I thought having a career, a house and a family would mean I'd made it.' She takes a huge sip of wine and rolls her eyes. 'My life would be complete.'

My fingers pinch the stem of my glass. Candy slops in more Cabernet Sauvignon.

'What more do you want?' I ask.

'I don't know, maybe that's the problem. There doesn't feel like there should be anything left to figure out, apart from where we're going to send Jake and Holly to school or what colours to redecorate the house with. Me, I'm supposed to be sorted.'

'But you're not?'

'Are we ever?' She shrugs, picks up her glass and taps it against mine.

Chapter Thirteen

The smell of the honeysuckle framing Candy's front door sticks in my throat. She hugs me goodbye. 'I promise we'll come and visit you in Greece. Give you a bit of respite from Alekos' Mum.'

'I'd like that.' The taxi's waiting. While the driver loads my suitcase into the boot I kiss Holly's damp cheek and acknowledge the sinking feeling of another long journey. I wave until Candy and Holly disappear from view around the corner.

'To the bus station then, love?'

'Yes please, but I want to make a stop on the way.'

Home is no longer the terraced house in Hazel Road. Candy would say I was soft, going back to my childhood home. I feel like a stalker wandering up and down our old road. The taxi driver's watching me through his rear-view mirror. The front garden's neater, almost regimental with its alternate red and white Busy Lizzies in the flowerbed. The shiny silver 7 screwed on to the front door is the same. There are net curtains up at the windows now, obscuring my view into our old living room.

My reminiscing costs me a fortune in taxi fare. I climb on to the coach and think of the hundreds of miles stretching ahead. Bristol disappears and Norwich edges closer. I'm unhinged. Talking with Candy took me away from thinking about the present and dealing with it. I hadn't thought what I was actually going to do when I got here. I was dumping myself on Mum without being invited. On top of being hurt she had to put up with me too. Stay for a while, had been my answer to Alekos. Stay. For what? I hadn't managed to stay for more than two days before escaping to Candy's house. I'd have to face Mum today. I'd have to be sure what I was going to do. Stay, for as long as it takes. But if she didn't want me to stay with her, where would I go? Back to Candy's across the other side of the country? I might as well go back to Greece. But what would that accomplish? Nothing.

I hadn't come back for nothing.

Two pinch-marks of colour dot Mum's cheeks. Half of me hoped Robert would be here with his over-familiar talk, but a part of me is glad he's not.

I take a deep breath. 'You look better.' I place the pot of chrysanthemums I bought on the way next to Robert's lavender.

'I don't feel it.'

'No?'

'I want to wash my hair, I want to shave my legs and I want privacy when I pee. I look a state. I hate people seeing me like this.'

'I can go if you want.'

'I didn't mean that. I need something to pass the time.'

I sit down. 'What about the other women in here? Do you talk to them?'

Mum lowers her voice. 'The woman next to me,' she motions towards the window, 'hasn't got her hearing aid in, so doesn't understand me most of the time. Doesn't stop her trying to talk to me. And she hums out of tune. Incessantly. It's driving me insane. The woman opposite has had her thyroid cut out, so it hurts her to talk. All she can manage is a slow nod and a manic smile. So the conversation in here is stimulating.'

This is the woman I remember, with her sharp tongue and

impatient streak. I'm surprised she's talking as calmly and quietly as she is, given the circumstances.

'I'm sorry I turned up like this.'

'It's been a long time.'

'I want to look after you for a while, if that's okay?'

'Robert said you're going to stay at the house,' Mum says, avoiding the question.

'It was his idea. I'm really sorry, I asked him not to say anything.'

'I guess it makes sense. The plants need watering.'

'You won't mind me staying there?'

'No. I don't like the thought of it being empty. Robert will let you know where everything is. The bread's probably gone off by now and check the milk just in case...' Her fingers play with the edge of the sheet and her eyes flit between me and somewhere over my shoulder. I'm not sure whether her attention's wandering or she can't look me in the eye. 'It's odd you never having been to my house.'

'Is it anything like Hazel Road?'

'It's a cottage on the edge of a village, not a paper-thin-walled terraced house in the middle of Bristol. I couldn't sleep properly for the first couple of weeks because it was too quiet. No cars, no doors slamming, no bloody next-door neighbours...'

'They were still arguing?'

'Until the day I left. Their problems were the only thing keeping them together. I think they lived for verbally abusing each other at two o'clock in the morning. The first couple of nights in Marshton I laid awake thinking something was really wrong not hearing Ella and Ken slamming and shouting their way upstairs. Funny what you miss.'

Thyroid lady is watching us; her beady eyes stare across from the opposite bed. I bet she loves to gossip. She's probably the kind of woman always leaning on the next-door neighbour's fence having a chat. I pity everyone on this ward when their visitors go home and they're left with each other for company, all a little too far away to sustain a proper conversation. They can sympathise, but none of them really understands what each other is going through. Thyroid lady sees Mum with her broken leg, fractured wrist, stitches and bruises, but she doesn't know about Mum's emotional scars, she doesn't know the history between us. I wonder what she sees. A loving daughter? A grateful mother? She doesn't know anything.

'I'm not going to his funeral,' Mum suddenly says.

I don't know what to say. I manage, 'Oh.'

'Even if I was welcome I wouldn't go.'

I play with the buckle on my bag.

Mum's eyes don't meet mine. 'I wasn't going to see him again after the weekend. I didn't want to spend any more energy on another relationship that was going nowhere. I should have finished it before he came down.'

'You weren't to know.'

'It was bloody selfish of me wanting a goodbye shag.'

It was this kind of talk that embarrassed me when I was a teenager. Too much information, too often. It was happening again, our roles were reversing. 'Did you know he was married?'

'Don't lecture me, Sophie.'

'I'm not. It's a question. Forget it.'

Mum reaches for her cup of water. Her cheeks have flushed redder. 'I had an idea, even though he didn't wear a ring. I saw a photo of his wife and kids in his wallet when he paid for drinks the weekend I met him. He admitted it a month later. It was too bloody late by then for it to matter.'

'Did you love him?'

Her good hand reaches up to her face and sweeps a loose hair from her eyes. She's cried herself dry. There's no privacy for emotions, not with thyroid lady watching and nurses and visitors padding up and down, back and forth. Even if we closed the curtains, people would just listen harder.

'How long have I been here?' Mum asks.

'Nearly a week. Since last Saturday.'

'I want to get out so badly,' she says. She reaches her arms slowly above her head and stretches. She winces as she brings her injured arm gently back down. 'You'll have to find sheets in the airing cupboard for the spare room. It'll probably be stuffy; it gets the sun throughout the day.'

'I really don't have to stay. The hotel's fine.'

'Robert wasn't sure when you were coming back. Now you're here he'll drive back today.'

'He's been waiting for me?'

Mum shakes her head. 'He's happy spending time with Vicky, but being Friday he needs to get back to the pub. There's food in the house and veg in the garden if you want to make yourself something. I suggest you have steak and chips at *The Globe*. It's the best. Robert will look after you.'

'Have they said when you can go home yet?'

'Another few days, whatever that means. Too long. I want a bath.'

'Hang in there.'

'I'll never get in a bloody bath with this fucking thing on.' She points to her plastered leg. I'm sure thyroid woman is reeling at Mum's language. At least Mum's lost none of her spirit. Maybe I should suggest she drops a few swear words into the conversation when her ward buddies ask too many questions. Then she might get the peace and quiet she longs for.

A slightly dirty Toyota Corolla is not what I imagined Robert would drive. I thought a shiny new Land Rover would be more his taste. He's uprooted himself from the city only to find himself stuck in the country. I might be doing him a great injustice but that's my first impression. Maybe it's something to do with his worryingly neat nails.

'She's looking better, isn't she?' he asks, heaving my suitcase into the boot.

'Much better.'

On the backseat of the car there's a box of tissues and a UK road map. An air freshener dangles from the rear-view mirror and a pair of sunglasses and a packet of sugar-free gum are in the central holder.

We'd both said goodbye to Mum and left her with our promise to visit on Sunday. I wonder what I'm going to do on my own for the next two days.

'Did you get a chance to talk to her?' Robert asks, turning on the engine.

'About what?'

He pauses for a moment. 'I guess you've both got a lot of things to sort out.'

'Let's just say we talked.'

'But you sorted things out?'

'A hospital's hardly the place to talk properly.'

We pull out of the car park and head in the opposite direction to the Travelodge. Robert puts his glasses on and drives with both hands clamped to the wheel. I'm glad his attention is on the road and not me.

'I said she'd be okay about you staying, though,' he says. 'She'll be glad to have you about for a while after years in Greece. I'm very lucky having both my children living close by.'

'And your grandchildren too,' I calmly reply.

'Only Vicky's newborn. The other two are in London with their mother.'

'Oh, they're not your daughter's?'

'No, Ben's.' He glances in the mirror before pulling into the outside lane to overtake a lorry. 'He's got a son and daughter.'

I can't picture Ben as a father. He seemed so single. I want to ask why they're in London while Ben's in Norfolk with his Dad. 'How long does it take to get to Marshton?' I ask instead.

'About forty-five minutes.'

Not what I was hoping for.

'It's a lovely drive mind,' he says, turning on the radio. He tunes it into a classical music station and I lean back against the headrest.

Our conversation dissolves into silence and I watch the countryside pass by as we head towards the coast. Everywhere looks green, the grass and the trees, patch-worked with yellow from the harvest. It is refreshing after the dryness of Greece, and the flat landscape is a novelty compared to the mountainous backdrop of *O Kípos*.

The sign for Marshton appears at the top of a gentle incline on a road that barely allows two cars to pass side by side. Robert slows to a crawl. Straight in front where the road curves sharply to the left is *The Globe*, a cream-fronted pub next to a great expanse of green leading up to the church. Picnic tables filled with families enjoying the sunshine dot the grassy area to the side of the pub. It's like a living watercolour.

'There she is,' Robert says. The pub is timber-framed and has a hand-painted sign hanging above the door. Red and yellow flowers fill window boxes along the ledges of the leaded windows. The wooden door is ajar but I can see only darkness inside because of the late afternoon sun.

'I fell in love with it the first time I came to Marshton.'

'You must get tons of holidaymakers,' I say. We dart past a row of flint cottages and head out of the heart of the village towards an open road lined with tall hedges.

'Can you blame them? Horse-riding and sailing is big business. And we're only a fifteen-minute walk from the sea.' He could write the holiday brochure. Robert brakes and we swing sharply on to a muddy lane obscured by trees, before bouncing through an open gateway. 'Here we are,' he says, parking next to a new Mini.

Mum wasn't kidding when she said it was different to our old terraced house on Hazel Road. I get out of the car and take a deep breath of fresh air. Mum's cottage is built of flint. It's almost identical to the row of cottages we passed, except it's detached and stands in the middle of a well cared for garden. The front of the house looks like a face, with a wooden front door in the centre and windows either side, top and bottom. An attic window breaks up the red roof. I stop and listen to the birds singing and the breeze rustling through the trees. Robert crunches across the gravel, dragging my suitcase behind him. 'It's a bit better than the Travelodge.'

Since being in Greece, I hadn't given a thought to where Mum was living, in Norfolk was all I knew. I had no preconceptions of what her home was like. I hadn't thought about it because at the time it didn't matter, I had my life and it was far removed from hers. The distance we'd created between us before I'd gone to Greece only intensified as the months and years passed. This is Mum's home and not mine and that's an odd feeling.

'Come on, I'll show you around,' Robert says. I wonder if he feels anywhere near as awkward as I do or if he hides it well. Maybe he's enjoying looking after 'Leila's daughter'.

I follow him up the stone path to the front door. There's a wooden plaque on the wall that says *Salt Cottage.*

'Unusual name,' I say.

Robert unlocks the door. 'After the salt marshes near Blakeney.'

It's cool and dark in the square hallway. Wooden floorboards disappear beneath the doors on both sides of the hall. I can't help thinking it's a big house for one person. The kitchen is as light as the hallway is dark and there's a pile of unopened letters on the kitchen table. Sun streams through the wide window. It's bright but stuffy with the door and windows shut.

'The milk's okay,' Robert says, closing the fridge door. The American-style fridge that always looked too big in our old kitchen looks at home here. 'There's powdered milk in one of the cupboards if you prefer that. Coffee and sugar here,' he points to the terracotta jars on the wooden work surface. 'Shall I show you your room?' He makes for the hallway.

'No, it's fine, I can sort myself out.' I want to explore, but on my own.

'Leila's room is at the front. You're in the spare room at the back. It's got great views.' He fiddles with his wedding band. 'Let's get some air in here,' he says.

He takes the keys from his jeans pocket and unlocks the backdoor before handing them to me. However lovely the rest of the house might be, I suddenly see its true selling point. I follow Robert out into the sunshine, down a couple of steps and on to grass speckled with daises. The lawn finishes at a weathered fence overlooking a field of horses and a further patchwork of fields sloping towards a wooded hill. The sun, still high in the sky, penetrates every area of the garden. Further down, on the right-hand side beneath the shade of trees, is a patio area with a brick barbeque and a green wrought-iron table and chairs.

'Leila's had some great parties out here,' Robert says with a smile.

There's too much history here that I'm not a part of. I retreat to the kitchen and start opening cupboards to see where Mum keeps the glasses and plates. When I look up, Robert is standing in the doorway with his hands on his hips, blocking the view and sunlight, watching me. He looks at home, as if his silhouette belongs in the kitchen doorway. I'm the trespasser. It's an unfamiliar house, filled with familiar things and memories – like the clay leaf I moulded and shaped, painted and glazed in an art class and proudly gave to Mum who used it as her favourite ashtray. She still has it, sitting on the kitchen windowsill with teabags and coffee grounds on it.

'I'm sure Leila would want you to make yourself at home,' he finally says. 'Remember to water the plants in here and the bathroom and Leila always double locks the front door at night.'

I open my bag and hunt for my mobile. 'I need to phone Alekos.'

'Alekos?' He frowns.

'My boyfriend. In Greece. I should phone him before it gets too late.'

We both stand and watch each other for a moment, my fingers poised to dial.

'Oh. Oh, okay. I'd better get off anyway. See how busy it is.' He makes his way out of the kitchen and through the hallway to the front door. I follow him, step by slow step.

'Thanks for the lift.'

'My pleasure.' He opens the door and turns to me. 'I think you'll do her a world of good being here.' He pauses. 'You'll come to the pub for a meal tonight, won't you?'

'I hadn't really thought…'

'Come down about half eight, it's on me.'

'You don't have to, I'm quite happy…'

He holds one hand up. 'No arguments – it's the least I can do.'

He's full of the right things to say that makes it truly difficult to refuse. I may well end up heading down to the pub but I'd like it to be my choice. He crunches his retreat across the gravel. I feel odd waving goodbye from a strange doorstep.

'By the way,' he calls, before getting in his car. 'I don't think there's any reception in the house. Try the lane.'

There's no reception in the house, the garden or the lane. I wander up and down, holding my mobile out in front of me, then towards the sky, waiting for even one bar of reception to appear. I try the neighbouring field and pad across the soft sandy soil while corn stalks scratch my ankles. About twenty paces in and I have success. I let it ring.

'*Ela.*'

'Hi, it's me.'

'Can I phone you back?' He shouts to make himself heard above the noise in the background. It doesn't sound like the restaurant.

'If you have to.'

What am I supposed to do? Wait for him here to call back

and cut my legs to pieces on the corn stubble in the process? He must be on the beach at that volleyball game. Is that why he was so reluctant to come with me because he'd miss out on the volleyball matches? It's hot enough here to be lounging on a beach. I fancy swimming in the sea, cooling down, floating in the shallows. There's quite a view from this field. I can't see the sea, although I swear I can taste a slight saltiness in the air. I can see the farm at the end of the lane and up the field towards a church. Down in a dip, Mum's cottage is half-hidden by the foliage clinging to the walls and the trees surrounding the garden. There's not another house in sight, just like the garden in Greece; the view stretches endlessly to the horizon, but it feels bigger there, more rugged, mountainous. Here it is peaceful and quiet. Empty. That rarely happens at *Estiatorio O Kipos*.

Chapter Fourteen

I take a look in every room of Mum's house, even her bedroom. It's as if Mum's lifted her bedroom from Hazel Road and put it straight into *Salt Cottage*. The colour, the bedspread, the layout is identical, only there's more space. Everywhere reminds me of her. The dressing table is cluttered with perfumes, creams, make-up, books and photos. There's a black-and-white photo stuck to the mirror of me on a swing and another of my grandparents, the edges curled yellow with age. *The Handmaid's Tale* by Margaret Atwood lies open on the bedside table, next to a half-filled glass of water. I don't open the wardrobe or chest of drawers. I leave everything untouched, even the unmade bed, particularly when I notice the second glass of water on the other bedside table.

I'm impressed by the way the towels complement the colour scheme in the bathroom. They never used to. There were always too many colours, too many ideas going on in our old house. The downstairs study surprises me too. It's sophisticated, with wooden floorboards, an open fireplace and black-and-white photographs adorning white walls. Maybe the house is not too big; I'd forgotten she works from home. It's something we've not talked about. The same way I kept my life in Greece to myself, Mum never divulged what she was up to either, and what I had learnt was via Candy. Her laptop sits on the black-stained desk in front of the window. I wonder how much work she gets done with a view like this. The room opposite the bathroom and next to the spare room is very different from the stark, business-like study below. It must be Mum's workroom. It's filled with light and colour. The window is large and curtain-less and sunshine pours across the honey-yellow walls. Sketches and plans of weddings and parties are strewn across the large worktable in the centre of the room, and apart from a leather armchair next to the window and a bookshelf, there are only flowers filling the space; dried and fresh arrangements. The smell is potent and heady in the heat.

I tiptoe from the room and close the door softly behind me. Devoid of any real statement, the spare bedroom is inviting. Mum's personality is only mildly stamped on it by the choice of blinds instead of curtains and the artistic nude on the wall. The chocolate brown bedspread and mushroom-coloured walls is toned down for Mum. This would be my room if I'd grown up here. I'd have overlooked the garden, just as I did in Hazel Road, but to a view that stretches towards a hill and not on to another red brick house.

Even with the windows open it's quiet. I put the radio on in the kitchen to fill the silence. A power shower, fresh clothes and a brush of mascara later and I'm in the mood to head down to the pub. I don't feel like cooking for just myself or trying to turn slightly green potatoes and frozen sausages into something appetising.

It's a warm, sticky evening, as if the earlier breeze has been sucked from the sky. I leave *Salt Cottage* and turn my back on the sunset and make my way along the lane to the road. The windows of the flint cottages are flung wide open. Smoke spirals into the sky from behind the last cottage and distant voices sound loud in the stillness. The barbeque smell is enticing and my mouth waters at the thought of a meal being cooked for me. I follow the road round the corner and the village opens up. A group of kids are playing rounders on the green and the people filling the picnic tables to the side of the pub have spilled on to the grass.

The pub door is open and I duck through and hover while my eyes adjust to the gloom. There's a low-beamed ceiling and an open fireplace at the far end of the room which is filled with dried flowers, much like the ones in Mum's workroom. I can't see an empty table anywhere. The bar is loud with conversation. The French windows at the back of the pub open out into a conservatory filled with people eating. I work my way to the L-shaped bar. The two women behind the bar look hot and flustered. A door to my right swings open followed by a gush of steam and a waitress carrying plates. What if Robert invited me just to be polite? Maybe I should leave them to it; the place is busy enough without me.

'What can I get you?' One of the bar women is in front of me, wiping the wood down with a cloth.

'Is Robert around?' I ask.

She glances at me and her eyes linger for a moment. Her cheeks are flushed and her forehead glows beneath the spotlights. 'You must be Leila's daughter,' she says, in a thick Norfolk accent. 'I'm Marcy. Robert said you'd be down for dinner. He's outside, but he'll be back in soon. Can I get you a drink?'

'Lager, please.' I reach into my bag and pull out my purse.

'Don't you worry about that,' Marcy says. 'Will Stella do you?'

I nod. She blows air from her lips over her face while she pours me my pint. She's not wearing any make-up; her hair is brown and streaked with grey, scraped off her forehead by a band.

'Take a seat at the bar. We've no spare tables tonight. It's Sophie, right?'

She leaves me on the end stool with a cold pint and a menu. Robert was right about it being busy. There are sunburnt families tucking into dinner, young couples holding hands, older couples deep in conversation, even a couple of local men with flat caps and wax jackets on the other arm of the bar, drinking their pints. I rarely drink pints in Greece, but it feels good, sipping a cold pint in a hot pub. It feels good actually being in a pub, a proper English pub with different beers and lagers to choose from and packets of scampi crisps and dry roasted peanuts on display at the back of the bar.

'Good, you've got a drink.' Robert says, appearing round the corner of the bar. 'Have you been here long?'

'No. It's a great place you've got here.'

'Not bad is it,' he says, with a broad grin. 'What would you like to eat?'

'I've heard the steak's good.'

'I'll let them know in the kitchen. How would you like it done?'

'Medium-rare, please.'

The other woman behind the bar shouts for Robert. He puts his thumbs up, nods and turns back to me. 'I feel terrible inviting you and leaving you by yourself.'

'Don't worry. I more than understand.'

I perch on my barstool and can see into the kitchen and behind the bar. Robert does a great job of working the room, not being too intrusive yet helping out with the orders. I can hear his booming laugh above everyone's conversations. My meal arrives and I eat it up at the bar. The steak is juicy, the chips crispy on the outside and soft in the middle. Marcy silently re-fills my pint mid-mouthful so I can only nod my thanks.

'I didn't realise you were here.' Ben appears in the doorway on the other side of the bar. He looks pale. His hair is ruffled, his T-shirt is creased and he's in grey tracksuit bottoms.

'Your Dad drove me down today,' I say with a mouthful of steak.

'I bet he invited you for a meal too.'

I wipe my mouth on my napkin and swallow. 'He insisted.'

He pours himself a pint of lemonade and drops an ice cube in. 'Like it's not busy enough.'

I don't quite know what to say to that. Ben watches me

from over the top of his pint glass as he takes a sip. 'Shame you've had to sit up at the bar with Itchy and Scratchy over there.' He nods his head towards the two flat-capped men at the opposite end of the bar.

'Who?'

'Watch them,' he says. 'Well, enjoy yourself. I've got paperwork to do for Dad. Just as well really, I can't stand it when it's busy. Too many obnoxious people.' And you're one of them, I think, as he escapes through the bar door. I'm shocked he didn't get rid of all the customers when Robert was in Norwich.

I finish the steak and mop the tomato and mushroom juice from the bottom of the plate with the last couple of chips.

'The pints are just going straight through me,' I say, when Marcy heads my way to re-fill my glass.

'What can I get you instead? Malibu? Whisky? Vodka?'

'Vodka and orange, please.'

It reminds me of being at University in Falmouth, although I drank cheaper vodka then. The kind of vodka that made me sick at the end of the night and left me with a thumping head, dizzy spells and unable to scrape myself out of bed until the middle of the afternoon.

I don't see Ben again until nearly eleven when he comes down and sits with me at the bar. He's changed into worn jeans and a long-sleeved top. His hair is still ruffled and his eyes are red.

'I didn't think you'd still be here,' he says. He seems in a better mood than earlier in the evening.

'I haven't got anything else to do.'

He leans across the bar and pinches Marcy as she goes past. She playfully slaps the back of his hands before chucking him a packet of dry roasted peanuts and pouring me another vodka and orange on the sly. She winks. 'One for the road,' she says. I bet she gets on well with Mum.

'It's always a late night on Fridays,' Robert says, pulling a barstool up. There are lots of people eating, some finishing off their blackcurrant cheesecakes and coffee, others still on their main course.

'Late?' I say. 'This is nothing compared to Greece. We're lucky if the last customers are out by two or three in the morning.'

'I like my sleep,' he says. His eyes are ringed by shadows and his hair looks greyer in the dull light of the bar.

'He overdoes it,' Marcy says, giving Robert a mothering look.

'I'm hands on,' he replies.

'He pulls pints like a demented robot on busy nights. Wears himself out, don't he Ben?' Ben carries on munching peanuts. Marcy wipes the last couple of glasses. 'Any plans for tomorrow, Sophie?'

'Not really. I feel like I should be doing something to the house, but it's tidy.'

'As soon as he heard about Leila he went and checked on everything, even put the Marigolds on and did the washing up, didn't you.'

Robert sighs and sips his whisky.

'I fancy going to the beach,' I say.

'Take a walk to Blakeney Point. It's beautiful up there,' Marcy says.

'It's going to be good weather tomorrow,' Robert says. 'You could buy a fresh dressed crab for your dinner.'

'I might just do that, after a good night's sleep.' I try to stifle a yawn.

'It's been a long day,' Robert says.

'It's been a long week,' I reply. 'All I've done is travel, from one country to another, then across England and back again. I'm going to head off. Thank you for the meal, Robert.'

Robert scrapes his bar stool back and stands up. 'Ben will walk you back.'

'There's no need, I'll be fine.'

Robert and Marcy glance at each other.

'If you say so,' Ben says.

Marcy flashes me a wide, toothy grin. 'See you again, Sophie.'

'Goodnight.'

I close the heavy wooden door on the warmth. I'm met by the glow from the lamps outside and the nip of autumn in the air. I shiver in my short sleeves and cropped trousers. I turn the corner past the pub and all of a sudden it's as if someone's switched off all the lights. The darkness is blinding. I look upwards but there's no moon or stars. It's disorientating and I might as well be walking with my eyes closed. Taking tentative steps forward I strain to make out anything ahead – the cottages or the hedges on either side. Did I leave a light on in Mum's house? It didn't cross my mind when I left the house in sunshine. How am I supposed to find the lane, let alone navigate my way through the front garden? I take tiny steps, edging my foot out, feeling for solid ground. I feel ridiculous taking my phone from my pocket and seeing how much light the white screen gives off. I wave my arms about in front of me but I can only make out my own hand and not the road ahead. Behind me the darkness smothers everything. I stand still and take a deep breath. I've never felt this isolated before. I step forward and a beam of yellow light joins me, splitting the darkness. I watch a circle of light bob towards me.

'We were taking bets on how far you'd get,' Ben says, bathing me in the torch beam. Despite the relief of being able to see, he's the last person I want saving me.

'I was going to turn back but couldn't see anything that way either.'

'Dad said if you were as stubborn as Leila you might be camping out here until dawn.'

'I can be stubborn but I'm not stupid,' I say. The torchlight leads the way and, side by side, we follow it along the middle of the road. 'I suppose you get to know these things after a while.'

'You have to adjust to your environment.'

'How long have you been living here?'

'A few months.'

'Not long then.'

'It feels like a lifetime.'

We fall silent, guided by the light piercing the darkness. The only sound is our shoes scuffing the tarmac.

'I love the beach at Salthouse,' Ben says after a while. We turn down the lane towards the house.

'What's it like?'

'Pebbly, and stretches as far as you can see. It's always windy there. The sea's cold, really refreshing.'

'Is it far?'

'Not by car. I'd take you tomorrow, except I've got to go back to London. But if you're around for a while...'

'I hope to be,' I say, glancing at him. His face is cast in shadows. 'What are you doing in London?'

We turn into the gateway and the soundless muddy lane turns into a loud crunching driveway.

'I've got things to sort out,' he says.

My mobile rings in my pocket. 'Sorry,' I say. The photo of Alekos holding the octopus flashes on to the screen. 'Hi.'

'Finally,' Alekos says. 'I've been trying you all night.'

'There's not much reception here.'

'Where are you?'

'At Mum's house. I'm staying here instead of the hotel.'

Ben shines the torch's beam on to the front door while I fumble with the keys. There's a click and the door swings inwards.

Ben looks at me with raised eyebrows. 'Okay?'

I nod. 'Yes thanks.'

'Who's that?' Alekos asks.

'Mum's friend. He just walked me home.'

Alekos is silent.

'It's so dark here you can't see any further than a foot in front,' I say.

Ben crunches back across the driveway and I wait for his torchlight to disappear.

'Where have you been all evening?' Alekos asks.

'I had a meal at the pub. What about you? What were you doing earlier?'

'At a volleyball match. We won again. Georgis gave me lift home from Olympic Beach.'

'You were celebrating instead of working?' I go inside, close the door behind me and run my hand across the wall to find the light switch. 'Aleko?' The line has died. I don't fancy going back outside to find reception again. I could phone him on Mum's landline. Instead, I put the kettle on and find some pear and apple flavoured tea in one of the cupboards. I let it brew, squeeze the teabag and leave it with the other dried teabags on my ceramic leaf on the windowsill. I drag myself upstairs and after a quick wash, undress and climb into bed. Alekos will have to wait until tomorrow.

Chapter Fifteen

I sleep well and wake to birds singing, their shadows disturbing the daylight through the spare bedroom blinds. It's only 07.00 but I feel awake and refreshed. I pad across the floorboards and open the blinds. A thin mist lies across the field at the end of the garden and the sun has almost reached the patio. Cool air blows through the open window. I get back into bed and listen: to the birds outside, to the stillness within the house. I've longed for this, no doors slamming, no shouting and no interruptions. I don't even feel guilty that it's Mum's house I'm taking advantage of because I know she'll be home soon and everything will change. The dynamics of a place always change with the arrival of someone else. I doze for a while and enjoy the rarity of being on my own.

After a cup of freshly brewed coffee, I take Marcy's advice and walk up the road to Blakeney. It's as if the place has come alive overnight. Cars rush past me, filled with families off on Saturday morning outings. The hill I can see from the cottage is deceptive. It's not steep but it steadily keeps on going up, winding round the corner beneath the shade of a wood before finally levelling off next to the church. I cross a main road and find myself on a narrow lane packed with people heading down to the patch of blue between the houses. It's the same here as in Greece with the last holidaymakers clinging to the remains of summer. Children pass by in shorts and sandals clutching fishing nets and buckets. Despite the peppering of clouds and the cool breeze, people are still dressed for mid-August. In Greece, the first hint of autumn sends the locals reaching for their winter clothes. I understand the need in Britain to hang on to every second of sunshine. I have so many memories of camping holidays with Mum. The sound of rain drumming on a window always reminds me of being huddled inside our tent.

I reach the end of the street and it opens on to a harbour filled with boats bobbing up and down on the channel of water. The marshes stretch so far out I can't even see the sea. The taste of salt is strong and seagulls squawk overhead.

I glance both ways along the quay and take the quieter way to my left, away from the car park, ice cream van and pub. The children who passed me earlier are squatting on the side of the quay with their buckets. The eldest girl holds a crab up for the others to see. I watch its pincers clutching at thin air. The sun struggles through the clouds, casting only patchy warmth along the front. I reach the end and take the stony path next to a cottage surrounded by a high flint wall.

Tall grasses line the sandy path all the way to the next village, which is hazy in the distance. There are a handful of people on the path, some walking, others looking through binoculars towards the marshes. I don't go far, only until I find a spot in the sun to sit. People's voices sound distant, almost an echo. I like the feeling of being removed from everything and everyone. I wish I'd brought a pencil and paper to sketch the view. I will next time, and a picnic to share with the birds.

I check my mobile for reception and return Alekos' late-night call.

His first words are: 'What happened last night?'

'We got cut off.'

'Why didn't you phone back?'

'I was tired. I wanted to sleep.'

'Who was with you?'

'A friend of Mum's.'

'Right,' he says slowly. 'When are you coming home?'

'Mum's still in hospital. I can't leave yet.'

'I think what you're doing is good.'

'Really? Your reaction to me coming here could've fooled me, particularly when only a couple of weeks ago you were telling me all about the importance of family.'

'I understand now you need to sort things out with your Mum.'

Two cream butterflies chase each other through the tall grass in front of me and skim over the sandy path. I stretch my legs out and lean back, resting my free hand on the mossy grass behind. 'Then why were you so reluctant about me coming here?'

'To be honest I thought you had an alternative motive, that you wanted to escape O *Kipos* rather than help your Mum. I'm sorry I thought that but I was surprised, that's all.'

'Why?'

'Because you rarely have a good word to say about her.'

'That doesn't mean I don't care.'

'Maybe not. It's only my opinion.'

'I think you'd like her.'

He sighs. 'I'm sorry I'm not there with you. I'm sure I'll meet her when she's well again.'

'You mean when she's able to come and visit you in Greece.' I pluck a blade of grass and flick it into the air.

'It is empty here without you,' he says.

'How can it possibly feel empty? There's no room to sneeze without someone hearing. There's always someone there. Always.'

I'm conscious of my voice rising. A young couple is walking towards me hand in hand along the path.

'There'll be a time when it's only us,' he says.

'When Aleko? When?' I don't get an answer and wasn't expecting one. We say goodbye. He's got things to do. Our lives and routines seem opposed to each other.

~

I do some shopping on the way back up through Blakeney. I buy bread, milk, cheese and tomatoes in the Spar before I find a man selling dressed crabs from a shed off the main road. I can't stop thinking about Alekos, but it's not because I'm missing him. I walk back down the hill towards Mum's house. It's quite a view across the fields towards the village and the church. Marshton is just a cluster of houses behind the pub and the green. *Salt Cottage* stands alone, with its back to the village. Its nearest neighbour is the farm at the end of the muddy lane.

I have crab salad for dinner with a lettuce from the garden. I eat it on the patio with my back to the cottage and watch the horses in the field. I don't hear Robert until he's almost beside me.

'Perfect timing,' he says.

'God you scared me.'

'Sorry, I came through the side gate; Leila always keeps an open house policy. These are for you,' he says. He puts a punnet of strawberries and a pot of double cream on the patio table.

I scramble to my feet. 'There was no need but thank you.'

'My pleasure,' he says. He folds his arms across his chest and gazes across the field. 'To think I wasted so much time living in a city instead of here.'

'Can I get you a drink?'

'No thanks. I was only popping around to make arrangements to visit Leila tomorrow. Does ten o'clock suit you?'

'That's fine with me.'

'Great, well, I'll see you tomorrow then,' he says, and makes his way back up the garden. He reaches the kitchen door and calls back. 'If you don't eat the strawberries and cream straight away then pop them in the fridge.'

'Of course!' I shout back.

Sleep comes easily after fresh air, sunshine and food. There's nothing to disturb the quiet, except an owl hooting and the occasional car passing by. I don't want to be uprooted tomorrow and heading back towards a city. I don't want to be making polite chit-chat with Robert on the forty-five minute journey. Most of all, I don't want to face the prospect of Mum coming home. I have no idea how I'm going to deal with her. The owl's hoots fade as I drift off into dreamless sleep.

Robert picks me up bang on ten o'clock. He hums along to the radio all the way to Norwich. We take the lift and I note how familiar I've become with the stark white walls and seemingly identical corridors of the hospital.

Thyroid lady's been replaced with an equally inquisitive woman on Mum's ward. Her knitting needles click against each other; she has a pale blue ball of wool that she's turning into some kind of oversized jumper. She smiles warmly at us when we pull up two chairs and sit down opposite. 'Your family?' she calls across from her bed.

Mum gives a drawn-out sigh. 'My daughter, Sophie, and my friend, Robert.'

'Oh lovely,' thyroid lady's replacement says before going back to her knitting.

'You've got new roommates then,' I say.

'Tell me about it,' Mum scowls. She's sitting up in bed reading *Take a Break*. The whole of her bed is strewn with magazines: *Woman*, *Hello* and *Now*.

'You're not bored then?' Robert asks.

'Not if you think reading about some woman's stomach stapling operation is exciting stuff. They're all over a year old. I'm catching up on dead gossip.'

Her previously ashen face has colour and there's a hint of make-up on her eyes and face, very subtle but it makes a difference. A week ago she looked ten years older, now she looks younger than her actual age.

I sit back and listen to Robert telling Mum about a villager's art exhibition further down the coast. The three of us together censors the conversation. Robert tries to include me but his talk is all about people and a life I don't know. One on one, we could talk properly, but this unnatural set-up forces us to be too polite. We avoid anything emotional or personal. Talking about Darren, myself or anytime before this week are strictly off limits.

'Ah, yes,' Robert says. He reaches into his bag, pulls out Mum's post and neatly arranges it on the bedside cabinet. 'I thought you might like to catch up with things.'

'I hope you left the bills at home.'

'I brought everything I'm afraid.'

'At least it'll be more exciting than *Take a Break*. Do I look like the type of person to read those kind of magazines?'

Robert shakes his head. 'No.'

'How's the cottage?' Mum asks, her gaze flicking between Robert and me.

'Being well looked after,' Robert quickly replies.

'It's lovely,' I say.

Mum smiles for the first time since I arrived in England.

'You did it all up yourself, didn't you,' Robert says in a fatherly voice.

'Almost.'

I don't get what she sees in him, even if he is just a friend. He's everything I thought she couldn't stand in a man... He reminds me so much of Despina.

'It wasn't hard making it look good in the state it was in,' Mum says. She reaches for the glass of water but Robert jumps up and hands it to her.

'What state?' I ask.

'Tobacco-stained walls, flowery wallpaper and threadbare brown carpets. Bloody disgusting.'

'But you fell in love with it,' Robert says.

Mum nods. She's beginning to look tired. Her energy seems to drain with our company. The ward is filled with visitors; nearly every bed has people chatting round it. It doesn't seem to be restful at all.

'Robert,' Mum says. 'Can you do me a favour and phone Pamela Swann about her daughter's wedding, let her know...'

He nods. 'I've already spoken to her. She phoned the other day when I popped round. I explained everything.'

'Call her back and tell her I'll be there on the day could you.'

'Are you sure?'

'They're releasing me from this hell-hole on Tuesday,' she says.

'That's earlier than expected, isn't it?' he asks.

'They can't wait to get rid of me. I made sure of that.'

I endure the forty-five minute journey back to Marshton by making small talk with Robert. But there's only so much we can say about the weather and the countryside. He seems to be afraid of a moment's silence between us. When we pull into *Salt Cottage's* gateway, I find out what he's being working up to say.

'Leila's told me about what happened between you.' Robert kills the engine and we sit awkwardly in the car, not looking at each other. 'I understand why things are difficult.'

'You know more than you let on in the hospital then,' I say. My hands are on the door release, ready to make my escape.

'I thought you might take it the wrong way if I blurted out that I knew the difficulties between the two of you.'

'And you don't think I'll take it the wrong way now?'

He's quiet. His hands tense on the steering wheel. The heat intensifies the longer we sit in the parked car. I open the door.

'I care about Leila,' he says. 'I don't want to see her unhappy, that's all.'

'It sounds to me like she's very happy here.'

'She is. But she misses you. She won't admit it but I can tell.' He unclamps his hands from the steering wheel and glances at me. 'I hope you can sort things out.'

'I screwed things up with her. It's not that easy.'

'She was in the wrong. I told her that. She didn't like it but it's the truth.'

    'You actually said that to her? And you're still friends?'

    'I was only telling her what deep down she already knew.'

Chapter Sixteen

I hear the crunch of tyres on gravel first. I'm upstairs in the bathroom cleaning the sink that was clean to begin with and is now spotless. I get to the window in time to see Robert pull up in his Toyota as close to the cottage as he can get. He's cleaned the car since we visited Mum on Sunday. By the time I've pulled off the rubber gloves, he's out of the car and round to the passenger side and opening the door for Mum. She looks much better in her own clothes – a loose tunic top and long skirt that hides the scar on her arm and the cast on her leg. She's so thin. Even from up here her cheeks look hollow. She needs practice on the crutches or simply enough energy to use them. Robert guides her towards the front door. I make my way downstairs.

'Hello Sophie,' Robert says in an overly cheerful voice. 'Everything all right?'

'Yes, everything's fine Robert, thank you.'

'Where do you want to go, Leila?' he asks. Mum struggles through the door, knocking the crutches on the side as she comes in. I step back and stay out of the way.

'Living room,' she says.

While Robert helps Mum get comfy on the sofa, I put the kettle on. I find three mugs and pop a teabag in one. I don't know what to do. Should I go in and try and help? I stand on the doorstep whilst the kettle boils and watch blue tits swoop across the garden and up into the safety of the trees.

'She's comfortable now,' Robert says, joining me in the kitchen.

'Does she want a hot drink?'

'No. She's going to have a sleep. I think the relief of coming home has taken it out on her more than she realised,' he says. 'I'd better get back. Are you going to be okay?'

'Of course I'll be okay,' I say. 'Why shouldn't I be?'

He doesn't say anything, but his dark eyebrows furrow. With a quick nod he backs out into the hallway.

'Tell her I'll be over tomorrow,' he whispers.

I open the door for him. 'I will.'

I feel the need to creep from room to room, aware that I'm no longer alone in the house. I take a deep breath and push the living room door open.

The bravado Mum had in hospital is gone. She's lying on the sofa with her eyes closed and her arms curled around a cushion. Her hair is lank against her pale face. Despite the warmth of the room she has a blanket wrapped around her. I tiptoe across the rug and carefully pull the blinds halfway down the window. The room darkens. There are two framed photographs on the mantelpiece above the open fireplace. The first one is of Mum and me on the beach in Falmouth. The other is Mum leaning against the backdoor of *Salt Cottage*, squinting in the sun. She's wearing paint-splattered dungarees and shading her eyes with one hand. The other hand holds a paintbrush. The cottage walls are a dirty white, the border along the house is bare and it's obvious how much time and love she has put into the house. Mum shifts on the sofa.

'Are you hungry?' I ask.

'A little,' she says without opening her eyes.

It gives me something to do and Mum time to herself. I shut myself in the kitchen and prop the back door open. At least I feel like I'm doing something useful, making Mum her first home-cooked meal in days. After all it's what I'm good at. I'm able to forget about everything when I'm cooking. I suppose it's the same with anything you enjoy.

The late afternoon sun is shining on the patio, so I set the table outside. It's shady beneath the trees but warm. The view of horses being playful in the field, rubbing their necks together, is enough to make anyone feel better. A fresh breeze wafts a ripe farmyard smell towards the cottage. It's a homely smell and reminds me of being at O *Kipos*, with its surrounding fields and farms.

Mum's asleep. I call her name twice from the doorway but she doesn't answer. I squat beside her and gently shake her good arm. 'Mum?'

She stirs, her eyes open and focus on me. 'What time is it?'

'Almost seven,' I say. 'You haven't been sleeping long. Food's ready.'

'Oh.'

'Are you still hungry?'

She nods and throws off the blanket. 'Where's the damn crutches?'

I retrieve them from the end of the sofa and help her to her feet.

'I thought we could eat outside,' I say.

'Fine.'

Mum hobbles out to the patio while I dish up. She looks at the tubs of geraniums at the bottom of the steps and the shrub filled borders edging the grass that Robert advised me to cut. I wait until she's settled at the patio table with her crutches propped against the nearest tree before joining her with two plates of food. We eat in silence. Mum picks at the salmon, taking tiny forkfuls and chewing until there surely can't be anything left in her mouth. We gaze off in opposite directions with Mum looking across the garden towards the cottage while I watch the horses in the field.

'Robert seems to really care about you,' I say, to fill the silence.

'He's a good friend.' She methodically cuts her salmon and potatoes into bite-sized pieces.

'I haven't met his wife yet.'

Mum stops cutting. 'His wife?' She looks at me. 'She's dead.'

'I didn't realise. He wears a wedding band, so I thought… You know.'

'She died when Ben and Vicky were teenagers.' She skewers a piece of potato on to her fork. 'Why do you ask? Did you say something to Robert?'

'No, no, nothing like that. I was curious. It's me assuming too much.'

'He always wears the ring but rarely talks about her. It's not a good subject to bring up.'

'I won't.'

She swallows her mouthful and says, 'Did you think I was having an affair with him as well?'

'You've taken me completely the wrong way.'

'Really?' She lets her knife and fork clatter on to her half-eaten plate of food and leans back in her chair. 'But you wouldn't have been surprised if we were?'

'Truthfully? No.' I move the salmon about on my plate. 'So, how did you find this place,' I ask, hoping *Salt Cottage* is a safe subject.

She tears her eyes away from the garden and looks at me, her blue eyes lingering on my face.

'On the internet,' she says.

'Why here?'

'I had a contact over this way who wanted me to arrange her daughter's wedding.'

'You moved for a wedding?'

'It was as good a reason as any. It was a toss-up between a city that had sucked me dry or a place like this.'

She smiles when she talks about the cottage. I'm not surprised. To have somewhere so beautiful, to have my own space and to do what I wanted, when I wanted, would put a smile on my face too.

'I'm amazed you left Bristol in the first place.'

'I had nothing keeping me there.'

'Honestly?'

'You'd gone. There was no family. Just a string of broken relationships.'

'You had masses of friends.'

'My friends were more obsessed with dieting and how to look good in a bikini than real life. I'm being unfair but I honestly didn't care about moving so far away from them. They've all got families of their own, kids and teenagers; I've got a grown-up daughter for God's sake. We spent less and less time together. I wasn't worried about not knowing anyone here. I'm not shy.'

'I saw the photo in the living room,' I say. 'The house looked a mess.'

'A bloody tip. Dirty. Stained walls. The oven didn't work, I couldn't find the microwave. I got a takeaway the first night. The nearest Chinese is a five-mile drive away, not round the corner like Hazel Road.'

'I'd have been scared I'd made a mistake.'

'I only moved house, not countries.' She stares at the cottage for a moment before saying. 'I was worried, but not for long.'

Mum stays sitting outside watching the birds darting between the trees as the sun begins to dip on the horizon. I wash up but it doesn't take me long. I find an old newspaper and sit down at the kitchen table to do the crossword.

It's dark by the time Mum appears in the kitchen doorway. She staggers in as if she's under the influence of alcohol rather than on crutches.

'It's cold out,' she says.

I fold the newspaper and scrape back my chair. 'Do you want to sit down? Watch TV?'

'I'm going upstairs,' she says, heading for the hall door. 'I've got things to do tomorrow.'

'Sleep will do you good,' is all I can think of to say. I follow her into the dark hallway, turn on the lights and stand helpless for a moment while she struggles up the first couple of stairs. 'Here,' I say, joining her. I half expect her to shrug me off but she allows me to guide her up the stairs. She pulls away from me when we reach the top step.

'Can I help with anything else?' I ask.

We stand opposite each other on the landing. A moth flits around the naked bulb above.

Mum puts her hand on her bedroom door. 'I don't care about cleaning my teeth or getting out of these bloody clothes. I just want to sleep, in my own bed.'

I shrug in defeat. 'I'll be next door if you need me.'

'I know where my spare room is, Sophie.'

She closes her bedroom door on me. I remain outside, half hoping she'll change her mind and want my help, but I hear nothing apart from the moth hitting the light bulb. I silently close the spare bedroom door behind me. I leave the blinds open on a clear midnight blue sky, the moon and stars glowing brightly. It's too still and quiet to sleep. I entertain myself by sketching a caricature of Mum with her bulbous cast and frown lines the size of craters across her forehead. I add steam coming out of her ears for good measure. I'm beginning to relax when something smashes against the other side of the wall behind my head. I drop my pencil and notebook on the bed and dash on to the landing.

'Mum?' I call through her closed door. I put my ear close and hear sobbing.

'Mum, can I come in?'

'Leave me alone,' she says.

'Are you hurt?'

'Of course I'm fucking hurt!'

I push open the door. She's perched on the bed, her broken leg stuck out, her head buried in her hands. The wardrobe door is open and a man's shirt is hanging on the back of it. One of the glasses from the bedside table is smashed on the floor. Water trickles down the wall.

'It's like he's going to fucking walk in any minute,' she says. She wipes her eyes with the back of her hand.

'I didn't want to touch your room,' I say.

'I thought I was okay about him. I coped too bloody well. But coming back to this.' She throws her hands in the air.

I notice his aftershave next to her perfume on the dressing table and the washing basket lid open. I can only imagine she found his dirty clothes mixed in with hers.

'I'll clear up,' I say.

'Leave it.' Her voice is firm. She looks at me. 'Just leave it, Sophie. It's out of my system now.'

'Do you want me to help you?' I motion towards the smashed glass.

She shakes her head. Before I close the door she quietly says, 'Thank you.'

I'm not tired so I lie on my bed and gaze out of the window at the stars. Alekos feels as distant as Mum had seemed until just a week ago. I've lost track of days and time and can't think what he'd be doing right now. Thinking of me? I hope so, because I'm thinking of him.

Chapter Seventeen

I emerge from the spare bedroom feeling lethargic from too much sleep. Going to bed early was a bad idea. I normally survive on five hours' sleep not ten. Mum's bedroom door is ajar and the bed is stripped of the duvet cover, sheets and pillowcases. Downstairs the washing machine rumbles and Mum's sitting at the kitchen table with a mug of coffee and a piece of toast.

'There's filter coffee if you want some,' she says.

'I should be doing this for you.'

'You don't have to treat me like an invalid.'

She's still in the same clothes as yesterday. I put a slice of bread in the toaster and join her at the table with my own mug of coffee.

'What are you going to do today?' I ask.

'Make phone calls. I've got a wedding to finish organising for Saturday.'

'Seriously?'

'Yep. I'm doing the flowers and the bride's make-up.'

'Is there anything I can do?'

'Not really.'

I was hoping she'd say yes. I don't want to be knocking around the house, getting in her way, killing time.

'You can weed out front if you like,' she says. 'And cook dinner.'

She gets the fork and trowel from the shed and shows me

where to weed. After getting washed and dressed she shuts herself in her study.

It's another warm, sunny day. I'm amazed by the run of good weather. It's as if I'm back in Greece, except the trees and fields are a more vivid shade of green. It's a different landscape but just as appealing.

I set about weeding the front garden. It looks immaculate but as I delve between the shrubs and flower beds I find healthy weeds poking through. It's satisfying ripping weeds up and working outdoors; being stuck in a stuffy kitchen all day and night in a hot country can get claustrophobic. At least Mum and I aren't getting underneath each other's feet. Perhaps that's why she sent me out here. Alone, with my back to the cottage and facing the trees that enclose the large front garden, I think about what I'd be doing back in Greece: marinating meat and making filo pastry for the evening; drinking a *frappe* on the patio with Alekos and Takis; chasing after a cat that's brought a lizard into the garden after a successful hunt in the field. I hear a car on the lane and glance at my watch and realise I've been outside for over an hour. Robert's Toyota pulls into the drive.

'Lovely morning, isn't it?' Robert says, getting out of the car. 'Leila inside?'

'In her study, working.' I stretch and I'm suddenly aware of the strain on my back from bending over.

'Really?' Robert says and frowns, before striding towards the front door.

'She insisted,' I call after him.

'Dad's a worrier,' Ben says, emerging from the passenger seat.

'Mum's not.'

'Do you fancy escaping for a couple of hours?' He leans on the open car door. He's clean-shaven, which makes him look younger, and wearing sunglasses. 'I want to make it up to you for being an arsehole the other night. I was tired and I had a lot on my mind, so sorry.'

I shade my eyes with my hand. 'I don't know if Mum needs me.'

'They'll be talking for hours. Trust me they won't even notice we're gone.'

It's an enticing thought to have a bit of time away. I stick the trowel in the soil. 'Okay. I'll get my jacket.'

Robert's talking to Mum in the kitchen and the kettle's boiling. I grab my jacket from off the hook in the hallway and close the front door behind me.

'What's the deal with them?' I ask, getting into the car.

'What do you mean?'

'They seem close.'

Ben shrugs. 'They were friends a long time before I got here.'

'And that's it?'

'What?' He glances at me as he turns the car sharply round, crunching over the gravel. 'You think there's something more?'

'Don't you?'

'Dad adores her,' he says. 'But as far as I know Leila's always been with someone.'

'That figures.'

I wind the window down when we reach the main road and let cool air buffer my face. I immediately feel more relaxed with Ben than Robert. It's got nothing to do with age, but his attitude. Ben is laid back, unlike Robert who always seems on edge, asking questions to fill the gaps in the conversation. With Ben the silences are comfortable. We listen to Radio One as we wind along the coast road away from Marshton. The land flattens and marshes spread towards an expanse of pale blue on the horizon.

We reach Salthouse, a village of flint houses lining the road facing the distant sea. The focal point is a triangular patch of grass full of parked cars next to a tiny fish restaurant and a Post Office. We drive past and turn left down a sandy track simply signposted 'Beach'. We cut through the marshland until we reach a stony car park in front of a bank of pebbles. The wind batters the car and when I get out its whistle mixes with the rumble of waves folding on to the shore.

'It doesn't look too busy,' I say, glancing round at the few cars lining one side of the car park.

Ben takes a rucksack from the boot. 'Most people head up to the sandy beach at Wells. I like it here.'

He throws the rucksack over one shoulder and strides towards the pebbly hill. We scramble up the embankment, our feet sinking and slipping with every effort to reach the top. It's worth it. The pebble beach stretches so far in each direction I have to squint. The sea is grey-green and churns rhythmically as it crashes on to the shore with a flurry of white foam. There are families and couples close by, camped out with their windbreaks and picnics. A young man walks with his dog along the edge of the shore.

'Come on,' Ben says.

The pebbles knock together like marbles as we half-run, half-slide down the embankment to where the beach levels off. It's difficult to walk, almost as bad as struggling across a sandy beach, but instead of my feet sinking it feels as if I'm dragging a dead weight behind me.

We find a quiet spot away from any families and screeching children. We struggle back up the pebbly embankment, almost to the top, so we can look down on the waves curling on to the shore.

'You've come prepared,' I say, as Ben reaches into his rucksack and pulls out a travel rug.

'Better than getting a cold arse.'

He flicks the rug out and the wind catches it, whipping it high into the air. I reach for one of the corners and together we bring it down flat on to the pebbles. We secure it with a large pebble on each corner and sit down.

Nearby voices are muffled by the wind and the waves breaking and bubbling on to the stones. I close my eyes and everyone around me, including Ben, peels away. The wind whispers and wraps itself around me. I shiver. I'm glad of my jacket and pull it tighter. 'That's quite a breeze,' I say.

'Straight off the North Sea. A bit of revitalising sea air. Toughen you up.' He pulls a bottle with a handwritten label from the rucksack and unscrews the lid. 'Dad's homemade elderflower champagne.'

Ben passes it to me. It has an overpowering sweet smell. He holds out two plastic cups and I pour us each a foaming cupful.

'To an hour's freedom,' he says with a knowing look.

We tap our cups together and I take a sip. It's sweet, cold and refreshing. 'That's so good,' I say.

'I told Dad he should sell it in the pub but he can't make enough of the stuff.'

'Something this good you should keep to yourself.'

He tops our drinks up. 'You have to come prepared for a day at the beach.'

'Did you grow up by the sea?'

'Hardly. I was born in Cardiff but we moved to London when I was seven. That's why I've got no accent. Dad was desperate to leave the city as soon as we got there.'

'I'm surprised Mum took so long to leave Bristol.'

'Dad only stayed in London because of work.'

'That was Mum's reason too. Actually Mum's reason was money, or lack of it at the time.'

'She's done well for herself,' he says. 'It must've been hard for her without your Dad.'

I glance at him but he's looking towards the sea. 'She had no choice but to cope.'

'How about you?'

'What about me?'

'How did you cope with no father?'

My fingers tense around the plastic cup. 'Depends on when you're talking about. I spent my childhood believing my father was a nameless, faceless person I would never meet. In some ways that was easier than at the age of twenty-one, just after I graduated, discovering that Mum knew who he was all along and not a one-night stand as she'd always said.'

'What made her own up?'

'She didn't mean to tell me. We were supposed to be celebrating my graduation but she'd come home late. She was drunk and ended up opening a letter from him, which took her by surprise and she was forced to tell me the truth.'

'Have you met him?'

The sea's rhythmic churn is mesmerising. I watch the next wave foam on to the pebbles. 'No.'

'Do you want to?'

I shrug. 'I don't think he's going to live up to my expectations.'

'I worry about that with Fraser and Bella – my kids.'

'What's to worry about, they know who you are.'

'I just don't want them to spend so little time with me that they don't get to know me beyond what their mother tells them.'

We fall quiet and sip our drinks. 'I love being by the sea,' I say after a while. 'Even if it's not bikini weather like in Greece.'

'I love coming here on cloudy days, when it's really windy and there's no one about,' Ben says.

'Windier than this?'

'You have to fight your way along the beach sometimes. It's funny watching the seagulls being smacked by the wind.' He glances at me. 'I'm easily amused.'

'What do you do, besides freeze to death?'

'Think about things.'

'A rare moment to yourself, eh?'

'It must be difficult in Greece, to find time to yourself?'

'Practically impossible.' I lean back and find a comfortable spot, resting my hands on two palm-sized pebbles. 'Alekos' parents are always there. We work together, eat together, practically sleep together the walls are so thin.'

Ben laughs. 'Sleeping with the in-laws, eh?' He nudges my arm with his elbow. 'Is there nowhere to escape?'

'There's this spot at the far end of the garden that's mine. Alekos has learnt to leave me alone if I'm leaning on the fence. I could stand and look at Olympus for hours.'

'That's your view?'

I nod.

'Beats this.'

'Not really. This is wild. It's beautiful.'

'You should see it in December when the sea's grey and churned up and the waves literally smash on to this beach. It's deserted here in winter. I can't stand packed beaches or anywhere that's been overdeveloped. But that's just me. I've always been a bit of a weirdo.'

'That's not weird,' I say. 'Alekos always moans when I drag him away from the crowds to the furthest end of the beach.'

'Hot and sweaty tourists. Not my idea of fun.'

'It's only when he wants to play volleyball that we end up next to loads of people. Once I'm floating in the sea I could be the only one there.'

'Great minds think alike.' He knocks his plastic cup of elderflower champagne against mine. 'I like my own company. Don't get me wrong, I like spending time with people but it's doing my head in living with Dad. He means well but he's treating me like a teenager instead of an adult with two children.'

'I know the feeling. I don't mean being here with Mum. I mean my life in Greece...'

Ben knocks a cigarette out from the packet in his jacket pocket, slips it between his lips and shelters the lighter from the wind with his hand. 'I started again,' he says, flicking ash into the empty bottle.

'You managed to quit?'

'For about six months. I started again on Sunday.'

'What happened on Sunday?'

'My soon-to-be ex-wife went off on one.'

'Is that why you're living here?' I ask.

He takes a drag on his cigarette and gazes towards the sea.

The stones are digging into my palms. 'Sorry, that's rude of me.'

'No, it's not. In fact, that's the truth. I moved here because it was the easy option,' he says. He takes his sunglasses off and chucks them on top of the rucksack. 'Dad offered, said he wanted me here. If only to keep an eye on me.'

'It must be hard.'

'I fucked things up and I have to live with that. But she's being a bitch. I moved out because we both needed space and now I get to see Fraser and Bella once a month if I'm lucky. She blamed me for being irresponsible and ruining our marriage. Now she's the one who's hooked up with some bloke.' He grinds his barely-smoked cigarette on one of the pebbles. 'This is miserable talk for a day like this. Let's go for a paddle.'

I can't blame him if he doesn't want to carry on talking but I understand his outburst. It must be so hard for both him and his kids to cope with their family life dissolving around them. At least I can't miss what I haven't got. I follow Ben's lead and roll my jeans up, kick off my trainers and edge across the pebbles. The water is icy cold. The shock to my skin sends shivers through me. Any leftover summer warmth has been dragged into the sea's depths with the current. The stones are smooth and round beneath the soles of my feet and clunk together. The waves breaking on the shore erase the noise of children playing on the beach. I close my eyes. I could be alone, the only person for miles...

Cold water splashes my face. I open my eyes and Ben is in front of me grinning. We stand opposite each other like sumo wrestlers, each waiting for the other to make a move. I drag my hands across the surface of the sea and throw water into the air, splashing Ben's T-shirt and jeans. He moves towards me, almost in slow motion, the sea churning in his wake. I back away but I can barely walk, let alone run on the stony seabed. I manage to get some momentum going and splash my way to shore, getting my jeans wetter than if I'd waited for Ben's attack. I collapse on to the pebbles and Ben sinks down next to me.

'I haven't done that for years,' I say, catching my breath between laughter. I turn on my side and rest on my elbow.

'Dad would say I'm too old to be behaving like a kid.'

'You've got children of your own, they're your excuse.'

'What's yours?'

I shrug. 'Do I need one? I don't feel any older than I did when I was a teenager. Do you ever get that feeling?'

'I did until Fraser was born.' He turns to me. 'That pretty much puts everything into perspective. It changes your life.' He stands, reaches out his hand and pulls me to my feet. 'Make the most of it now.'

We drive to *Salt Cottage*, sun-kissed and wind-battered but refreshed. The drive back is as quiet and comfortable as the journey there. Where the sea meets the horizon the sky is darkening with rain clouds and I'm glad we're heading towards the sunshine. It doesn't take long and I'm already familiar with the crossroads at Blakeney and the road that dips down the hill past the tree-shrouded church towards the cottage.

'Thanks Ben,' I say as he halts in the driveway next to Mum's car. 'I really enjoyed myself.'

'Me too. It makes a change.'

I close the car door and wave.

'Don't be a stranger, Sophie,' he calls before driving off.

Mum and Robert are in her study. I can hear muffled conversation through the closed door. I don't disturb them by saying hello.

The spare bedroom feels like my own – a bit of private space, more than I have at *O Kipos*. I throw the clothes I'd chucked over the back of the armchair on to the bed and sit down next to the window. It's been a strange day and an even odder week. There's been no time to sit back and reflect.

When I was on my own in Mum's house there were things to do, even if it was just discovering the cottage and the surrounding area or unannounced visits from Robert.

I don't have a book to read. I've nothing to do besides think and look at the view. The sky is darkening over Blakeney now, slate grey clouds rolling in from the North Sea. The promise of autumn blustering towards us. I'll have to raid Mum's bookcase and start something new. Kate Mosse's *Labyrinth* is lying half-read on my bedside table in Greece.

A rainbow arcs across the sky. There's a feeling of limbo between night and day with the sun shining on the garden and the darkening clouds gathering on the horizon. I push the window up and stick my head out. The air is fresh and cool. And then I see them, their cream wings flickering in the sunlight, butterflies, making patterns in the air directly below the window. They make me think of Alekos; my best friend, my fiancé. There was the promise of so much more – but somewhere our promises have disintegrated, been lost to the wind like those butterflies below. I hug my knees to my chest. The expanding black cloud extinguishes the sun but Alekos remains imprinted on my thoughts.

Chapter Eighteen

When the clouds swamp the sun and the butterflies disperse, I venture downstairs to start dinner. There's the threat of rain in the air and I'm glad I enjoyed the sunshine while it lasted. I'm in the kitchen peeling potatoes when Robert pokes his head round the door.

'She's a stubborn one,' he says. He closes the door behind him, stands next to the table and looks out through the back door.

'I'm sorry?' I let the peeler clatter into the sink.

'She's insisting on doing everything for this wedding on Saturday. They've paid her already, see, and she doesn't want to let anyone down. Typical of her. So we've put you on her car insurance,' he continues. 'So you can drive her to and fro.'

'You do realise I've not driven in four years? At least not on the correct side of the road. Anyway, meeting a donkey in the middle of a narrow track up a mountain put me off for good.'

'Oh, I see. Well, it's only horses you're likely to meet on these roads.'

'Robert, I'm joking, I'll be fine.'

He laughs. 'Good. I see you have your mother's sense of humour.' He looks away from me to the garden. 'They want the flowers delivered early in the morning. Plus she's got to do the bride's and bridesmaids' hair and make-up. She's going to need your help.'

'Why do you think I'm here?'

'I know, I know, I'm just making sure. I don't want her running herself into the ground.'

'I'm doing my best. She's not the easiest person to help. She's always been like this. A broken leg and me being here isn't going to change that.'

He nods; his face is drawn and pale and the strain of everyone else's problems shows in the bags beneath his eyes and the lines across his forehead. 'Did Ben go home?' he asks.

I nod and start peeling another potato.

'Did you both have a good afternoon?'

'Yes, thank you, I loved your elderflower homebrew.'

'It's good that Ben's got someone younger around, you know, to talk to.'

Robert drums his fingers on the table: tap, tap, tap, pause, tap, tap, tap... 'Ben's going through a difficult patch at the moment, with his wife and the divorce.'

'I gathered, but he didn't seem to want to talk about it much.'

'He lost his job too,' Robert continues. 'He had a great job as a photographer for a travel magazine.'

'He didn't say.'

My scraping joins his nervous tapping. Robert takes an audible deep breath. I'm on the last potato.

'I'm an eternal worrier, that's all, and Ben doesn't talk to me which makes me worry all the more,' he says. He rolls up his shirtsleeves. 'I've got Ben and Leila to worry about now.'

I'm worried he's going to cry. Instead he neatens his rolled up sleeves, gives me a weak smile and makes for the door. 'I'd best let you get on.'

I drop the last potato into a pan of water and wipe my hands on the towel. 'Don't worry about Leila so much. She's tough. And as for Ben, I don't really know him, but it was great spending time with him. He took my mind off things too.'

'I'm glad you're here, Sophie,' he says as he leaves.

I sit down on the steps leading to the garden and take a deep breath. Dark clouds fill the sky and the breeze is fresh and cold. There's dampness in the air. The butterflies have gone, danced their way into oblivion. My walk up to Blakeney seems a long time ago, before Mum came home. Even though she's only in the next room, the distance between us feels greater than it did when we lived thousands of miles apart.

Tears build in my throat – I put it down to PMT. I wrap my arms around my knees and hug them to my chest. I'm more confused than I was before I got here. I don't know what I was expecting – a magical cure or that it would be easy to kiss and make up with Mum. I can't forget the past and know she can't either. Too much has been said and done to simply erase it and start over.

The backs of my hands are damp and sobs catch in my throat. I feel in limbo, unsure of where I belong or where I want to be. At least it's peaceful here. I'm sure Mum and I could manage not to see each other all day if we chose not to. I wipe away my tears. Goosebumps steal across my arms. The wind has picked up and rustles through the leaves, catching some and twirling them on the breeze before allowing them to float to the ground.

I close the back door on the grey sky and turn on the kitchen light. I'd like a kitchen like this: homely, warm, countrified but with a sleek stainless steel cooking range. It's a proper kitchen, with wooden work surfaces and normal sized pots and pans unlike the O *Kipos* kitchen that we use whether we're cooking for a hundred people or just the four of us. It's a simple meal tonight at Mum's request: ham, boiled eggs, new potatoes and salad and it doesn't take me long to prepare it. It's raining by the time I knock on Mum's study door to tell her dinner's ready.

'I'll eat it in here,' she says.

She's at her desk, working on her laptop. She barely looks up at me.

'You don't want to sit at the table?' I ask.

'No, I've still got emails to send and then I'm going to bed.'

That's the extent of our conversation for the rest of the evening. Ignoring me is not going to make me go away. I eat in the kitchen on my own, clear away and wash up. Afterwards I sit down in the living room and choose one of Mum's DVDs to watch. She's replaced all our old videos with DVDs and bought a load more. I'm not in the mood for anything sad so that rules out *Braveheart*, *Beaches* and *ET*. I want something to take my mind off things and I finally decide on *Friends*. I curl up on the sofa and snuggle into the soft cushions. An hour later, at nine o'clock, Mum's study door creaks open. There's a brief silence before a slow rhythmic thud as she makes her way upstairs. Despite wanting to make sure she's okay, I stay put and only relax when I hear her bedroom door slam shut.

The flowers arrive the next morning. I open the front door to find a shrivelled looking man with broken veins in his cheeks and a tobacco-stained grin. He stands on the doorstep, not with a bouquet of flowers, but a van-full in the drive.

'Is Leila not in?' he asks. I thought Marcy's accent was strong but his beats it, drawn-out and thick Norfolk.

'She's still asleep.'

'Terrible, terrible what happened.'

'You've heard?'

'Word gets around,' he says. 'Is she?' He gestures with his hands, which I take to mean 'is she coming down?'

'She's not up yet.'

'Oh,' he says. 'Best get these flowers in.'

I follow him out to his van. *Wilde's Flowers* is written on the side in green. He slides open the side door and climbs in. The smell is sweet and potent. I recognise some of the more common flowers: roses, lilies and carnations, but there are exotic ones too. He passes Mum's order of flowers to me in buckets and I put them down on the gravel.

'I'll give you a hand taking them in,' he says after handing me the last lot.

'It's okay, I've got nothing else to do.'

He shrugs. 'You're the boss.'

'Do I need to pay you now?'

'No, no need, Leila will settle up with me later. Tell her there's no rush.'

After taking the third bucket of flowers upstairs to Mum's workroom, I regret being so generous with my time. No wonder he gave me such an odd look. I'm not unfit but I'm no wonder woman – certainly not after the fifth trip upstairs.

The workroom looks like a florist's by the time I'm done. I tentatively clear a space on the table, ensuring I don't muddle up any of the paperwork and drawings in the process.

The door creaks open and Mum thumps in on her crutches. 'You should have called me.'

She surveys the room. Her cheeks have more colour than when I saw her last night. Her hair is loose around her shoulders and she looks cool and comfortable in a cardigan and floor-grazing summer skirt.

'How many flower arrangements do you have to do?' I ask.

'A lot,' she replies, hobbling across the room. She inspects the flowers one by one and sniffs them. 'They want things done in style.'

'It's a big wedding then?'

'The bride's mother is a social animal. She wants this wedding to be talked and no doubt written about. The reception is in a marquee in their garden. You'll see it on Saturday.'

We work in silence for a while. She even trusts me to cut the flowers to the right length. It's satisfying snipping and crushing the stems.

'I'm surprised you're not married yet,' she says.

I bite my lip and don't say anything. Despite the fact I have every intention of inviting her to our wedding saying anything now will seem like an afterthought. I try to judge the comment and tone. I can't tell if it's an honest question. History makes me think otherwise.

'I had you down for calling within a year saying you were Mrs Kakawhatsit and you had a bun in the oven.' She looks at the flowers and not me.

'That's ironic, considering the last thing you said to me before I left for Greece suggested you didn't think we'd stay together.'

'I remember the last thing you said,' she says.

'With good reason.'

Her face flushes. 'Pass the scissors, would you.'

'It'd been building up for years,' I say. I pick half a dozen pink carnations from the bucket by my feet and start snipping the ends. I look across at her. 'Why did you lie to me?'

'About what?'

'Don't play dumb. You know exactly what I'm talking about.'

'I've always done what I felt was right at the time.'

'Even if it meant deceiving me?'

She bites her lip and focuses on the arrangement she's working on. Her fingers grip the thorny stalk of a pink rose. I watch her across the leaf- and petal-strewn table. So much for tiptoeing round each other these last few days. If she wants to ask awkward questions then I can play that game too. 'Do you ever think about him? My father?'

She sweeps the discarded leaves and petals off the table into a bin. 'Not in a long time.'

'Were you ashamed?'

She glances at me. 'Of what?'

'Of what I'd think about you, having an affair with a married man.'

'You really think I'd care about that?'

I snip and crush the stem of the last carnation. 'I guess not. I thought you might have some shame about him and his wife being best friends with Gran and Grandad. No wonder you fell out with them. It was a bit more complicated than Gran disowning you because you were pregnant.'

She looks at me sharply and her blue eyes narrow. 'How do you know?'

'I do occasionally talk to Gran.'

She catches her breath as if I've just winded her with my words. She places her hands palm down on the table; blue veins are prominent through still fragile skin.

'She hates me because she's had to keep our affair secret to save his marriage. Elliot chose his wife. Mum was happy. She didn't make me leave. Elliot managed that by himself. I'm no angel but it takes two.'

'Why did you wait so long to tell me about him?'

'I'd as good as erased him from my life and I wanted to keep it that way. I didn't want you asking awkward questions. If he didn't exist, then there was nothing you could do. No chance of you wanting to contact him. It was easier. I've never said it was the right thing.' She busies herself again, cutting a roll of pink ribbon into lengths.

'When you opened his letter that night, why did you destroy it?'

She shakes her head. 'I was angry with him. It was unexpected. I hadn't seen or heard from him since I left Sheffield, pregnant with you. I'd kept my promise and stayed out of his life and then he did something like that.' She snips angrily at the ribbon. 'I wasn't going to write back. What was I going to say? Your daughter, the one you've never met, is doing fine. Finished university. Just graduated. I'm proud of her. Hope you are too. Waste of bloody trees.'

'You could have let me read it.'

'It was an accident that I even told you that night. I was drunk and his unexpected letter shocked me into saying something.'

'Otherwise I'd never have found out?'

'By telling you those stories about not knowing who your father was made me almost believe them myself. Except he's always played on my mind. You remind me of him so much. The older you got, the more you looked like him. He said in his letter how proud he was of you. He's never even met you.' She sniffs hard to fight back tears. The arrangement she's working on is taking shape: pink and cream miniature roses woven into a circular display. 'He's an architect. Well respected. Intelligent, creative, focused, impulsive. You're alike, I can't deny that. You're more like him than you are me.' She puts the rose she's holding on the table and looks at me. I mean really looks at me, her eyes searching my face. 'That night, when you walked out, I was devastated. I felt I'd failed you.'

I suddenly realise how tense I am. I move beside her and slide my arm around her slight shoulders. She shudders, whether from my touch or her tears, I'm not sure.

'Until you have a child of your own, Sophie,' she says after a while, 'you won't understand the amount of responsibility, time and love they take. They're your life, your whole fucking world.' She pulls away from me. 'I'm going to lie down. I'll finish this later.'

I close myself away in my bedroom too. We're walking away from each other yet again. There's a lump in my throat but I'm all cried out. Ironically, when I was growing up there was only one person I would turn to at times like this. I haven't thought about him in a very long time but right now I can't get him out of my head.

Before the night Mum told me the truth about my real father, I often daydreamed about my Dad. He was real in my mind, not the nameless, faceless one-night stand Mum described him as. He always stayed the same age, somewhere around the age I am now, I guess. I invented a father when I realised I was different from my friends. Even the friends whose parents had split up still had a dad. He might not live with them anymore but he would take them to the park or watch them play football, give them presents on their birthdays and at Christmas. So I invented a father figure that I'm sure no man could live up to. I called him Dad: his surname was Keech, the same as mine of course and if anyone asked I said his name was Mikey, after Sean Astin's character in *The Goonies*.

He always sided with me whatever I'd done wrong. I had his green eyes and red hair. He was quieter than Mum, didn't embarrass me, didn't show me up in front of my friends or get me drunk on my fifteenth birthday. In fact he frowned on all of that. He was a voice of reason when I needed him. Mum came to school plays and parents' evening, friends' parties and sports days. Dad was there when no one else was, during my exams, when I was alone, when I was sad.

He was real until the night Mum destroyed him. I never got him back. Instead I was given a poor replacement, a stranger with a meaningless name, a man far removed from the perfect father I'd constructed since the age of seven. I don't know how I can forgive her for that.

Chapter Nineteen

I stall the car on the first attempt and then when I do get it going my right hand automatically reaches for the gear stick and finds the door handle instead. Mum fidgets in the passenger seat. We crunch out of the gate and bump up the lane and on to the road. It's a much newer car than Alekos' hand-me-down and doesn't sound anywhere near as rough.

'Nice car,' I say.

'I should have bought a van.'

It's true; there are flowers everywhere, squashed into the boot, obscuring the rear window, piled high on the back seat, even on Mum's lap and arranged around her leg cast.

It's good to be driving again, even if it is with silent company. Mum only speaks to give directions. We drive the few miles to the church along a fast main road and then down winding lanes not wide enough to pass two cars. Each lane looks identical to the last, with tall grasses on either side speckled with hogweed and mugwort. The fields beyond are varying shades of green and yellow and misted with the morning light. Last night's dusk and pink sky promised a sunny day, but there's a nip in the air.

'Pull over here,' Mum says when houses begin to line the sides of the road. I do as I'm told and stop on a grass verge. Through closed gates I spy a church with a clock tower soaring above the trees.

'Let's get to work,' she says.

Armed with flowers, I follow Mum up the path to the entrance. Inside it's dusky and cool with enough dark wooden pews to seat a hundred guests on either side of the aisle, but it's still small enough for an intimate service. I place the flowers on one of the pews for Mum to deal with and go back for more.

By the time we finish the church smells of roses and the darkness of the wood and stone is offset by the pink and cream petals. I can imagine the scene in a few hours' time when the sun streams though the stained glass and the pews are filled with guests in suits or dresses and wide-brimmed hats. The bride and groom will emerge from the church to be showered by confetti. Mum places two large arrangements on either side of the gate. Variegated ivy trails down and entwines itself around the bars of the fence.

'We'll drive to the house,' Mum says. She hobbles back to the car and eases her way on to the front seat. 'It's not far.'

Next to wrought-iron gates, the sign reads, *Kingfisher Hall.* We drive along a sweeping gravel drive. *Kingfisher Hall* is obscured by trees, until the drive curves and the house finally comes into view. I'm not sure what I was expecting but it wasn't this. It looks secretive – if a house can be described as that – reminiscent of a National Trust property. The walls are covered in creepers, trained around the many windows. I park alongside a BMW, Porsche and Land Rover. The front door is ajar and Mum pushes it open and goes in. The entrance hall houses a staircase that curves to the first floor. Our shoes tap across chequered black and white flagstones. There are distant voices coming from different parts of the house.

'Pamela?' Mum calls.

Doors bang upstairs before a shock of blonde hair appears over the banister.

'Leila, honey, how are you?' The blonde hair belongs to a fifty-something woman who clatters down the stairs in pink high heels and a black Japanese print dressing gown. She hugs Mum and plants a kiss on her cheek. 'You poor, poor thing.'

She pulls away from Mum. 'But you're looking well, you really are.' She glances over at me. 'And who's this?'

'My daughter, Sophie,' Mum says. 'She's come over from Greece.'

'Greece. Fabulous.'

Mum turns to me. 'This is Pamela, mother of the bride.'

'I just love it – mother of the bride!' She rolls her eyes at me. 'It's my youngest daughter, Sylvie, who's getting married. My eldest has sworn off marriage and is living in sin with a man twice her age.'

Pamela is already in full make-up. Up close, when she kisses my cheek, I can see the tell-tale lines around her eyes and the way her jawline is beginning to sag. Even so she's a beautiful woman, confident and unforgettable.

'The girls are in Sylvie's room,' she says, ushering us upstairs.

The first floor hallway runs the length of the house, from east to west with the stairs in the centre. Pamela leads us down the left-hand side corridor and we creak our way to the end room at the back of the house.

'I'll leave you to it,' Pamela says, before heading into another room.

We're engulfed by women screeching, laughter and Britney Spears' "Oops!... I Did It Again". A muddle of perfumes stick in my throat. Three girls are dancing around the room. It's a teenager's bedroom with teddy bears propped on the bed and pictures of horses on the wall. As for the bride, I wouldn't put her past her early twenties.

'Hi Leila,' Sylvie says, still swirling. She's a younger version of Pamela and sickeningly pretty, even without a touch of make-up on.

'It's a pink theme,' Mum whispers. 'I tried everything to dissuade them.' She shrugs. 'It's their wedding, their photos.'

Pink it certainly is. Sylvie's dress on first glance is cream, but a fitted bodice leads my eye towards a full skirt with swirls of pink chiffon sewn on to the cream satin. Her hair is strawberry blonde, almost certainly dyed, as it's too perfect and obvious a colour to be natural.

Mum unloads a bag heaving with foundation, lipsticks, eye shadow and blusher. There's commotion at the dressing table with the first bridesmaid until Mum gets herself on the right level to do the girl's make-up.

Sylvie twirls towards me. 'Hi.' She holds out her left hand and I shake it, aware of her engagement ring with a diamond the size of a cherry glinting at me. 'Are you doing our make-up too?'

'No. Mum only trusts me with the flowers.' Any memories Mum might have of encouraging me, aged twelve, to experiment with make-up when I would rather have smeared my face with mud probably don't help.

'You can start putting the table arrangements in the marquee, Sophie,' Mum says.

'It's going to look so totally amazing out there,' Sylvie says.

'What music shall I put on now?' One of the bridesmaids calls across the room.

Pamela pokes her head round the door. 'Anyone for Bucks Fizz?'

I escape the singing and constant squirt of perfume and leave Mum to transform Sylvie and her two pink-cheeked bridesmaids. The bridesmaids are more fortunate than Sylvie. Their dusky pink floor-length skirts and bodices are actually quite flattering.

The house is intriguing and doesn't quite fit with an over-the-top pink wedding. The decorations and furniture betray the owner's tastes: alongside fireplaces and wood-panelled walls are white leather sofas and flowery wallpaper that overpower the history. I'd love to explore it, to rip away the modern touch and discover the past. Back in the entrance hall, I find the hallway that leads to the rear of the house. My footsteps on the flagstones merge with the voices and laughter echoing from other parts of the house. I slip silently out of the back door and on to a patio the size of our entire back garden in Hazel Road. It is weed-free and the stone looks polished, as if someone's given it a good scrub. A raised border divides the patio from the lawn. The marquee is huge and white, with pink balloons hanging above the entrance. It's set in the middle of a large lawn that reaches towards weeping willows and a meandering river at the end of the garden. The grass looks newly laid. With no moss, weeds, daises or clover, it looks artificial but is spongy underfoot. The grass in Greece shrivels in the sun and is constantly trampled on by customers and children playing. I feel I should take my shoes off and not ruin it; it's like walking on a new carpet.

It's warm inside the marquee and it will be warmer by the time the guests arrive. Two girls in black trousers and fitted white shirts are laying the tables round the dance floor. I set a centrepiece of miniature pink and cream roses on each table and place two larger ones on the head table, next to jars of dolly mixtures, jelly babies and flying saucers. There are bottles of pink champagne to wash everything down and even the place names are handwritten on pink cards.

By the time I've finished in the marquee, the two girls are putting up tables and chairs on the lawn. Music floats from an upstairs window and when I recognise Rihanna's "Umbrella" I presume it must be Sylvie's room. I go back through the house and meet Pamela at the bottom of the stairs. Still in her dressing gown she clasps two champagne glasses. Her long nails are now shocking pink.

'Sweetheart,' she says. 'I was coming to find you.' She hands me one of the glasses. 'Buck's Fizz. We'll start the day as we mean to go on.' She pulls me to one side. 'Leila's an absolute trouper. I told her that man of hers was no good. To think what could have happened. I'm sorry for the poor guy but at least she's shot of him now. She needs someone decent. Someone to take care of her.'

'She's never expected a man to look after her.'

'Tsch, tsch,' she says, leaning towards me. Her hazelnut eyes are framed by lashes thick with black mascara. 'We'll see.'

It doesn't take long to empty the back seat of the remaining flowers. There are more cars in the drive now, more family members filling the house with laughter and chatter. I take the buttonholes and Sylvie's bouquet up to her room. Hairspray clouds the air masking the perfume. It resembles an impromptu karaoke bar with hairbrushes in place of mikes as the two bridesmaids sing along to Abba at the top of their voices. The Buck's Fizz is certainly flowing. Mum is curling Sylvie's hair. She glances up at me, raises her eyebrows and shrugs towards the two girls. Pamela is clapping along to the music. This is my idea of hell. I was never the kind of girl to dream of white, let alone pink weddings, or to have named my future children by the age of thirteen. I always thought there was something twisted about schoolgirls discussing how many kids they were going to have before they'd even kissed a boy.

'Do you need any help?' I ask Mum over the noise.

'No,' she says through a mouthful of hairpins.

'I'll check outside again.' I leave the noise and fumes and head back through the house and into the garden. The grass slopes towards the riverbank. I crouch down and let the coolness of the fast-flowing water caress my hand. Forget everything that's going on behind me, this is the centrepiece of the garden. The sound of the water trickling over rocks is soothing. A dragonfly hovers millimetres above the water. My fingers are frozen and I shiver. The sun is shining but weak; the breeze wraps itself round me and through the slender branches of the willow trees.

I sit cross-legged on the grassy bank and phone Alekos.

'Hi stranger,' I say when he answers. 'I tried calling you yesterday.'

'I know. I had a meeting at the bank.'

'Oh?'

'I had to work straight after,' he says.

'Are you working today?'

'What do you think?'

I ignore his comment. 'I've been helping Mum.'

'Doing what?'

'The flowers for this wedding. You should see it, all pink and showy. Your Mum would love it.'

Our conversation dissolves into silence. A boat with peeling white paint is moored on the other bank. I wonder where the river would take me if I set sail. Out into the wild, unpredictable North Sea?

'I'd like to be my own boss, like Mum is,' I say. 'Run my own kitchen one day.'

'Look, Sophie, I can't talk long,' Alekos says.

'I know, you're busy.'

'When I said about coming home, it's because I miss you. I'm hoping you'll be home for your birthday.'

The light from my mobile dies as he hangs up. I hadn't given my birthday a thought. It's next Sunday, a week tomorrow. I'll have been here three weeks by then.

'Sophie!' Mum's voice calls across the garden. 'I'm done.'

She's standing next to Pamela who has changed into a suit even more shocking pink than her nails. I slowly walk over to them, leaving behind tranquillity for fake glamour.

'You've both done a super job,' Pamela says, linking her arms with ours. 'Promise me you'll come back this evening and have a drink or two with us.'

'We'd love to,' Mum says.

Pamela leads us through the house and out on to the driveway where a number of people have gathered. The men of the family are smart in grey suits with waistcoats the colour of the bridesmaid's outfits.

The BMW on the drive has been dressed with pink ribbon ready for Pamela and the two bridesmaids. There's a horse and carriage waiting for Sylvie and her father, smart in his top hat. The grey horse flicks its tail and pounds the gravel impatiently with its hoof before they move off in a convoy towards the church and Sylvie's husband-to-be.

Back at *Salt Cottage* Mum sleeps for a couple of hours. She looks drained, the busyness of this morning and the past couple of days finally catching up with her. At seven, as befits the planner of a pink wedding, Mum chooses her outfit to match the flower arrangements: a pale pink knee-length skirt and cream top; she even finds a pink necklace.

'There's not a lot I can do about this bloody leg,' she says, looking at her white cast in the full-length mirror. 'I'm going to need my other leg waxing soon.'

Even with a broken leg she looks more glamorous than I do. I make do with cream linen trousers, a halter neck top and a cardigan borrowed from Mum because I feel exposed with autumn definitely in the air.

We miss out on the three-course dinner, the speeches and the toasts to the bride and groom, but make it back in time for the jazz band, dancing and the buffet. The pink theme continues into the night. The trees lining the edge of the garden and river are floodlit with a pink gel, turning the leaves a strange colour. Tall lanterns flicker light across the patio where a never-ending supply of drinks is available.

Sylvie's mother and new mother-in-law are trying to outdo each other: Pamela in fuchsia pink to match – or more likely from what I've seen of her – upstage her daughter. The mother-in-law's dress is bright turquoise, with a matching feathered hat. They both remind me of a version of the woman I met on the plane. They have the same immaculate hair, make-up and clothes. But there's something ever so insincere about both of them. Rula wasn't like that. Her look was effortless and understated and there was a woman beneath I really wanted to get to know. I don't feel like that with these two. Would it be the same with Mum and Despina?

To the left of the marquee there's a popcorn and candyfloss stand. Guests have spilled out on to the lawn clutching thin-stemmed glasses of pink champagne. The photographer is still here, trying to get as many different combinations of family and friends together as possible. I even see him make the two poor bridesmaids jump into the air and land on spongy grass in five-inch heels.

Sylvie is tipsy; she concentrates hard putting one heeled foot in front of the other as she walks towards me. 'Isn't this the most incredible day,' she says, leaning on me. 'I'm so lucky. I'm going to the Maldives tomorrow. I chose the holiday. Mattie was happy as long as he could watch football. He can watch football while I sunbathe.' She rolls her eyes. 'My best friend said I was too young to get married.'

Her arm is heavy around my shoulders. 'How old are you?'

'Twenty-two. She's just jealous. It's only because she'll be losing her pulling partner.' She turns to me. 'What do you think?'

Her breath stinks of peach schnapps and garlic chicken from the buffet. I shrug. 'If you love him, what difference does it make?'

'Exactly. Are you in love?'

'I am, but we've lost our way.'

She frowns and her arm drops from my shoulder. 'Come and dance.'

'No thanks, I'd best find Mum and I'm sure your husband will be wondering where you are.'

She gives me a wave and makes her way slowly from the patio towards the marquee.

'Only the best for my princess,' Sylvie's father says as she joins him. He's smoking a cigar and talking to his new son-in-law who's built like a rugby player.

'Did you get me a drink, sweetheart?' Mattie says.

'Oops, I forgot!'

Sylvie's father is still talking, loud enough for everyone around him to hear. 'I wanted a bigger marquee. But that's the largest one they do. About £4000 with the lighting.'

I look around at the strangers' faces in conversation on the patio, at three little girls in pink dresses dancing in a circle by the candyfloss stand. Pamela is laughing loudly with an elderly couple and I spy the best man by the river kissing a lanky brunette in a red dress. Mum's alone on a bench beneath one of the willow trees. I walk over and sit beside her.

'Why do people throw ridiculous amounts of money into a wedding when it's clear it's all going to go wrong,' I say.

'You think so?'

'Yeah, she's a trophy girl for him and he's good-looking but sounds a bit of a twat.'

'Maybe it will last then.'

'I swear that rock on her finger is just a status symbol. She cares more about the honeymoon than she does about him.'

'See this.' Mum shuffles over and points to the plaque on the centre of the bench. 'Some things do last.'

For Pamela & Raymond
On your 25th Wedding Anniversary

I look at my bare ring finger. The understated but gorgeous diamond ring Alekos had given me four weeks after his proposal is in its box in our bedroom in Greece. It had taken him that long to find it and it was perfect. I wave my hands towards the marquee and the guests and swallow back tears. 'All these people, all this attention, the big dress, the money spent on this wedding, I couldn't think of anything worse.'

'Good. I'm glad.'

I glance at her. 'You planned all this.'

'It doesn't mean I have to like it,' she says with a smile. 'I'm just good at my job. I organised one wedding reception on a boat. Now that was classy. They only invited twenty guests and after the actual service they all piled on to the, oh God what was it called...' she looks up into the pink-tinged leaves for a moment. '*The Marauder*, that was it. They went seal spotting first. Then they moored up at Wells for a Lebanese buffet and drinks late into the night. It was low-key. The bride and groom would have been happy with bangers and mash as long as it meant being together.'

'I like bangers and mash.'

'So do I.'

We fall silent and look across the lawn towards the marquee and its backdrop of *Kingfisher Hall*. The garden is floodlit like a football pitch. The jazz band is playing inside the marquee. The sound of saxophone, bass guitar and piano washes towards us. Behind us the river flows idly by on its way to the sea while we try not to look in the direction of the best man and the woman in red.

'I'm sorry about yesterday,' Mum says. 'For having a go at you. I was tired, but truthfully I don't know how to behave around you. I've been on my own for so long. I don't mean that in a lonely pity me kind of way. It's just we've had our problems and it feels like we've picked up right where we left off.'

'I'm sorry too. But I'm glad we talked, we need to, you know, talk about him.' I leave it, unable, unwilling to say much more. We sit side by side, gazing out over the spectacle Mum helped create and I'm content with just that for the moment.

We yawn all the way home and it's gone midnight by the time we get in. Mum flicks on the light and steps on an envelope. She picks it up and glances at the name on the front before passing it to me.

I rip it open and unfold the piece of paper. It's handwritten. All it says is:

I've got nothing to do tomorrow and I hope you've made no plans because I'm going to pick you up at 10am, Ben.

P.S. Bring wet weather gear (just in case) and walking boots (if they fit, Leila's got some, otherwise trainers will do).

'From Ben is it?' Mum asks. She's waiting at the bottom of the stairs.

I look up and nod. 'Inviting me out tomorrow.'

'Uh, uh.' She makes to go, then turns back. 'Just watch yourself.'

'What's that supposed to mean?' I call up the stairs after

169

her.

She shrugs and closes her bedroom door behind her.

I'm left bemused in the hallway with Ben's letter still in my hand. I'm unsure what Mum was implying but I realise I don't actually care. I'll be my own judge of Ben's character. I tuck his letter into my trouser pocket and go upstairs to bed.

Chapter Twenty

I wake up thinking about Ben. It's eight-thirty on a Sunday morning. Mum's still in bed and half of me wishes I could lie in too. The more adventurous side of me likes the idea of being told to be up for a certain time, not knowing what the day ahead will bring.

I'm ready way too early. I'm showered, dressed and waiting for him by quarter to ten. I make a pot of filter coffee, hoping the smell will entice Mum down to continue last night's conversation. The coffee tastes bitter and I have to stir in three spoonfuls of sugar before I can drink it.

Mum's walking boots are lined up by the front door and my waterproof is hanging on the stair post. I peer out through the living room window and wait. He arrives bang on time. I gather my things together and meet him outside.

'You got my note then,' he says through the open car window. 'I had a horrible thought I'd have to come in and wake you up. Actually, it was quite a nice thought.'

'I was really pleased.' I say, getting into the car. 'The days here are endless. I have nothing to do besides help Mum. I don't begrudge her that but I hate being bored.'

'Well Keech, you're not going to be bored today,' he says.

'God – nobody's called me that for years.'

We pull out of the drive, on to the road and head up towards Blakeney.

'Really?' he says. 'It's too good a surname not to use.'

'My friend up the road in Bristol always called me Keech; in fact he used to chant "Sophie Keech got a bum like a peach".'

He laughs. 'I must check that out.'

'I was only eleven or twelve at the time.'

Ben has a Norah Jones CD playing today. I've kept up with British music by listening to Radio One online. It was my daily treat, listening to half an hour of Fearne Cotton before having a siesta.

'Is it your CD?' I ask.

'Dad's actually. A lot of his taste in music has been influenced by Leila.'

'Do you know, I haven't heard her sing once since I've been here.'

'Why? Did she use to?'

'Constantly, whatever she was doing round the house she always had the radio on and would sing along.'

'Maybe she's self-conscious because you're here.'

We turn left at the top of the road and head away from Blakeney, past the crab hut and out along the main road towards the next village. We park and walk down to a moored boat. Ben slings his camera round his neck. A small group of people is gathered on the muddy bank. The smell of fish is strong on the breeze, whipping inland from the North Sea.

'What are we doing?'

'We're going on a seal trip. Then the pub,' he says. We stop before we reach the group of people. 'I wanted it to be just us but my plans fell through.'

'This'll be great.'

He frowns. 'At least the kids have gone back to school. I'd never do this in summer.'

'Then why now?'

'Because you'll enjoy it.'

I smile. This must be hell for him, spending time trapped on a boat with a load of strangers. I reach out and touch his arm. 'Thank you.'

It's a grey morning but clear. Clouds blanket any warmth from the sun but at least there's no mist. I peer down into the murky water; it's the same brown as the mud banks on either side. A seagull squawks from its perch on the mast of a moored boat.

'Are you cold?' Ben asks.

'A little.'

He stands close in front of me and I realise how tall he is. Taller than Alekos. He rubs his hands up and down my arms to warm me up. I start laughing.

'What's so funny, Keech?' He lands a playful punch on my arm.

'You,' I say, blocking him. Our arms lock together for a moment before I drop my arms back to my sides.

'I was going to buy a boat yesterday,' he says, changing the subject. 'Dad persuaded me not to.'

'Really?'

'I've always wanted to go sailing, just a small boat, big enough for me.'

'No company?'

'I think there's something appealing about being alone at sea.'

'Are you going to get one?'

He shrugs. 'Mandy's not so keen.' He looks at me. 'My wife. She's not happy letting Fraser and Bella visit if I have a boat. She doesn't trust me.' He picks a round pebble off the ground and skims it into the water. It bounces three times before disappearing. 'I'm not going to let her dictate my life.'

'What if she doesn't let you see them?'

'She'll have to take me to court.'

'You could end up seeing even less of them.'

'It's a risk I have to take.'

'Over a boat?'

He shoots me a dark look, his eyebrows scrunching together. 'It's the principle of it.'

'I didn't mean it like that,' I say. 'Alekos was sailing boats when I met him on Cephalonia. For a couple of summers he took tourists round the islands and made a fortune in just a few weeks.'

The crowd of people starts moving on to the boat. I nudge Ben and we slowly walk towards them.

'It's just she's fighting me over everything: our home, money, Fraser and Bella,' he says. 'I'm out of her life, that's what she wanted. I get pretty pissed off when she starts interfering.'

Our conversation trails off as we reach the boat. The wooden benches around the sides have already started to fill up with people wrapped up in waterproofs, hats and gloves. One of the crew takes my hand and I board the boat and sit down. Ben joins me and we all shuffle along the bench. Ben taps me on the shoulder. I turn round and he takes a picture, really close up.

I slap his shoulder. 'Warn me next time so I can at least smile.'

'I like the natural look.'

We move off from the bank, along the muddy channel and out towards the point. We're the youngest on the boat; the majority of our fellow passengers are past retirement age, out enjoying themselves after the summer rush.

We reach open water and salt spray rains down cold against our skin. I'm glad of my waterproof and the thick socks inside Mum's walking boots. We're packed tight together, about twenty of us, all staring out to sea, straining to catch a glimpse of a seal. Ben's thigh is squashed against mine and as the boat rocks with the current so do we against each other.

'Can you see them?' he says close to my ear.

He's not the only one who's spotted something. Twenty heads strain in the direction of the open sea and it's worth the cold, the damp frizzy hair and the numbness from the hard bench. Two grey seals swim, their bodies rippling as they glide together just off the point. I lean forwards so Ben can get a good shot of them close to the boat. They're mesmerising to watch, floating and playing, skimming and diving. As we get closer to Blakeney Point I begin to make out at least ten seals lying on the pebbles, their whiskers inches away from the gentle lapping of the sea. It was worth getting up early.

Back on land, my legs feel like jelly. I walk a few paces and my head spins.

'Are you okay?' Ben asks.

I sit down on a nearby bench and drop my head towards my knees. 'Haven't quite got my sea-legs.' I bring my head up slowly and the dizziness fades.

Ben sits down next to me. 'Are you up for a walk?'

'Lead the way and as long as it's on solid ground I'll follow.'

We take the coastal path towards Stiffkey, although there's so much marshland veined by streams, the actual coastline is out of sight. The varying green of the grasses and the mustard yellow of the flowers between nettles marble the landscape. It's sheltered away from the blustery North Sea and after a good ten minutes walking I stop to take off my waterproof.

'Are you working up a sweat?' Ben asks.

'Something like that,' I say, tying it around my waist.

'As soon as we get to Stiffkey we can have a drink.'

The sun strains through white clouds dispersing the grey of early morning.

'I'm going to buy a place out this way. I'm not trading this life for the city again,' Ben says. 'Fraser and Bella love it up here, whatever their mother says.'

'She can't complain about them visiting you by the sea. It'll be a holiday for them every time.'

'What are you going to do?' he asks.

'What do you mean?'

'Do you regret living so far away?'

'From here?'

'From your Mum.'

I kick the soil with the toe of my boot. 'I'm beginning to. There are too many bad memories mixed with the good ones in Bristol. But here there are possibilities. I don't know, maybe we can start over.'

'I'd be happy with a little two-bed cottage. Enough space for the kids and me when they come to stay. A sea view perhaps... I can dream.' He takes a tripod out of his rucksack. 'What do you want, Sophie?'

'Space,' I say, flinging my arms into the air. There's not a person or house in sight. 'A place of my own without anyone's parents. I want to be allowed to do what I want, when I want. It seems such a simple thing.'

'On your own or with your boyfriend?'

'With Alekos of course.'

He clicks open the tripod and screws on the camera.

'You could have done the photography at the wedding yesterday,' I say.

'Leila asked me.'

I look at him. 'You turned it down?'

'I don't want to be a wedding photographer and force family and friends to smile when really they hate each other's guts because the bride's two months pregnant.'

'That's one way to look at it.'

'This is the type of photography I want to do.'

He sets the camera and tripod on a flat grassy ridge overlooking the salt marshes. I'd be happy spending hours alone here, watching for wildlife, taking photographs of birds, the heather and the hidden streams winding their way through the marshes. I should have brought a drawing pad with me and sketched the landscape while Ben captures it on film.

'I've all the time in the world for animals or birds, but very little for most humans,' Ben says. He peers into the camera, adjusting the focus.

'Why spend time with me?'

'I liked the look of you.'

I laugh.

'I loved the way you smiled at me when I first met you,' he says.

I remember him walking into the hospital restaurant, a stranger with a face I wanted to get to know.

'Here,' he beckons me over. 'Have a look.'

The distant stream cutting through the marsh fills the lens. The focus is on a gorse bush pinpricked with delicate yellow flowers.

'Adjust the focus if you want and take a picture,' he says. His hand shadows mine; his palm warm over the back of my hand. He shows me how to adjust and zoom in and out. He lets me experiment on my own but I can sense him behind me, not quite touching, but close enough. All I have to do is lean back against his chest. My concentration wavers. I'm treading on dangerous ground. I zoom in on the gorse bush until the image is crisp. I can see a bee hovering over a flower, its stripy body blending with the yellow. I take a picture.

I pull back from the camera and brush against Ben. I step away.

'Just the one?' he says.

'I'm a digital camera girl. I like to see the image.'

'It's far more satisfying watching them develop.'

'Do you have a darkroom?'

'I used to. Mandy's turned it into a spare bedroom.'

'She's taken everything away from you.'

'I'm better off without her. We were destroying each other. It's not how I imagined life would turn out but I don't regret leaving. It's Fraser and Bella I care about.'

I sit down on a patch of grass by the side of the path and watch Ben take pictures. Surrounded by tall grasses, I'm warm and sheltered from the breeze. I feel at home here, watching the birds and insects. The colours are vivid: the blues and greys of the sky, the green of the marshes pinpricked with yellows, white and the occasional bright red.

'Thirsty?' Ben asks after a while.

I nod and shake the dirt off me before we continue our

walk along the salt marsh path.

The pub at Stiffkey is larger than *The Globe* but it is still cosy with a low-beamed ceiling and dark stained wooden tables and chairs. Ben gets the drinks and I sit at a table by a window that looks out across the road to a field of cows. There's no music playing and I can hear the thump of darts over the conversation filling the bar. I don't even look at the menu after seeing what the couple on the next table is eating: roast beef and Yorkshire puddings. Ben returns from the bar clutching two pints.

'Aren't we being traitors to your Dad's pub?' I ask.

'A pint here won't kill him or us.'

Ben's finished his pint before our food arrives. He goes to the bar to get another one and by the time he gets back there are two large plates in front of us brimming with meat, roast potatoes, vegetables, Yorkshire puddings and stuffing.

'This is the life,' I say, dipping my Yorkshire pudding into gravy. 'Do you know I haven't worked for just over two weeks. At least not proper work.'

'A change of country is as good as a rest,' Ben says. 'When are you going back?'

'I see you want to get rid of me already.'

'Far from it.'

'I'm in no rush,' I say.

Ben takes a gulp of his pint before starting on his food. 'Most people would kill to live in Greece. I loved it.'

'It's always different visiting a place to living there.'

'I guess so,' he says. 'I'm always wishing I was somewhere else.'

'Maybe I've got itchy feet. I lived in Falmouth for three years, went back to Bristol for another three, then Greece for four. Maybe it's time to move on again.'

'Would your boyfriend want to live here?'

I shake my head. 'His whole life is his family.'

'Even without you?'

I shrug. 'I have no idea what Alekos would do or say if I

didn't go back. I can't see him living here and speaking English every day. He'd have no job, no friends. I'd have to start afresh too but that would be exciting, a new challenge.' I cut into a roast potato and pop it in my mouth. 'I'd love to buy a house and do it up, have a kitchen to cook what I want in and a garden I don't have to share with hundreds of other people every day. I'm just worried what I want is different to what Alekos wants.'

'I think you were brave to go live in another country and learn the language to begin with,' Ben says.

'Mum thought I was foolish leaving everything behind for Alekos.'

'Isn't that what everyone does when they're in love? That's what I did. It's just sometimes it doesn't work out.' He mops the last of the gravy up with a roast potato and puts his knife and fork together on te plate. 'And there aren't many people who'd turn down the chance of living in Greece. Athens is such an exciting place. When I went there on assignments a few days was never enough. I love travelling but it didn't exactly help my marriage.'

'I always felt lost in Athens, even as a visitor.'

'And a place like this you feel exposed.'

'I feel invisible. It's just what I want. No one knows me.'

'Everyone knows you.'

'Yes, as Leila's daughter. No one knows *me*. I could re-invent myself here if I wanted to.'

'I like the Sophie I've m.et very much.' He taps what's left of his pint against mine. 'Do you want another one?' he asks, scraping his chair back.

'Why not.' I down the rest of my pint and watch Ben weave his way to the bar. He's a mixture of city and country in his Levi's, walking boots and sweatshirt. Sitting here with the smell of beer, roast dinner and smoke reminds me of Sundays with my flatmates in Bristol, having a pub lunch so we didn't have to cook. One pint would turn into four and eventually a Monday morning hangover. More recently days off at *O Kipos* are rare and when we do have free time we never do this: go out and relax, eat out and talk. We used to, a lot. At least I feel like I'm living life here.

Chapter Twenty-One

After lunch we have a game of pool. I win and Ben challenges me to a rematch, which he wins. We can't leave it at that so with another pint to keep us going we battle it out. It ends when Ben pots the black.

'The more I drink the better I get,' he says. I can hear the slur of his words.

It's his fifth pint and I'm struggling with my third. Even a full roast dinner hasn't soaked up the alcohol.

'We'd better get going,' I say. I take the cue from him and lean it against the wall with mine. He downs the rest of the pint I've left on the side. 'Thirsty are you?'

'Can't waste a good pint,' he says.

The earlier blanket of cloud is patchy and the path switches between shade and sunlight as we walk. There are more people around, out for their Sunday afternoon stroll. Ben clamps his arm across my shoulders when we reach the salt marshes and we set off along the path at a fast pace, our hips knocking against each other's before we settle into a rhythm. A new confidence oozes from him and I wonder if it's just the drink talking. His laugh is louder and he's more upbeat.

'Dad swears a walk every day will keep him healthy,' Ben says. 'Has he given you that advice yet?'

'Not yet. He's given me plenty of other advice though.'

'Ben, tidy your room for Bella and Fraser; Ben, remember

it's Vicky's birthday,' he says, doing a very convincing impression of Robert. He throws his hands in the air. 'I'm thirty-four!' he shouts. He startles terns hidden in the undergrowth and they squawk and flap into the air. 'He's disappointed in me. He can't understand why we're divorcing. He has such high moral standards. Fuck him!' He grins at me. 'Race you to that boat.'

He's off before I have time to digest his words. I run after him, my legs pounding the grassy path. By the time I catch up with him leaning against an upturned boat, I'm out of breath.

He punches the air with his fist. 'That felt good!' he shouts.

'That was unfair,' I say. 'I wasn't ready.'

'You want a rematch?'

'I'm knackered.'

'How about a piggyback?'

'Now you're talking.'

I take a run up, grasp his shoulders and launch myself on to his back. It's warm pressed against him and I curl my arms around his neck. He staggers along the path with my legs resting on his arms. 'Great view from up here,' I say. He heads straight for the muddy stream and I scream when he pretends to tip me in. We end up in a heap on the sandy soil, our legs stretched out towards the water. We're sheltered from the wind and hidden from the path by a sand bank with reeds growing on it. We're leaning in towards each other, our shoulders touching. I've forgotten what this feels like, this closeness with someone I'm just getting to know, the excitement of the unknown, imagining what it would be like to touch him, to kiss him. Or for him to touch me. I dare not look at him; I don't want him to read my thoughts. I don't want to see if he's feeling the same way. I begin to scramble up but he reaches for my arm and pulls me back. He touches my face, his fingertips smooth against my skin. He presses his lips hard against mine, his tongue probing, the taste of beer and cigarettes strong. His hand moves to my neck, his touch gentler than his kiss. I close my eyes and kiss him back, teasing him with my tongue. His hand drops further, moving above my clothes until he reaches my breasts. My head is heavy with drink, my body longing to be free, passionate. My hands follow his lead, travelling from his face and down the length of his torso, until I'm tugging at his belt buckle. My eagerness gives his hands permission to dip under my top and skim across my skin. He effortlessly unhooks my bra and kisses my neck, while all the time his hands are eagerly reaching forward until he's cupping my breasts. He manoeuvres on top of me and I rest my head in the sand. I open my eyes. Everything's unfamiliar. His pale forehead and the flecks of grey in his gelled hair. His taste. His caress. The blueness of his eyes as he looks at me in-between kisses. And then, over his shoulder, I see two children chasing after a Labrador along the edge of the stream. They're heading towards us. I nudge Ben but he's concentrating on undoing the buttons on my jeans.

'Ben,' I whisper and point. He glances over his shoulder. The children's parents have just come into view.

'Shit,' Ben says as we begin to untangle ourselves. We look dishevelled with his belt and jeans gaping open, my top riding halfway up my stomach. The children run past us, oblivious, and we manage to tidy ourselves up by the time their parents stroll past.

'Afternoon,' the father says before quickly looking away.

'Afternoon,' we chorus like naughty schoolchildren before falling back into the sand giggling.

'I feel like I'm fifteen years old and have been caught in an uncompromising position by my mother,' I say.

'Me too.' He strokes the sand from my hair.

'Except when I was fifteen it was usually my mother in the uncompromising position.'

We fall silent and look towards the once again deserted landscape. Had he been waiting the whole day to make a move? It's like I'm living an alternate life here. Alekos filters into my thoughts. I stand up and shake myself. 'I've got sand everywhere.'

Ben reaches out his hand and I pull him up. 'We'd better walk home,' I say.

Salt Cottage is quiet and the study door is ajar. The smell of baking is sweet and strong. In the kitchen there's a tray of flapjacks cooling on the work surface. The back door is open, and I spy Mum sitting on the patio. I go upstairs and lock myself in the bathroom. I lean on the edge of the sink and stare at myself in the mirror. My hair is windswept. I gather it up into a ponytail. I can still taste Ben and smell his aftershave on my skin and in my hair. I swear my lips and chin are red from him kissing me. I splash water on my face and clean my teeth before patting my skin dry with a towel. Walking out into the garden I feel self-conscious as if I've just come home after my first kiss. 'Hi,' I call across to Mum.

She looks up and waves.

'You look relaxed,' I say.

She shakes a tall glass filled with ice and a clear liquid. 'Fancy a G & T?'

I shake my head and sit down. 'You made flapjacks.'

'I fancied getting off my arse. And I wanted something sweet to eat.' She looks at me over the top of her sunglasses. 'Where've you been?'

'To see the seals and then we walked to Stiffkey,' I say.

Mum sips her drink and places it carefully on the patio table. 'Why are you getting involved with him?'

My cheeks begin to burn. 'I'm not involved. We've been to the beach and gone for a walk. What's the big deal?'

'What would Alekos say?' Mum asks.

'You're a right one to talk.'

'I just don't think you want to get attached to him and his problems.'

'Give him a break, his marriage has broken up.'

'Did he tell you why?'

'It's none of my business. Or yours.'

'Ben makes it everyone else's business. He's not the victim

he makes out to be.' Mum swirls her G & T around, rattling the ice.

'Does Robert know you don't like his son?' I ask.

'I never said I didn't like him. Robert's fully aware of my feelings about Ben. He feels the same,' she says. 'Don't look at me like that. I speak my mind, Sophie. Always have, always will. I stuck up for Ben when he first moved here. We spent a lot of time talking and I defended him when Robert was being too harsh.'

'What changed then?' I ask.

'Him putting himself before his kids.'

'I turned out okay, didn't I?'

She sucks her breath in sharply. 'He had a drink problem,' she says. 'It's not the best place, living above a pub, but Robert keeps an eye on him. His marriage broke down because of *his* problems.'

'A breakdown of a marriage can't be blamed on one person.'

Mum shrugs and wraps her cardigan tighter around her. 'Did he drink today?'

'He's an adult; he can do what he likes.'

'He's going to lose his kids, Sophie. Mandy's going to fight him all the way for sole custody and she'll be bloody ecstatic if he doesn't get any visitation rights. That'll break Robert's heart.'

'What about Ben's?'

'I'm sure Ben will be cut up about it when it happens, but he's living in denial. Robert lost his wife. He doesn't want to lose his grandchildren too.'

'Maybe it won't come to that.'

'Why would she want to make things any more complicated for herself? If she wants Ben out of her life that means Robert too. Ben needs a kick up the backside. He needs to be responsible for his actions or he'll end up with a lot of regrets.'

I'm stuck in the middle. I feel dishonest, tainted by secrets.

I shiver. 'I'm going inside. Do you want another drink?'

She shakes her head.

'Are you warm enough?' I ask.

She nods.

'I'll have a flapjack,' she calls, before I go through the kitchen door.

I make us a simple dinner of pasta and pesto. Mum doesn't comment on my half-eaten meal. We watch some TV but I can't keep my eyes open.

'I'm going to call it a night,' I say, forcing myself off the sofa.

In a daze I change into my nightclothes, get a wash, clean my teeth, brush my hair, then cleanse, tone and moisturise. I go to bed feeling tired and grumpy with a niggling feeling at the back of my mind. My period hasn't started yet.

I wake to ringing. I reach for my mobile, then realise it's the house phone. I glance at the bedside clock – 7:30 – before snuggling back below the duvet and hugging my pillow. I listen to the muffled sound of Mum talking on the phone and the wind banging a door downstairs.

'Sophie!' Mum yells from her bedroom. 'Phone!'

'For me?' I call back.

'It's Alekos.'

My hands sweat at the mere mention of his name. With effort I sit up and swing my legs out of bed. I put my jogging bottoms and a T-shirt on over my shorts and vest top and pad on to the landing.

'Take it in the kitchen,' Mum says.

I creak down the stairs in the dark and pick up the receiver. 'I didn't know you had this number,' I say. I release the blind to a view of the field shrouded in low-lying mist.

'I don't. I found it in your address book. I can't get hold of you on your mobile.'

'It's very early, Aleko.'

'Sorry, did I wake you?'

'Yes. And Mum. What's up?'

'I want to talk to you.'

'You're two hours ahead of us. You could have waited until midday.'

'I'm helping Demetrius and Katrina move.'

'They've finally found somewhere?'

'Apartment in Thessaloniki.'

'Nice.'

'Katrina's decided they're going to have a party there in two weeks,' Alekos says. 'I can't believe they're moving so far away. He's lived here all his life.'

'Thessaloniki is hardly far away. Anyway, it's about time they moved out of her parents' house,' I say.

'Also, I wanted to know if you're coming home for your birthday?'

'I haven't given it a thought.'

'Will you be home?'

'It's this Sunday, Aleko,' I say. 'I'm not ready to leave. There's still so much I want to sort out.'

There's silence. 'Then I'm coming to see you. I want to see you, Sophie.'

'I thought there was no way your Mum could cope without both of us?'

'Don't worry about that. Anyway, it's time I met your Mum.'

I can't argue with that. For someone who is such a permanent fixture in my life it is odd that Mum has never met him. I don't think she's even seen a photo.

'It's not up to me whether you can stay,' I say. Two weeks ago I was begging him to come with me.

'But you could ask.'

'She's had an accident, Aleko.'

'I know that.'

I can't imagine him here, in Mum's home. He'd be the talk of the village – Leila's daughter's Greek lover. I wonder how he'd find it. Cold? Quiet? Lonely? Or feel at home, like I do.

187

'I'll ask her,' I say eventually. I shiver in the dark kitchen.

'I've checked the times from Thessaloniki to Heathrow and Gatwick on Saturday,' he says. I can hear the smile in his voice. 'Which airport will be easiest?'

'Aleko, let me ask first,' I say. 'But Heathrow's better.'

We hang up – Aleko to go and move our friends into a place of their own and me to find an opportunity to ask Mum if he can stay for a few days. It's not that she'd mind a boyfriend of mine staying, in fact she used to encourage it, but I never took her up on her liberal offer. She had enough boyfriends to stay for both of us.

I'm up now, so I might as well stay up. I get a pot of coffee brewing. I always wished coffee tasted as good as it smelt but this morning it turns my stomach. Its richness smells bitter and I go outside for air.

I can see my breath, only slightly, but it's visible in the chill of dawn. I can't imagine Alekos here or myself back in Greece. I've discovered freedom and I'm not sure if I'm willing to part with it. I'm beginning to feel alive again. When did I stop loving life?

When Mum finally appears the coffee is cold and the mist has cleared. 'It feels like time stands still here,' she says.

She's silhouetted in the back doorway. Her pose is the same as in the photo of her standing outside the cottage. Now I'm an insider looking out I know exactly what she means. This place envelops you and makes you feel safe from the outside world. Time ambles along, there's no hectic rush of city living and there's space to get away from summer holiday crowds.

But there's still work to be done. After toast and a mug of reheated coffee Mum gets on with the flowers ordered for a golden wedding anniversary and I play housekeeper: cleaning, washing and shopping.

Mum and I rub along together. Daylight turns to dusk. I stay awake to watch a film while Mum spends two hours on the phone to an old friend from Bristol. I'm in bed by midnight. I'm enjoying these earlier nights drifting off to sleep to the sound of an owl hooting.

The next morning brings a lie in with no wake-up call. The day eases by but there's no chance to ask Mum about Alekos. Mum has a steady flow of visitors. First a red-cheeked woman in jodhpurs and riding boots brings round half a dozen freshly laid eggs. Late afternoon, a mother and daughter turn up to discuss the daughter's wedding planned for next year. I make them a pot of tea and escape to the garden with my sketchpad.

We walk down – aided by a torch – for dinner at *The Globe*. A fire spits and crackles in the grate as Robert feeds it another log. Mum is greeted by a chorus of hellos from people sitting around the table near the bar. I'm introduced to everyone but faces become a blur and their names get muddled and forgotten. Everyone knows Mum and she's swamped by well-wishers and goes from one conversation to another.

Marcy brings us drinks. She hugs Mum. 'How are you girl?'

'I'm on the mend.'

'I've missed you propping up the bar.'

Mum laughs.

'Keep an eye on her, mind,' she says, winking at me.

'What's it like living in Greece?' is the question everyone asks me: Mrs Laker, the dairy farmer's wife; Sheila, the mother-of-two who lives in the cottage next to the pub; the elderly lady with white hair and youthful skin whose name I've forgotten. They all ask, they all make me feel welcome, and they all say, 'Aren't you lucky,' before starting a conversation with someone else.

Ben's serving drinks and the bar's lined with customers clutching twenty-pound notes. He catches my eye and beckons me over.

'Having fun?' he asks.

I nod. 'You?'

He shrugs. I can barely look at him without blushing. He leans across the bar and puts his hand on my arm. I glance round but Mum has her back to me and I can't see Robert anywhere. Only Marcy is close by. She winks at us. 'I'm off tomorrow night and I thought you might like to do something...' he says. 'I meant to ask you earlier, but... you know...'

'I wanted to ask the same thing. See if you wanted to go somewhere.'

'A meal out maybe.'

'I'd love that.'

'Ben, get us a double whisky and a glass of red, would you,' someone shouts from the table.

He lets go of me and I work my way back to the table. Mum's leg cast is being signed by a round-cheeked Len Laker. His wife giggles and grabs the pen off him to sign her own message.

Robert squeezes on to the bench next to me. I shuffle along until I'm sandwiched between him and Mum.

'I hear it's your birthday on Sunday,' he says. 'Don't look so surprised, Leila would hardly forget. Is it a special one?'

I shake my head. 'Twenty-nine.'

Robert whistles through his teeth. 'Oh to be that age again,' he says. 'It's wonderful that you've been able to stay here so long.'

'Alekos doesn't think so.'

'Oh?'

I lean towards him. 'He wants to come over.'

'That's great.'

'I haven't said anything to Mum. I think it might be a bit much, considering.'

'Don't be silly, she'd love it.'

'It's never the right time to ask.'

'There's no time like the present,' he says and before I can stop him he's reached behind me and squeezed Mum's shoulder. She looks up from the leg signing.

'Alekos wants to come over for Sophie's birthday,' he says. 'That's okay with you, isn't it?'

'I already told him he could.'

'He asked you?' I say. I spill some of my pint as I bang it on the table.

Mum smiles smugly. 'I wondered how long it would take you to ask me.'

'I can't believe he asked you.'

'It's about time I finally met him.'

'Well,' Robert says. 'If that's all decided, we'll have to have a party.'

Chapter Twenty-Two

I have nothing suitable to wear to go out. Maybe I shouldn't worry and just dress casually tonight, after all is there any need to make an impression? My nervousness grows with dusk. It feels as if I'm going on a first date. I try on and discard numerous items of clothing before settling on jeans and a black V-necked top. I slick on lip gloss, brush mascara over my eyelashes and go into the kitchen.

'You're going out?' Mum asks. 'You kept that quiet.'

'I didn't think you'd approve.'

'You're seeing Ben?'

'Who else?'

She tuts.

'Mum, he's a laugh. What's the crime in going for a meal with him?'

'It's a bit complicated, isn't it? Seeing Ben tonight and Alekos coming over for your birthday.'

'Not really,' I say, with very little conviction.

Two children are sitting on stools up at the bar, their legs dangling and kicking air as they sip their drinks through straws. They must be brother and sister. They have the same pale skin and chestnut-brown hair – the girl's in loose curls with a red shiny clip pulling it off her face, and the boy's short and spiked. They don't seem to belong to anyone.

'Hello Sophie,' Marcy says when I reach the bar.

The children stop drinking and look up. I glance between them and Marcy.

'Hi. I'm supposed to be meeting…'

She nods. 'He's outside with Mandy.'

'Oh.'

'Sophie, this is Fraser and Bella.'

'Hello,' they say in unison.

Bella looks at Marcy. 'Are Mummy and Daddy going to be long?'

'No, sweetheart,' Marcy says. 'What can I get you, Sophie?'

'A pint of Stella, please.'

'Grandad!' Fraser calls and slides off his chair. Bella scrambles down after him and they both fling themselves into Robert's arms. I've never seen someone smile so much.

I wander across the bar. The smell of steak and ale pie is inviting as I pass an elderly couple eating. It's distorted through the conservatory glass, but I can just make out Ben with his back to me and the woman he's with, tall and slender with dark, wavy hair like Bella's. Her smart grey trouser suit detaches her from her surroundings. She clasps a black handbag in front of her, as if to protect herself. She's the one doing all the talking. Her features look pinched, mean, maybe because she's frowning, it's difficult to tell. Ben's dressed to go out in jeans and a shirt. They look uncomfortable together. My conscience gets the better of me and I go back to the bar. Robert, sat at the nearest table with a grandchild on each knee, is all smiles. I perch on a bar stool.

'She arrived two days early.' Marcy lowers her voice. 'Wants to go away for a long weekend with this new man she's been seeing.'

'Ben said she was seeing someone.'

'She doesn't know about you, though,' she says.

'What about me?'

'You and Ben.'

I feel my cheeks go hot. 'There is no me and Ben.' I'm too quick to respond.

'But you are on a date tonight?'

'A date makes us sound like we're fifteen. We're eating out.' I don't like the way she's looking at me knowingly. I glance over at Bella and Fraser, laughing as Robert bounces them up and down on his knees. I wish my life was as uncomplicated as theirs. 'I enjoy his company, Marcy.'

'If you say so,' she says with a wink.

Marcy can see right through me, Mum's warning me off him, Robert's oblivious and I have no real idea how Ben feels.

'I didn't think we'd see you tonight,' Robert says. He lifts Bella back on to the bar stool and Fraser jumps off his other knee and clambers on to the bar stool next to his sister. 'Isn't Leila with you?'

I shake my head. 'Ben asked me out. Just to get something to eat,' I quickly backtrack. 'That's all.'

'Oh right.' He shoots a look towards the conservatory then back to me. 'I hope you didn't mind me suggesting a party last night?' he asks. Bella's blowing bubbles through her straw. Her foot taps rhythmically on the barstool leg.

'No, of course not,' I say.

Robert squeezes my shoulder. 'Good. Oh and Sophie, could I ask you a favour?'

'Go for it.'

'I wondered if you'd like to cook some Greek specials here Friday night?'

The conservatory door bangs open and Ben storms into the bar followed by Mandy. 'Robert, I'd love to,' I manage to say before finding myself in the middle of a domestic with a family I barely know. Fraser and Bella are giggling, oblivious to the tension. New customers are beginning to fill the pub and I don't resist when I'm forced to give my seat up. Ben catches my eye and mouths, 'sorry'.

Robert keeps talking, trying to defuse the situation, asking how Mandy is, when it's obvious all she wants to do is make sure her children are okay and leave. Ben stands awkwardly between Robert and me.

'Where are you going tonight?' Robert asks us, when conversation dries up with Mandy.

Ben tenses. 'I don't know.'

Mandy looks over at me.

'Sorry,' Robert says. 'This is Sophie, my friend Leila's daughter.'

She doesn't smile. Her eyes flicker across my face before returning to focus on her children. She bends down and kisses them both. 'Be good for your father,' she says.

Fraser and Bella are more interested in their fizzy drinks than their departing mother. They give her a quick wave but don't watch her leave. The oak door thuds shut.

'I'm so sorry, Sophie,' Ben says. He moves closer to me. 'She wasn't supposed to bring them over until Friday.'

'That's fine. It's great you've got them an extra couple of days,' I say, unsure whether I'm upset or relieved that our chance to be alone has gone. Marcy's taking orders, pulling pints and keeping an eye on us.

Ben turns to Robert. 'Dad, can you look after Bella and Fraser for a couple of hours?'

I look at Ben in disbelief. Robert nods, his attention focused on Bella. Fraser slides off the stool and tugs at Ben's trouser leg. Ben slowly shifts his attention from me to his son.

'What is it, Fraser?'

'Can we go to the beach tomorrow?'

'Of course we can. Whatever you want.'

'We should all go out,' I say.

'To the beach?' Ben frowns at me.

'No, for dinner tonight. They've got an extra couple of days with you, make the most of it.'

'Or you could just stay here,' Robert says, joining our conversation.

'Can we?' Bella asks. She holds Robert's hand and stares wide-eyed up at Ben.

'Table seven's free,' Robert says.

'Is that okay with you?' I look at Ben.

'I have no problem staying here.' He places his hands on top of Fraser and Bella's heads and manoeuvres them through the bar to the empty table near the open fire. 'What do you want to eat, you two,' he asks them on the way.

'Sausage, beans and chips,' Fraser says without hesitation.

'Are you joining us?' I ask Robert.

'On and off,' he says. 'I'll ring Leila and let her know you and the kids are here. She might want to come down and see them.' His face reddens. 'I'm sorry if they've spoilt your evening.'

I glance across to where Fraser, Bella and Ben have settled at the table near the glowing embers of the fire. 'They've made my evening.'

'They are gorgeous, aren't they?'

I touch his arm. 'Come and join us when you can.'

I sit opposite Ben and think it's going to feel odd playing happy families with him and his kids but Fraser and Bella diffuse the awkwardness as only children can. Fraser refuses to look at the menu now he's got it into his head what he wants: sausage, beans and chips. Bella can't be swayed either except she wants peas instead of beans. I decide on tenderloin pork in a creamy mushroom sauce and Ben chooses the steak and ale pie. It's lemonade all round.

'You can drink if you want,' Ben says.

'I'm fine, really.' I quickly finish the pint I had up at the bar, aware of it on the table between us. 'I don't drink that much in Greece anyway. It's not in the Greeks' nature to go out to get drunk. Beats having a hangover.' I'm talking too much, justifying why I'm not drinking because I know he can't drink with his Dad around. He catches my eye and I smile weakly. He knows Mum's talked to me. I am sorry he's missing his children growing up. Seeing the smile on his face and the way he looks at them, with his arm round Fraser's shoulders, laughing at Bella trying to stab a runaway pea with her fork, makes me sad. They're still at the age where each day they're changing, growing, discovering and learning. It must be awful for him to miss out on all that.

'So,' Ben says, once he's mopped his plate and Bella and Fraser are engrossed in the dessert menu. 'Dad said your boyfriend's coming over.'

'Apparently so. He had the cheek to ask Mum when he phoned the other day.'

'How long is he here for?'

I shrug. 'I don't even know for definite when he's arriving.'

He takes a sip of his drink and looks at me over the rim of the glass. 'Are you going back with him?'

'We'll see. I'm not ready to go back yet. It's like I'm getting to know Mum all over again. I've had time here to think about my life.'

'Daddy,' Fraser says, grabbing Ben's shirtsleeve. 'Can I have sticky toffee pudding please? With ice cream.'

'And custard,' Bella says.

'Custard as well?' Ben asks.

Bella nods enthusiastically. Ben puts his arm around her and kisses the top of her head before reaching his free hand across the table and taking hold of mine. The warmth of his touch is comforting. I wonder what Mum would make of this family tableau if she walked in now. 'I'll miss you when you go back,' he says quietly.

'Look,' Bella says, tugging at my sleeve. She takes a necklace from her skirt pocket and lays it on the table. 'I made it myself.'

'It's beautiful,' I say. Red, blue, green and purple beads are strung together on gold string. 'Do you want to wear it?'

She nods and turns her back to me.

I lift up her curly hair and place the necklace around her delicate neck. I tie it in a loose knot and arrange her curls on her shoulders.

'Thank you,' she says, turning to me with a grin. 'Now I'm a grown-up.'

It's still early and I follow Ben, Fraser and Bella upstairs to

Robert's spacious flat above the pub. Bella and Fraser run ahead into the living room screeching, '*Nemo, Nemo, Nemo!*'

'Make yourself comfortable,' Ben says, patting the back of the sofa. 'I'll sort these two out.'

I kick off my shoes, slump on the sofa and curl my feet beneath me. Like the pub, the upstairs ceiling is low and beamed. The room is large and open plan with the kitchen visible behind me with only a breakfast bar separating it from the living area. There's an unlit log fire set in the grate and the two windows in the living room overlook the road at the front of the pub to the field beyond. Fraser and Bella have plonked themselves on the rug in front of the TV and Ben is kneeling between them searching through DVDs.

'I've found *Toy Story*,' he says, holding a DVD up.

'I want *Nemo*,' Bella says. She looks at Ben with wide eyes. How can he refuse? He goes back to the stack of DVDs on the floor next to him. I know Alekos will be a natural with children: they'd always come first, the same as his family does. Maybe that's what's wrong; I can't imagine myself a part of family life in that way. Family for me has always been Mum and that's it. Alekos, Candy, Ben and even Mum's upbringing was with two parents and brothers or sisters or both. I've always been an outsider. I felt it with Candy and her family and again now with Ben and his children; it's a part of life I've missed out on. I can't imagine how Ben must feel when he has to say goodbye and watch them being driven back to London. He finds *Nemo* and Bella quietens down and watches it with her brother. Ben sits down next to me and rests his arm on the back of the sofa with his fingertips grazing my neck.

'It wasn't quite the romantic night out I imagined it would be,' he says quietly.

We're whispering like young lovers on the back seats of a cinema. 'I don't know,' I say. 'I enjoyed myself. It's good seeing you with your kids. They remind me of Alekos' nephew, Yannis – he's all the entertainment we ever need on a night out or at a party.'

'It's true. I think me and Mandy would have split way before we did if it wasn't for Fraser and Bella keeping us laughing and sane. If it had been just the two of us we'd have stopped communicating years ago. The only reason why there was any fun and laughter in the house was because of these two. At least something good came out of our marriage.' His fingers start to stroke the back of my neck. 'I miss this,' he says, motioning towards Fraser and Bella and then back to me.

I suddenly see myself through his eyes. 'You still love her, don't you?' I say.

His fingers freeze on my neck and I know it's a yes. He's been displaced and is floundering in no-man's land: no home, no woman, his family split up. And then I walk into his life; someone as emotionally messed up as he is.

'I didn't appreciate what we had at the time,' he finally says. 'I guess I thought I could get away with not paying our relationship much attention. It probably would have been okay if someone else hadn't been paying her the attention instead.'

'We're a right pair, aren't we?' I say. My God, I'd gone out thinking I might be having sex with him by the end of the night, not a heart to heart with him on his sofa while his kids happily watch TV. The passion I felt with him during our walk has dissipated and I sense the same with him. I'm still longing for him to touch me but I'm not sure if it's more to do with comfort rather than desire. Footsteps sound on the stairs and when Robert appears in the doorway we separate like fumbling teenagers.

Chapter Twenty-Three

I feel nauseous the moment I wake up. I'm sick in the bathroom toilet and it's certainly not because I drank too much at *The Globe* last night. The feeling I've had for the past couple of days, ever since my period was late, is confirmed. Five days now and that's unusual – my periods are like clockwork, with or without the pill – I can one hundred per cent rely on the day and usually pinpoint the time too.

I had a scare once before, when I was in Falmouth. I was nineteen years old and too much alcohol and a one-night stand got the better of me. My period was twenty-four hours late and I panicked. I thought history was going to repeat itself – like mother like daughter. I was stupid but lucky. I was given a second chance.

I take a walk. I want fresh air and need to get out of the house. Mum doesn't ask where I'm going and I don't say. It's blustery out and dried leaves are beginning to coat the driveway. I do my jacket up and wish I had a scarf, hat and gloves. I shove my hands into my jeans pockets and battle up the hill against the wind. It's amazing how quickly things can change in only three weeks.

I push open the Spar door and go in. It's busy inside and cramped; I have to squeeze past people to get down the aisles. I go back for a basket and add meaningless things to it: a bottle of water, a sandwich and a *New Woman* magazine before I find the toiletries shelf.

Shit. I hadn't thought the cashiers might know Mum. Small villages like this talk. I finger the box. My stomach churns but it's not the feeling I want. What I would give for a bad, horrible, painful period right now. I can't believe I'm doing this. I pick up the pregnancy test and slip it beneath the prawn sandwiches and magazine, like an embarrassed sixteen-year-old.

This is what we talked about, a little more than a year ago. This is what we wanted, what I wanted.

'Sophie. What a pleasant surprise.'

'Robert.' I nearly drop my basket. He's right behind me in the queue and I can't escape.

'I'm just picking up some milk,' he says.

My face is getting hotter and hotter.

'What are you here for?' he asks.

'Nothing. I wanted some fresh air.'

'It's certainly that. Fresh.'

'Next,' the girl behind the counter says. She looks at me lazily as I place the basket next to her. It's painful to watch her pick up the bottle of water and swipe. Robert's still not being served. Sandwiches, swipe. Magazine, swipe. Pregnancy test. She turns it over to find the barcode. Swipe.

'Can I help?'

Robert steps forward to the next till and glances across. So much for worrying about village gossip. The cashier puts my items into a bag, one by one. Robert finishes at the same time and we walk out of the door together. A gust of wind nearly knocks us off our feet.

'Do you want a lift?' he asks.

'No thanks, I fancy walking.'

'If you're sure.'

However much quicker the journey to *Salt Cottage* would be, I don't want to give Robert an opportunity to ask questions. I stuff the plastic Spar bag into the bag slung across my shoulders and start walking.

I'm halfway down the hill when it spots with rain and by

the time I reach the cottage my hair is plastered to my face and my jeans are stuck to my legs.

I quietly shut the front door, creep past the closed study door and up the stairs. I'm learning where the creaks are. In my room I tip my shopping on to the bed.

This is ridiculous. I'm on the pill. I'm pre-menstrual; I've been moody. I lock myself in the bathroom and open the box. Only a couple of days ago I was sitting on the back doorstep in floods of tears over nothing.

There's a chip on the corner of the sink. My cleanser and toner lines the shelf next to Mum's apricot facial scrub; my green toothbrush keeps her purple one company in the holder with a near-empty tube of toothpaste. I should have bought some more. I neaten the towels hanging on the rail.

My fate is sealed by a colour.

I don't know how to react. It's sudden, unexpected. Unwanted? A mistake. I don't feel any different from how I did an hour ago.

There's no going back. But how do I possibly go forwards? I should be hugging Alekos not dripping tears on to Mum's bathroom floor. This was never meant to happen like this.

Despite me staring at it, the stripe remains defiantly blue.

I'm not ready. We're not ready. I tear the box into pieces and stuff them and the test into the empty Spar bag and chuck it away in the kitchen swing bin. I don't want to deal with anything right now but I can't stop thinking about the enormity of a baby. I move through the rest of the day on autopilot. Mum suggests a lazy night in, so I drive to Holt for an Indian takeaway and a DVD. I should phone Alekos but I can't bring myself to call him. Doing that would make things real. It would mean I'd have to make a decision. Sleep does not come easily. I play my future over and over in my head, like *Groundhog Day*: what would happen if I made certain choices. If I got rid of it. No one would ever have to know. Nothing appeals. All of them involve a screaming baby less than nine months from now. I throw the duvet off. I'm hot one moment and then wake up later shivering. I feel sucked dry and lifeless by the time my alarm goes off.

'Are you all right?' Mum asks the next day at breakfast. I haven't said a word since I got up.

'I've got a headache. Do you mind if I go for a walk?'

'Do what you like.'

I scrape my chair back and clear away my plate. I'm halfway out of the kitchen door when Mum says, 'It's cold out.'

I close the door behind me. She sounds just like Despina, making sure I'm wrapped up the very second a cloud shades the sun. Mothering instinct. I wonder if I'll end up the same.

I take her advice though and layer a couple of tops underneath my denim jacket, put thick socks on with my boots and borrow one of her scarves. The wind curls itself around me the moment I leave the cottage. Leaves are falling heavily now, carpeting the grass a mottled brown and yellow.

I head down the muddy lane, away from the road. I don't have to walk far before the occasional swish of a car going past the cottage disappears altogether. The footpath sign at the end of the lane points over a stile and across a ploughed field. The soil is sandy and soft and I leave deep footprints as I walk the length of the field up towards the wood at the furthest end.

I've longed for this, away from the heat and intensity of home. The scent of autumn hangs in the air with the freshness of damp soil and the promise of rain. The chilly fingers of dawn, dissolved to dew with the sun, cling to each blade of grass. The wood is dark and cool, the soil underfoot turns to damp leaves and with each step I add the sound of snapping twigs to the birds calling and the sigh of the wind in the trees. It's a tranquillity I'm not used to, either as a child growing up in a city or as a woman living in a country where everyone knows your business and the only quiet time is the siesta, and that's only because everyone else is asleep too. Here, peace surrounds me: it's everywhere, in the cool breeze, the diluted sunlight – isn't it the very nature of the British to keep themselves to themselves. Mum doesn't pry, doesn't question. Not so in Greece, however laid back they are, they want to know what I'm up to, where I'm going, what I'm thinking: Alekos, Despina, Lena, aunts, uncles, grandparents, even Takis.

Through the trees the sun makes dappled patterns on the damp ground. Beneath my feet baby crab apples lie discarded like unloved toys, befriended by fawn mushrooms poking through the moss. I'm alone, unwatched, un-judged. Only my footprints give me away, imprinting the ground with my private pathway.

I emerge the other side of the wood and find myself at the bottom of Marshton Downs. I follow a rough path through stinging nettles and ferns and climb to the top. I can see across to Cley and the windmill, gleaming white in the morning sunshine. Beyond, a strip of dark blue sea meets the pale blue sky. Marshton village dots the landscape, snuggled between fields and trees. There's no one for miles. I'm all alone but desperate to talk to someone.

She's my oldest and best friend, and after telling Lee she was pregnant she told me. Well she can be my first. The Downs is full of sandy hollows in-between the gorse bushes. I find a sheltered one and sit down. It's a naturally formed seat and I rest my legs in the dip.

There's reception up here. I call Candy's mobile. Please, please, please answer…

'Hey Sophie, how are things going with your Mum?'

'Can you talk?'

'Yep, they're not filming at the moment,' she says. 'God, you sound like you're up a mountain.'

'I'm outside. It's just windy.'

'What's up?'

Time slows. A seagull glides on the wind, pale grey against

the rich brown of the ploughed field below. A lone butterfly settles on the ground next to me, its red and black wings beaten by the wind and then it's off. An orange ladybird crawls across my knee; I watch it begin its journey down my leg. All in a heartbeat.

I take a deep breath. 'I'm pregnant.'

There's absolute silence from Candy. The wind whistles around me. The seagull doesn't falter, the butterfly keeps fluttering and the ladybird reaches my trainers, orange against the white. The world keeps turning, same as before. It's only me that's changing.

'I saw you, less than two weeks ago,' she says.

'I know.'

'You had no idea?'

'None,' I say. 'I didn't want this. I'm not ready.'

She pauses. 'Alekos must be thrilled.'

The soil is so soft and pale like a sand dune. I want to roll down into the smooth hollow at the bottom. I dig my feet into the soil instead. 'I haven't told him.'

'I can't hear you, you're breaking up.'

'I haven't told him,' I say again.

'Sophie, you've got to.'

'Jesus Candy, I can't have a baby and still be living with his parents. They smother me enough as it is. This has to happen on my own terms.'

'What are you going to do?'

'I haven't thought that far ahead,' I say. 'What would you do?'

'That's a pointless question. I've been in your position, but I wanted it. We wanted it. It was planned, I was ecstatic. We both were.'

'I know, I know.'

'You didn't have a clue?'

'No. I'm on the pill,' I say. 'How the fuck could this happen?' I whack my free hand on the ground. It smarts and I bring my hand up stuck with soil and twigs.

'Did you forget to take it?'

'No.'

'Are you sure?'

'I was the one who decided to go back on it. I didn't want a baby. It didn't feel right.'

'When was your last period?' The line fades, she sounds distant.

'A while ago. I skipped one,' I say loudly, hoping she can hear me.

'Well if that's the case it's meant to be. It's fate. Did you take a pill late?' she suggests. 'Were you sick after taking it?'

The realisation of her words smacks me in the gut.

'Candy – what have I done?'

'I take it your Mum doesn't know.'

'No.'

'Are you going to tell her?'

I laugh. 'Telling her she's going to be a grandmother – can you imagine?'

'When are you going back to Greece?'

My ladybird friend is working its way towards the undergrowth. The day is undisturbed by voices, only the violent gusts of wind. The air is fresh and cool. I rest on my elbow and gaze up at the watery blue sky marked only by the tell-tale signs of a plane's trail. 'I'm not sure I want to go back,' I say. 'I feel at home here.'

'Is that because it seems like the easiest option?'

'No Candy, there is no easy option. I just love being here. There are quiet places, the countryside is stunning. I feel inspired by the people here, Mum included. She's made something of herself. I feel like I moved to Greece but didn't move on from who I was when I first arrived.'

'Sophie, you have to talk to him,' she says. 'Whatever you decide is going to affect the rest of your life. And his.'

'He's coming over for my birthday,' I say. 'He probably thinks I'll go back with him.'

'You should. Don't throw what you've got away.'

It's chilly sitting on the ground. I stand and stretch my legs.

'I've got to go,' Candy says. 'I'm needed on set. I'll give you a call later. It's been hectic going back to work and spending time with the kids in the evenings.'

'I understand. I've been busy here too. The days are running away from me.'

'Time flies when you're having fun...'

'I wish that was the least of my problems.'

'Call me, any time.'

'Thanks, Candy.'

'And talk to him,' she says before hanging up.

A dog barks and I am no longer alone as a Spaniel bounds through the gorse bushes towards me. Its owner, an elderly lady with a scarf tied around her head, a padded riding jacket, grey trousers and sturdy boots, swiftly follows behind. The dog's wet nose nudges my hand.

'Lovely morning isn't it,' the lady says, nodding a greeting, before she heads off to the wood.

I've so little time to think things through. What am I waiting for? I strike up a fast pace along the Downs and head for home.

Chapter Twenty-Four

It's nearly lunchtime when I get back from the Downs. I will time to slow down. I don't want to face Alekos tomorrow. It's too soon. But time refuses to slow. I hover in the kitchen, unsure what to do next. The sun is straining through thick, white cloud. Mum's in the garden, feeding the birds. The leaves on the trees are turning from green to yellow. A sycamore has red-tinged leaves already. I wave when Mum sees me but go upstairs before she comes in and has a chance to talk to me. In the airing cupboard Mum's laid out a clean bedspread, pillows and a sheet, ready for Alekos. I make the bed and hang up the clothes that are slung over the back of the armchair. Mum fusses around: wiping and re-wiping the kitchen surfaces. She makes me vacuum the living room carpet and furniture while she brings flowers in from the garden and arranges them in a vase, before baking a tray of flapjacks and chocolate brownies. All of this from a mother who used to be more interested in painting her toenails bubblegum pink and having a sneaky spliff with her twenty-year-old lover.

I move through the day as if it's a dream. Everything's vivid and real around me: the smell of coffee, the dampness of the soil, but I'm an onlooker, not quite involved. Mum asks me questions: 'Are you going to be okay driving all that way? What does Alekos like to eat? Does he drink beer? Does he speak much English?'

By the time she leaves the room I've forgotten what my answer was. 'Yes. Everything. Sometimes. Lots.'

I forget Mum wants help delivering flowers to a client and I'm in the bathroom again at the time we arranged to leave.

'Sophie?' And again. 'Sophie? What are you doing?' Mum shouts up the stairs.

I flush the toilet, go to the sink and splash my mouth with water.

'I need to get these flowers to Mrs Viner by five,' she calls.

'I'm coming!' I brush my teeth again to get rid of the bitter aftertaste.

This morning's walk cleared my head yet now it feels filled with smog. I touch my stomach, unsure whether it feels different. I remember having a conversation with a girl at school who couldn't understand why I didn't want to have children. I was adamant. But as for my reasons why... Maybe I was battling against what was expected, what everyone else seemed to want to do. I didn't want to get knocked up or married. I liked the name Keech.

Mum's waiting at the bottom of the stairs, her good foot tapping against the floorboards. A sharp breeze rushes through the open door.

'Mrs V's a bitch for being on time,' Mum says with an edge to her voice. 'Not the calmest of women.'

'I'm sorry.' I follow her out, picking up the flower arrangements on the way. 'Where does she live?' I ask as I start the engine and pull out on to the lane.

'Only in the next village. Turn right at the end.'

We pass *The Globe* and head down a narrow lane by the church.

'You've seemed a bit out of sorts these past couple of days. Are you alright?' Mum asks.

'I'm fine,' I reply.

'Are you missing Greece?'

I shrug. 'Not so much.' I keep my attention on the road

but sense Mum watching me.

'At least you'll see Alekos tomorrow,' she says. 'I can't wait to meet him.'

'Really?'

'I'm intrigued. I've never got to know any of your boyfriends.'

'There haven't been that many.'

'You're choosey, that's why.'

'Surely that's a good thing?'

'God, yes,' she says. 'Think of my track record. Bloody nutters.'

'Good-looking nutters though.'

'Not all of them. You wake up the next morning with a hangover, and Brad Pitt's turned into, well someone who doesn't resemble Brad Pitt in the slightest. Daylight's cruel. Pull over here, Soph,' she says.

I do as I'm told and stop on a grass verge next to a closed five-barred gate. Mum leads the way up the path and I follow behind with the flowers. Mum rings the doorbell. A dog barks. I hear muffled voices. The door opens and an elderly lady with glasses around her neck smiles at us.

'I thought you were never coming,' Mrs Viner says. She takes the flowers from me. 'They're wonderful, Leila.'

'I'll wait outside,' I say and leave them to it. I wander back down the path to the secluded lane and perch on the warm car bonnet. Whenever I think of the baby, my thoughts race to Alekos and then Ben filters in. The thought of him makes me feel dirty. I'm dragged down by the weight of this baby I haven't asked for. But maybe I can turn it into a positive mistake. A baby is what Alekos wants. We can't stay at *O Kipos* now; the apartment above the restaurant is too small for all of us and a baby. I know Despina will dispute that. Takis will just nod and Alekos shrug. There has to be a compromise now.

My mobile rings. I hesitate when I see Alekos' face flashing on the screen. I take a deep breath and answer.

'Hello.' It sounds forced, too enthusiastic. I'm conscious

my voice will give me away.

'I'm so glad I got hold of you,' he says. 'I've found a direct flight tomorrow. It arrives in Heathrow at 2.30 in the afternoon.'

'That's fine. I'm cooking at the pub tonight so I'm glad it's not early. It's a good three-hour drive from Mum's.'

'How are things going?'

'Better. We've talked a bit.'

'I'm nervous about meeting her.'

'Why?'

'You've made her sound like a monster.'

'I've been angry with her for years. I've said lots of unfair things.'

'So I've nothing to worry about?'

'She's looking forward to meeting you,' I say. 'You coming over here is no worse than me moving to Greece and meeting the whole of your family.'

'You didn't seem nervous.'

'I hid it well.'

'You hide lots of things well.'

Two hearts skip a beat.

'Like what?' I say.

'Everything. The last few months I've no idea what's going on in your head. When you handed the ring back I didn't know what to think. I don't want you unhappy.'

The car bonnet has cooled and I shiver. I stand and stretch my legs on the grass verge. The spiky husks of conkers lie littered beneath the trees. In the washed-out evening light, Mrs Viner's cottage looks inviting with a yellow glow spilling from the front window. I wish Mum would hurry up; I want to be at home, looking out on the day, not stuck out in it.

'How've you been?' he asks.

'Fine.' How can I tell him? It doesn't feel right, not over the phone. Candy will be disappointed in me. I'll wait until he's here. Seeing him will be different, being able to look at him, touch him and talk to him properly.

Leaves scuttle across the lane, collecting along the verge. I crunch one with my foot. It makes a satisfying sound as it disintegrates.

'How was Demetrius and Katrina's move?' I ask.

'Their new place is great. One of the top apartments in the block – they can see right over Thessaloniki. We only had two cars to move the lot. Katrina's got many, many things. Her family bought them everything: new cooker, fridge, bed, sofa. They have so much space and it's cheap because it's on the outskirts.'

'You sound jealous.'

'Why would I be?'

'Your best friend with a place of his own, in the city,' I say.

'*You've* always said you never want to live in a city again.'

'That's not the point.'

'What is then?'

'I'm jealous of them,' I say, kicking the fallen leaves. 'It's what I want for us.' The word 'us' holds more meaning now.

'They're in a different situation from us, Sophie. It's no good being bitter,' he says.

'I'm not bitter...'

'Mama's waiting,' he says. 'We're all going into Katerini to buy a present for your Mum. What does she like?'

'Wine. She's always liked wine. Red. But she can get that here. Get her something Greek. Olive oil or the hot feta from the delicatessen. I don't know. Use your imagination. Or ask your Mum.'

A car horn blasts in the background. Despina, I'm sure.

'Sophie,' he says.

'Yeah?' The wind rustles the fallen leaves.

He pauses and I hear the blast of the car horn again. 'Nothing. I'll see you tomorrow,' he says.

Chapter Twenty-Five

The Globe is quiet. It's the first time I've seen it empty. Not even Marcy is about, just a girl I don't recognise behind the bar. I hook my jacket over a chair and sit down next to the fireplace. On the wall are two black-and-white photographs of birds: a flock of ducks, dark against a pale sky, and a swan with its wings spread, charging towards the camera. There are footsteps and then a voice behind me.

'Do you like them?' Ben asks.

His voice alone makes my hands sweat. 'They're really good.'

He pulls up a chair and sits opposite me at the table. 'I took them earlier this year.'

'There's something so striking about black-and-white photos,' I say, not allowing myself to look at him. 'Have you ever thought about selling them?'

'Are you offering?'

'I would if I had somewhere to put them.'

'Dad wanted pictures for the pub, something natural.'

I'm conscious of him looking at me. He's as intense as Robert, rarely dropping eye contact. He's unshaven and his T-shirt and jeans are creased, but there's something pleasant about his dishevelled appearance. I shift in my seat. It's been less than forty-eight hours since I last saw him and so much has changed.

'Where are Fraser and Bella?' I ask.

'Playing in the garden,' he says. 'We're going to the beach again tomorrow. Do you fancy joining us? We're taking a picnic.'

'I can't. Alekos is arriving.'

'Oh.'

'For my birthday.'

He fiddles with a drinks mat. 'I don't want to lose you so soon.'

I hold his gaze and slowly say, 'You can't lose what you haven't got.'

He leans forward, his hands edging across the table towards mine. He smells of smoke. 'Even if Mandy changed her mind,' he says, 'I wouldn't go back, not now.'

'Not even for Fraser and Bella's sake?'

'We weren't happy. I don't want to lead a miserable life any more. I'd rather have less but quality time with Fraser and Bella than have to hide any more arguments from them. I want to be with someone I can have fun with. Life's for living.'

Our fingers are nearly touching and I pull my hands away and tuck them beneath my thighs. I can't touch him; I can't let the feeling I had in those sand dunes creep back into my body. Life is for living. That's how life used to be. Maybe Alekos' arrival tomorrow will be a turning point for us. After all he's coming here whether Despina wants him to or not.

'Ben,' Robert says, joining us, 'why didn't you tell me Sophie was here?'

'Sophie's here.' Ben scrapes his chair back and looks at me. 'I'll see you later.'

The chalkboards in the bar and the conservatory read: *Greek Salad*, *Pastitsio* and *Stuffed Peppers*. The kitchen is a miniature version of the one I'm used to at *O Kipos*, and with head chef Steve, his team and me, we constantly get in each other's way.

'Your specials are going down a storm,' Steve says, slapping another steak on the grill. He listens to classical music when he cooks. It's on in the background, behind the sizzle of food and the waft of conversation when the kitchen door opens. He doesn't look like he'd be into Beethoven or Brahms, with his shaved head, goatee beard and beer belly, 'from too much food rather than beer,' he claims.

'It keeps me calm,' he says, turning up the volume when the music goes quiet. 'The music soothes my nerves, but the chatter of arriving customers makes my hands sweat.'

'It's been nearly three weeks without this pressure,' I say to Steve. 'And you know what, I miss it.'

Robert's pub ticks along like a finely tuned machine, the waiters only coming into the kitchen to collect plates of food and deposit empty ones for washing up. I don't see Ben all night. Even Mum's not allowed to say hello. Robert simply tells me, 'Your Mum's here. She's having stuffed peppers.'

I barely have time to think in the steamy confines of the kitchen. It's only when the last special's been taken out that I become aware of the nagging pain across my stomach. Steve's busy with the dessert orders. I wipe my hands on my apron and take it off. My cheeks are burning in the heat. The kitchen is stuffy even with the outside door propped wide open on to the small car park. The change in temperature is startling as I go outside. It's dark out here. I lean against the wall and take deep breaths. The pain spreads across my stomach, low down like a dull throbbing period pain. I cross between the cars and sit on the far wall, shadowed by looming trees. I can see my breath, a puff of white in the moonlight before it disappears. I press my fingers against my stomach. It's too late to phone Candy. Maybe I'm imagining things, making myself worry – it's probably nothing to do with the baby.

Blocks of light from the conservatory windows throw colour over the pub garden. The grass looks luminous, inviting. Darkness folds around me in the shadowy car park, but it feels protective, not creepy. A couple is eating at one of the tables by the window, tucking into the food that I've prepared. A candle flickers between them, glinting on the full glasses of red wine on the table. Even from this far away I can see the woman's smile. Her lips move in a silent conversation I'd love to overhear. She takes a mouthful and looks intently at her partner, nodding as she chews. Her blonde bobbed hair curls neatly against her chin and her shirt is black with the top two buttons undone, enough to give a hint of cleavage yet remain classy. The man reaches his hand across the table and touches hers. Her smile grows. I turn away. The night sucks me back into its grip, with only the stars and honey-lit windows of the pub injecting any warmth. I run my hands across my stomach.

'I was wondering where you were.' Robert makes me jump. I turn and see his silhouette in the kitchen doorway. He walks over. 'Are you all right?'

I nod. 'A bit of stomach ache, that's all.'

'You should have said you weren't feeling well.'

'It's only been the last few minutes.'

'The *pastitsio* has gone down well. I wish I could have you cooking every night.'

'It's been good. I've missed it.' I wince and press my hands to my stomach again.

'I think you should go home, Sophie.'

I look up at him. 'Fresh air is good. I'm fine.'

'You don't talk to your Mum much, do you?' he says.

'We've been talking, I promise you that.'

'But not about yourself.'

'There's nothing to talk about,' I say.

Robert perches next to me on the wall. He clasps his hands together and rubs his thumb against his wedding band.

'I saw what you bought the other day,' he says.

The warmth of *The Globe* seems a greater distance than a few footsteps away. I glance at him but he's staring at his hands.

'I don't want you to feel you've got no one to talk to,' he says, still without looking at me. 'I know you and Ben get on... but there are some things... you know...'

'Better left unsaid.'

He looks at me. 'No. I think it's best to talk things through. From experience I know what it's like to bottle things up and pretend they're not there, whatever it is, anger, confusion, sadness… It's not healthy, Sophie. I went on like that for years, hiding my feelings, pretending I was okay, when really I was a mess. I still do. I've got better, but I don't find it easy talking about Jenny, my wife. I've got better at showing my feelings, though.'

'Mum said you didn't like talking about her.'

He shakes his head. 'Not with just anyone, no. But Leila's always been there for me. I felt at ease with her the moment we met. You should talk to her.'

'I don't think we've quite reached that stage in our relationship yet,' I say.

A family noisily leaves *The Globe* through the conservatory door and we watch them find their beaten-up Land Rover. The two boys fight their way on to the back seat, their voices disappearing into the night.

'You can always see a doctor,' Robert says, as the Land Rover pulls on to the road with a squeal.

'It's only tummy ache.'

'Are you pregnant?' He asks so matter-of-factly I automatically answer with a nod.

'You don't look happy,' he says.

'You don't say.'

'It wasn't planned?'

I shake my head. 'It was a shock.'

'I believe these things happen for a reason,' he says.

'Not always for the right reasons, though.'

'A child is a huge responsibility.'

'You're not helping,' I say.

'Ben and Vicky were the best things to happen to us.'

'That's what Ben said about Fraser and Bella.'

'He did?' Robert's eyes search mine, as if to check I'm telling the truth. 'Ben's not a talker, either. But I'm glad you told me.'

KATE FROST

'You were the one who asked.'

'I did, didn't I?' He smiles. His cheeks look grey in the moonlight, his eyes brighter, less tired.

'I don't want Mum to know,' I say.

'I won't say a word.'

'Alekos doesn't know either. I couldn't tell him… not over the phone.'

'It'll be different when you see him.'

'I'm not so sure.'

His hands are tense pressed against his trousers. He's the last person I imagined I could confide in. But I'm glad. He'll keep his word. My secret's safe. Mum doesn't have a clue – why would she? I didn't until two days ago.

'Jenny told me she was pregnant with Ben on our fourth wedding anniversary,' Robert says. 'She'd known for two days and nearly went demented keeping it secret. We went away for the weekend and she told me while we were walking along Hadrian's Wall. I tell you, I scared the sheep with my shouts. I remember every single detail about that moment. Alekos will feel the same.'

'That's not what I'm worried about,' I say. 'I know he's going to be happy. It's the whole situation that's wrong. It's not what I want.'

'A baby?'

'How our life is at the moment.'

The dull throb across my stomach seems to have numbed.

'You love him, don't you?' he asks.

I manage a nod but it feels like a shrug.

'I love Leila,' he says.

He's so sincere. It's not a throwaway comment. If anyone could see us sitting in the dark, perched on a wall, shivering – an odd couple divulging secrets.

'Have you told her?' I ask.

'No. I'm not too good at things like that. Out of practice.' The grip on his trouser legs loosens. 'I'm not sure how she feels about me.'

'There's only one way to find out.'

'She's always been with someone.'

'Not anymore.'

He looks at me with a frown. 'I know what it's like to lose someone.'

'She wasn't in love with Darren, if that's what you're wondering. She was going to finish with him that weekend,' I say. 'I'm sorry, that makes her sound heartless, but she's not, she's been cut up about...'

'I know,' he says. His fingers tense again, his knuckles whitening in the pale wash of moonlight. 'She talks to me.'

'I suppose you know her better than I do,' I say. The wind curls round the branches of the trees with a sigh; another car pulls out of the car park, its red lights puncturing the darkness until they disappear round a corner.

'Well,' Robert says, a smile coating his voice. 'This has been quite a night for revelations. I didn't mean to tell you, and I'm sure you weren't planning to spill the beans to me. I've been dying to tell someone.'

'I'm glad you did. And I won't say a word either.'

The kitchen door bangs against the outside wall and we both look up.

'What the hell are you two doing out here?' Mum says. 'It's bloody freezing.'

'We're made of strong stuff,' Robert says.

'I can understand what with you coming from Wales, but Sophie's been living in Greece for years.' She hobbles over on her crutches; her features look small and delicate in the moonlight.

'It does get cold there,' I say.

'Not like here it doesn't,' she says. 'Anyway, I've been wondering where you disappeared to.' She looks at Robert. 'And I'm sorry, but I walked through your kitchen.'

'I'll forgive you,' he says. Their eyes are fixed on each other. 'I came to find Sophie, to thank her for tonight.'

Mum shifts her focus from Robert to me. 'Bloody

delicious food,' she says. 'I think we'll be having a few Greek nights at home.'

I'm reluctant to go back inside despite being numb from sitting on the cold flint wall. I trail after Mum and Robert across the car park. Robert turns and smiles at me before ducking through the door into the steamy heat of the kitchen. I smile back and curl my arms around my stomach.

Chapter Twenty-Six

I open my eyes to sunshine streaming through the blinds. I stretch my arms and legs out before snuggling back into the pillows. The cobwebs clouding my thoughts these past few days have lifted – I'm ashamed to admit that last night's talk with Robert might have something to do with it. I laugh out loud with the realisation I'm excited about Alekos' arrival. I want to tell him about our baby.

Mum's stacking plates in the dishwasher when I finally make it downstairs.

'Do you want any coffee?' she asks, waving the pot at me.

'I'm trying to cut it out.'

'Sod that,' she says, pouring the dregs into her mug. 'I gave up smoking, that's enough willpower to last a lifetime. I'm not giving up caffeine. Or alcohol. Does Alekos smoke?'

'Occasionally.'

'I don't want to catch him hanging out your bedroom window having a sneaky fag.'

'He's thirty years old, Mum, not a teenager.'

'I'm dead excited about meeting him,' she says. 'I thought I'd make apple crumble for after our roast.'

'Only if you feel like it. You should still be taking it easy.'

She waves a hand at me and takes a sip of her coffee. 'I can't believe he's never had a proper roast.'

'He has.'

'Not with Yorkshire pud and gravy.'

'He is Greek.'

'How do I say hello again?'

'*Yasas.*'

'*Yasas.*'

I nod. 'It also means goodbye.'

'Bloody complicated language.'

I want to get going. All this waiting around is making me nervous. I have nothing to do. My room's tidy, the whole house is spotless and I've already planned the journey. I must be getting on Mum's nerves because she sends me down the lane to pick blackberries for the crumble. It's a perfect September day with sun filtering through high white clouds. I dodge puddles by stepping on the flint embedded in the muddy lane. I glance at my stomach. I still can't believe it. Maybe I shouldn't tell him at the airport. I could choose my moment like Robert's wife did and take Alekos somewhere memorable: the windswept beach at Salthouse or up to the Downs with its view to the sea. I don't have to go far before I find brambles heavy with fruit. I stretch into the hedgerow and take my pick of fat blackberries until I have an ice cream tub full.

It's time to go. I get into Mum's car, adjust the seat and start the engine. The UK road map lies on the passenger seat with a piece of paper and scribbled directions lying on top. There are ham and mustard sandwiches in the glove compartment and a bottle of water within reaching distance.

'Are you sure you'll be all right?' Mum asks through the open car window.

'Mum, really. How do you think I've managed on my own for the last few years?' I put the car into first and she taps the roof as I drive off.

Marshton disappears from view and soon I'm driving on wide, fast roads heading away from the coast. I'm tempted to change my route, to explore the long, straight road that veers off to my left through a canopy of trees, signposted to

Grimes Graves. But I keep going and slowly the countryside dissolves into Little Chefs, pylons and a horizon filled with grey buildings and windows glinting in the sunlight.

The radio's playing songs from the eighties: Kylie and Jason and Wham. It reminds me of Mum and I dancing around our kitchen in Hazel Road, using wooden spoons as mikes. I thought she was the coolest Mum; none of my friends' parents danced with them round the house or took them to see Madonna. She impressed all my friends when we were teenagers, and sleepovers at our house meant she cracked open a twelve-pack of lager and joined us watching *A Nightmare on Elm Street*.

Best of all I loved the stories Mum read to me at bedtime. She used to get side-tracked and ad-lib – even C S Lewis and Roald Dahl were given the Leila touch. I'd find myself in these stories: it was *Sophie and the Chocolate Factory*, not Charlie. I was the one riding high inside a peach, sitting on the shoulders of the BFG or walking out of the wardrobe and into Narnia with Peter, Susan and Edmund. Every night was a performance. Mum created characters, landscapes, stories and I painted them in my mind. That's how I started drawing. The next day, sitting at the kitchen table with crayons and pencils strewn across it, I would illustrate the previous night's story. I wonder if Mum still has my pictures or if they got lost during the move to Marshton. I took so little to Greece. My past is here. I wonder if my future is too.

The thunderous roar of aeroplanes deafens me as I arrive at Heathrow. I can see a plane's belly, shiny and white, coming in to land. There's a constant stream of planes taking off and landing. I'm envious of all those people who are able to forget reality for one or two weeks. A month. A lifetime perhaps.

I wonder what Alekos can see right now. The brown stretch of channel merging with land or green fields petering out into rows of suburban terraced houses. Will he like it here? With patchy sunlight and a vicious wind whipping leaves off the trees, it will certainly be too cold for him. I hope he can see past that to the beauty I've discovered in the short time I've been back.

I miss the entrance of the short stay car park and end up slamming my brakes on in the middle of the road when I spy another way in. There's no one behind me and my moment of dangerous – Greek – driving goes unnoticed.

My legs feel heavy as I walk towards Terminal 2. There are flights due to land from Milan, Athens, Cairo and Thessaloniki. This is where it all started just a few years ago when on impulse I jumped on a plane and escaped to Alekos and Greece. Our roles have reversed: this time I'm on home turf and Alekos is the one travelling to a new country to see me. I'd liked to have witnessed his conversation with Despina. To see him stand up to her, now that would have been quite something. I'm sure by allowing Alekos to leave *O Kipos* she's realised how much we need this time together. I watch another load of people arrive back from Malaga. The flight from Thessaloniki flashes up: delayed.

I can't stand it any more, leaning my weight from one foot to the other, watching tanned and smiling strangers emerge through the arrivals gate. The crowd around me disperses as friends and family find each other. But there's no sign of Alekos. I make my way to the nearby café and order a hot chocolate with marshmallows. I'm allowed; I'm eating for two. I perch on a stool up at the bar that overlooks arrivals and wait. I stir my hot chocolate until the marshmallows melt into a swirl of pink and white.

The first time I saw Alekos he was onboard *Artemis*, throwing a rope to another crew member. I was standing on the edge of the dock, waiting for Candy, who was bartering over a shell necklace, when I saw him. He was as toned as a Greek sculpture but instead of being pale like marble he was dark as honey. His shorts were slung low on his waist; the rest of him was bare, even his feet. He didn't see me, but that first sight of him is mine to keep. Candy, with her new necklace tied round her neck, dragged me away from the sea towards one of the cafés. The next day I knew his name, the day after I knew the taste of his lips, the day after that I just knew.

How can such strong emotions lead to so much uncertainty? Over this past year I have questioned if I fell in love with the place as much as with him. We've never gone back but it feels as if we left a part of ourselves there. It felt more than just a holiday romance. It is more. We've moved on, changed, grown and got to know each other. That takes time. We went from a romance on Cephalonia to the reality of living and working together at *O Kipos*. The Alekos I glimpsed that summer is a fading memory. The life he had, the passion, the independence seems to have been sucked out of him. It's his fault. Despina only rules him because he lets her. I'm hoping today is the start of something new. We need to do more than just survive. Ben was right when he said life is for living.

I take a sip of my hot chocolate and the melted marshmallow sticks to my top lip. The arrivals board flashes 'Thessaloniki: landed'. No one's come through the arrivals gate yet. He'll have to wait for his luggage. That'll take a while. In-between blowing on my hot chocolate, I take deep breaths. My jeans fit fine and my top's not too tight. There's no bump showing. I don't feel pregnant. I could quite easily start believing it isn't true. I used to be very good at make-believe when I was a child, out of necessity, lacking a father; out of boredom in physics lessons; out of loneliness as an only child with a working mother. Not that I blamed her, at least now I don't. I understand why she had to work long hours, sometimes in two jobs, or why we always had a lodger. 'It's useful having a man about the house,' she used to say. As if she had any choice. She'd never admit she *needed* a man about the house, as well as a man in her life. There was always someone – their faces became a blur, their names muddled. I gave up trying to remember. The ones I liked never seemed to last and then I'd get upset, so I learnt it wasn't worth getting to know them in the first place.

A few people emerge through the arrivals gate. The dregs of my hot chocolate are cold but I stay rooted to my seat as people flood into the terminal. I see his dark hair first, and then the white and grey stripes of his favourite shirt – the one he wears when he wants to make an impression. I glimpse his face between strangers: tanned skin, arched eyebrows and a long nose. But I also recognise the hair-sprayed blonde hair behind him and the thick fur coat only brought out when it snows. Alekos sees me, his smile only faltering when I don't smile back. Then the woman emerges from Alekos' shadow.

Chapter Twenty-Seven

Despina is in her fur coat, fully made up, looking unruffled despite a four-hour flight. '*Yasou*!' she calls, smiling as they walk towards me. 'You look surprised. Aleko didn't tell you I was coming?' she says, kissing my cheeks.

This changes everything. I take a deep breath and smile. 'No, he didn't.' I slip effortlessly back into Greek.

Alekos moves in front of her and hugs me. 'I'm sorry,' he whispers. His skin smells of the beach, hot and salty and so familiar. We hold on to each other for a moment and I don't want to let go of his familiarity and the comforting way he rests his hand in the small of my back. We pull away and our eyes briefly meet.

'How was the journey?' is all I can think of to say. Everything else will have to wait. For when, I don't know.

'Long,' Despina replies. She buttons her coat right up despite the fact we're still inside. 'I've been worried about you, Sophie. I had to come.' She pinches my cheek, a habit I detest, particularly as she seems to only do it to five-year-old Yannis and me.

'That's kind of you, but I'm fine. I wanted to stay to help Mum.'

'Your poor mother, how is she?'

Another planeload of people emerge through the arrivals gate before I can answer. The three of us are in the way with suitcases and bags surrounding us.

'Let's go.' I begin to drag Despina's suitcase towards the car park.

'Sophie, wait. Where's the bathroom?'

I stop and point her in the direction of the ladies. We both watch her clatter in her heels across the tiled floor.

I turn to Alekos. 'Are you insane?'

He was waiting for this. His forehead is already creased in a frown, his hands shoved deep in his trouser pockets. 'I couldn't say no.'

'You never can.'

'She's worried about you. And your Mum. She wanted to come. You know when she gets an idea in her head, you can't stop her.'

'This time you should have.'

I want to walk away from him. Leave him here with no option but to go back to Greece with his mother. I fold my arms across my chest and fight back the tears forming in my throat. I'm not going to cry in front of him or have to explain myself to Despina.

Alekos' hand gently brushes my cheek. 'I didn't know how to tell you.'

This isn't the man I met on Cephalonia. He's too preened and polished, with his hair gelled, smart without jeans and too much tanned flesh on show. I wonder if Despina made him wear trousers and a shirt. The man I met on Cephalonia would have stood up to her.

He steps closer me. 'It's so good to see you, Sophie.'

Our lips are inches apart. I want to kiss him.

'This was your chance to make everything right,' I say. 'Forget any past promises, I just wanted to be with you for a couple of days, somewhere other than O *Kipos*. I want some kind of commitment from you.'

He takes my hands. 'Sophie, I have committed to you. Whenever you're…'

'Not that kind of commitment. Commitment to our future, the physical things in our life, the practicalities. I was hoping we could move on.'

'We can.'

I shake my head. 'Your mother's with you. That's not us moving on.' I begin to walk away. 'I have to phone Mum.'

It rings for ages. Alekos stands by the luggage and fiddles with the address label.

Mum answers: 'He arrived safely?'

'Yes. And his Mum. Despina turned up too.'

There's silence. 'Oh.'

'I'll sort everything out when we get back. Despina can have my room and me and Alekos can sleep downstairs.'

'There's a camp bed in the attic,' she says calmly.

'Great. Perfect.'

'You sound pissed off.'

'I am.'

'I hope she likes roast beef and Yorkshires.'

'I'm so sorry. If I'd known she was coming... This is the last thing you need.'

'I should have learnt more Greek.'

'We'll be home before eight.'

'Drive carefully.'

Alekos' watchful eyes make me feel exposed. Does he know something's changed? Do I look different?

'I didn't bring her,' he says when I rejoin him. 'She told me she was coming.'

'Why didn't you tell me?'

'I was going to but I thought you wouldn't want me to come at all if you knew.'

I'm silenced by Despina emerging from the ladies with her coat still done up to her chin. Red lipstick has been freshly applied to her lips.

'I bought your mother silver earrings from Lena's friends' shop in Katerini.' Despina says. 'Alekos said...'

'I said I didn't know, Mama.'

'He thought she had her ears pierced.'

'She does,' I say. 'But you didn't have to buy her anything.'

She looks at me sternly. 'Of course I did.' She starts dragging her suitcase and I pick up her bag of duty free.

It's a trek out of Terminal 2. It's difficult to hold a conversation on the move but Despina insists on firing questions at the back of my head as we walk single file along corridors and up escalators. She shivers the moment we step out of the warmth of arrivals and into the car park. She pulls on her fur-lined leather gloves.

'It's only the end of September, not winter,' I say.

'I remember how pale you were, Sophie, when you first arrived. Don't tell me it's not cold in England.'

'It's very built-up,' Despina says as we start our journey north towards the M25. 'Very dull and grey. Not at all like the images of London shown on the television.'

'That's because we're not actually in London,' I say. 'We're on the outskirts. It's like us driving from your cousin's house on the edge of Thessaloniki to *O Kipos.*'

Despina reaches into her handbag for a nail file and begins to tidy up her nails rather than look out of the window.

I keep glancing at her in my rear-view mirror. 'How on earth is the restaurant running without you?'

'I've employed a new chef,' she says, without looking up from her nails.

'You have?'

'He's a young chef with glowing references from an award-winning restaurant in Athens. I need reliability.'

'Meaning?'

'Meaning I need reliability.'

Alekos remains quiet in the passenger seat next to me and doesn't catch my eye.

'I'm sorry if I left so suddenly and made things difficult for you but Mum was pretty badly injured, I needed to be here. I still need to be here.'

'There's no need to apologise, Sophie, I'm glad you put family first for once, just as I felt it was my duty to put my family first, which is why I'm here. We must all make sacrifices.'

Alekos sinks further into the passenger seat and I bite my tongue. Despina finishes filing her nails and takes a bottle of red nail varnish out of her handbag. 'The only problem I envisage is leaving Takis in charge. He's too soft. Goodness knows what mess we'll go back to.'

Fields, motorway junctions and roadworks all pass in a blur, as do signposts for Watford, St Albans, the A1 and eventually the M11. Despina finishes painting her fingernails and starts looking out of the window. Ninety minutes into the journey, dual carriageway merges into fast, straight roads and we pass the wooded picnic site at Mildenhall and Lakenheath army base. This journey is new to me, yet it feels like I'm going home. Despina is silent and watchful in the back, her face turned to the window. I can see her profile, high cheekbones and a long, straight nose. Her best assets are highlighted with blusher and lipstick. She's still wearing her coat but her gloves and scarf are neatly laid on the seat next to her.

Alekos remains silent as we crawl through Swaffham's bustling town centre. I turn the radio on low and Alekos glances at me before settling his gaze back to the window. He has defined cheekbones too, but his features are softer, like Takis'. Yet he's as handsome as Despina is beautiful.

'I've not been outside of Greece since our one and only holiday abroad in Italy before we had children.' Despina breaks the silence. 'Did you used to go on holiday with your mother?'

'We went camping every summer to Yorkshire or Wales. We never went abroad. We attempted to go to Scotland once but our car broke down so we only made it as far as Northumberland and we had to be rescued by a friendly AA man.'

'Camping, as in a tent?'

'Mama, what's wrong with that?'

'I loved it,' I say. 'Spending time with Mum, warming our hands over the gas stove, eating fish and chips out of newspaper, walking arm in arm to the toilet block at night, guided by torchlight. What's not to like?'

'But it rains here all the time. I couldn't think of anything worse.'

'It's not raining now,' Alekos says.

My legs are aching and I can't stop yawning. I turn off the main road and head down a lane that cuts through fields on either side. I scare a pheasant and it dashes into the hedge, in a flurry of red and brown feathers.

'Nearly there,' I say.

We drive through a wood and the lane narrows. The trees on either side are so close together their branches interlock and prevent the sun from penetrating. The flint-clad cottages are a familiar sight now and they look cosy with the odd window lit up as we pass. As I drive up the incline to Marshton, I realise how Robert must have felt driving me here, knowing I was about to get my first look at his village. I hold my breath until *The Globe* comes into view, with the lamps on in the windows. I can't see Robert's car. I wonder if Ben kept his promise and took Fraser and Bella to the beach.

'*Po, po!*' Despina exclaims as we pull up outside *Salt Cottage*. 'I never imagined... you always talked about living in a city.' She slams the car door and startles wood pigeons in the trees. It's perfect timing; the retreating sun spreads orange and marshmallow pink across the horizon. The front garden is ablaze with colour, the grass and trees a richer green than anything in Greece, the flowers a vivid yellow, red and white. Alekos points to the sky and we look up. A dozen or so ducks, black against the sky, flap across in arrow formation, quacking as they fly over.

The front door scrapes open and Mum appears on the step supported by her crutches. She's smiling. This is my homecoming, how I wished it had been three weeks ago.

'*Yasas*!' she calls.

Despina claps in delight. 'You speak Greek?'

'No, only one word,' Mum says, beckoning us inside.

She's been busy while I've been away. In the hallway she's placed a vase of pale pink roses from the garden and the lamp on the sideboard is switched on giving a welcoming glow. But it's the smell of roasting beef that entices. The kitchen door is open and the sound of cooking filters into the hallway.

'Mum, this is Alekos.' I shrug off my coat and take Despina's. We head into the kitchen.

'I'd love to say Sophie's told me all about you but I'd be lying,' Mum says. She firmly shakes his hand and looks him up and down. 'Better late than never.'

'It's very good to finally meet you,' Alekos says in English.

'And this is Despina.' Despina launches forward and kisses Mum on both cheeks. Her hands fly everywhere as she tells Mum, in Greek, of the shock the family felt when they heard about the accident. Alekos translates. Mum nods and allows Despina to clutch her hand as if they're long-lost friends rather than strangers.

'Sophie,' Mum says. 'Sophie.' All three of them are looking at me. 'Dinner's nearly ready, so if you want to show Despina to her room and get the camp bed down…'

'*Pame pano*,' I say to Despina and Alekos and they follow me out of the kitchen.

'Alekos, you're tall enough to open the trapdoor to the attic,' Mum calls after us. 'Top landing.'

It seems so long ago that I was exploring this house on my own. Now it feels crowded. Despina's and Alekos' feet hit every creaky spot on the stairs. I push open my bedroom door. Her bedroom now. There's no sense in calling it my bedroom, after all it's only Mum's spare room. My wash bag sits on top of the chest of drawers and my clothes are still hanging in the wardrobe, although I've cleared them off the back of the chair.

'Sophie, I can't take your room,' Despina says.

'You must.' Although I really mean, 'You should have thought about that before coming unannounced.' She has no clue about the commotion she's caused, or if she does she hides it well. Or doesn't give a shit. I notice Mum's taken the tasteful nude off the wall and replaced it with one of Ben's black-and-white bird photographs. I leave Despina to unpack.

I rejoin Alekos on the landing. He's already opened the hatch to the attic and pulled the stepladder down.

'Your Mum's great,' he says.

'I never said she wasn't.' I step on to the ladder.

He grabs my hand. 'I'll get it.'

I continue up the steps. 'I'll pass it down.'

I reach the top, crawl into the attic space and feel around for a light switch. I find it and squint when the naked bulb flickers into life. It's dusty up here and uncomfortable on my knees. Thick beams, so low I have to crawl under them, cut across the attic. Mum's packed the space with individually marked boxes: *Christmas Decorations*, *Hazel Road Curtains*, *Sophie's Stuff*. It's the box I dumped on her before I left for Greece. I'm tempted to open it – it's like a time capsule, a reminder of my past. But I don't. The dust is tickling my nose. I sneeze.

'Can't you find it?' Alekos says poking his head through the hole.

I have. It's just behind the Christmas box, wrapped in a plastic cover. Between the two of us we drag it out of the attic, down the stairs and into the living room. It's only a single bed and old, the mattress thin. Mum's already laid out sheets, pillows and two duvets on the coffee table.

'I'll take the sofa if you want the camp bed,' I say.

'There's room for two.'

'Yeah, if we don't want to have any sleep.'

'That's what I'm hoping.'

'I was too.' I chuck him a single sheet.

It's a surreal sight seeing Despina sitting in the kitchen with

Mum. The food she's brought is spread across the table amongst dishes and plates of roast potatoes, carrots, swede, cabbage and a juicy beef joint on a carving dish.

'This,' Despina says, handing Mum a slice of pie, '*spanakopita*...cheese and...' she turns to me. '*Pos lene spanaki?*'

'Spinach,' I say.

Mum takes a bite. 'My God that's good.'

Despina beams.

'They're my favourite,' I say.

I watch Despina carefully. She cuts a tiny square of Yorkshire pudding, pops it into her mouth and chews. Her expression doesn't change.

'You don't have to eat it,' I say in Greek. Mum looks at me, questioning.

'Is very good,' Despina says with a smile. I don't believe her but at least she's making an effort. She doesn't have seconds.

Mum and Despina go to bed early, leaving Alekos and me alone in the sitting room. I've already made myself comfortable on the sofa with a duvet and pillows. Alekos is sitting at the end, squashed against my feet, his hand resting on my legs. I want to erase everything that's happened and just live in this moment. He switches off the TV.

'Do you want to talk?' he asks.

'I think enough's been said already.'

'Are you still angry with me?'

I shake my head. 'Not angry, disappointed.' I turn on my side so I'm facing away from him and tuck my hand beneath the pillow. I close my eyes and try to ignore him but I sense him watching me. His hand strokes my leg, creeping higher until he's massaging my thigh. I can't sleep but I pretend to. I'm not sure how long he stays up watching me because eventually I drift off, his advances ignored.

Chapter Twenty-Eight

'Sophie? Are you awake?' The camp bed squeaks as Alekos shifts and sits up. He's a solid black shape in the grainy darkness. His warm hands slide beneath my vest top and across my breasts. I freeze as his hand moves towards my stomach. I keep my eyes closed and stay very still.

'I know you're awake,' he says. His fingers tickle my side and I squirm away. 'Happy Birthday.'

'It's early,' I say.

He switches the lamp on and scrabbles around in his bag. 'I've got a proper present to give you later,' he says, 'but I thought you might want this back.'

I wriggle into a sitting position and rub my eyes. Alekos kneels next to the sofa and unclasps his hand to reveal my engagement ring. 'I know I said all the wrong things on Santorini…' he says.

'Aleko, no.'

'I want to make you happy, Sophie.'

'I took the ring off for a reason, Aleko. Why you think giving it back to me now is a good idea is beyond me. Your mother's here. Have you not listened to anything I've been telling you over the last few weeks? Us getting married is not the problem.'

'Then why won't you wear it?'

'Because putting it back on is not going to change anything.'

~

Alekos is quiet at breakfast. Despina makes up for his silence by telling Mum all about the restaurant and the family in Greece and it's left up to me to translate. Despina sips at a very strong mug of coffee and tucks into a croissant thickly spread with strawberry jam. I butter my toast and reach across the table for the marmite.

'Alekos, you didn't give Sophie back her ring?' Despina asks. 'You said you were going to give it to her this morning.'

'I know what I said, Mama.'

'He did. But I'm not wearing it,' I reply in Greek.

Despina puts her half-eaten croissant back on her plate. 'Why not?'

'Why don't you ask Alekos.'

Mum takes a sip of her coffee and glances between the three of us.

Alekos stands up. 'Because the ring was never lost on Santorini, Mama, and me telling you and Baba the other day that I'd found it in the suitcase pocket was a lie. Sophie took it off and we have a lot to talk about before she'll be wearing it again.'

'But I don't understand… the wedding… what's happened for you to feel like this Sophie?'

'That's between Alekos and me. And if I'm honest, our problems would have been a lot easier to sort out if Alekos had come here on his own.'

Silence. Alekos leans his hands on the edge of the sink and looks out of the window. Despina fiddles with the gold cross on the chain around her neck.

Mum coughs. 'Does anyone fancy translating what's just been said?'

'Mum really, you don't want to know.'

Alekos turns to face us and says in English. 'I asked Sophie to marry me in July last year.'

'You're engaged and you didn't think to tell me?' Mum says, glancing at my ring finger.

I hold my hand up. 'Why I'm not wearing my engagement

237

ring is what we were discussing.'

'And why aren't you wearing it?' Mum looks at us. Despina, unable to understand, scrapes her chair back from the table and folds her arms across her chest. 'Do you love each other?' Mum asks.

I look at Alekos. 'Yes,' we both say quietly.

'Then what else matters?'

Despina pours herself another mug of coffee. '*Eiseh kakomathemenos*, Sophie.'

'What did she say?' Mum asks.

'She said I was spoilt.'

'Spoilt?' Mum laughs and looks at Despina. 'That's one thing Sophie's not. Opinionated, passionate, angry, unforgiving, yes, but not spoilt.'

Despina frowns and stands up. 'It's not all about you, Sophie. You need to think about the people who love you, my son in particular before you hurt him too badly.'

Alekos places his hand on her shoulder. 'Mama, let's go for a walk.' He steers her out of the back door and I watch until they disappear from sight.

Mum puts her hand on top of mine. 'It's your life, Sophie; I'm not going to say another word. I can't understand half of what she says but I think Despina says enough for all of us.'

The Globe smells of roast dinners mixed with beer and log fires. It's six o'clock and the last customers have left and the waiting staff are clearing away. Despina, Alekos and I follow Mum out of the patio doors and into the garden. Smoke streams into the air from a barbeque made from half an oil drum. Robert's standing over it turning sausages and burgers and wearing an apron with 'I'm the chef' written on it. He seems to have invited the whole village as the garden is filled with people. Ben's here, minus his children who must have been picked up by Mandy. Marcy is chatting with another woman from behind the bar. She looks relaxed with her usual scraped back hair loose around her shoulders.

'Ah, the birthday girl!' Robert calls. Mum cuts across the

grass towards him and we follow her.

'Happy Birthday, Sophie!' Robert says, and pats my shoulder.

'Robert, meet Alekos and Despina,' Mum says.

He shakes Alekos' hand but Despina insists on a kiss on both cheeks. She's charmed by him. 'A English man cook!' she says in broken English.

'I can cope with hotdogs.'

'Don't put yourself down,' Mum says. She touches his arm, briefly, but I notice the smile her gesture brings to his face. 'Can we help?'

Robert turns a row of skewered onions and peppers. 'Absolutely not. All under control. Help yourselves to a drink.'

'I make salad,' Despina says.

Robert looks at her, frowns and then looks at me. 'Greek salad?'

Despina nods. '*To kouzina?*'

'She means the kitchen,' I say.

Robert shrugs and points her in the right direction. 'Our chef's still here...' But Despina's halfway across the lawn. I catch Ben looking at me as she passes him. He doesn't smile, but holds my gaze. He's talking to Marcy and she glances between the two of us and nudges him.

'So, Alekos,' I hear Robert say, 'how do you like England?'

'I like it a lot,' he says. I feel my cheeks flush as I turn away from Ben and back to Alekos warming his hands over the barbeque.

'Too cold?' Robert asks.

'Mum,' I say. 'I'm going to make sure Despina's not bullying Steve out of his kitchen.'

She nods but doesn't turn her attention away from Robert and Alekos.

I skirt the lawn to avoid Ben, and find Despina in the kitchen with her sleeves already rolled up and Steve staring at her.

'My name Despina.'

'Steve, this is my boyfriend's Mum,' I say.

She's opening cupboards by the time I've finished introducing them. Steve looks at her with his mouth open.

'I'm sorry,' I say, as Despina brushes past him with a large bowl in her hand.

'*Dhomates, pu ica?*' she demands.

Steve's cheeks flush red. '*Dhomates?* Tomates? Tomatoes?'

Despina looks at him and frowns. '*Ne*, to-ma-toes,' she says really slowly.

He points her in the direction of the salad compartment and raises his eyebrows at me. 'I need a smoke,' he says and heads outside. He sits on the same spot of wall where I sat with Robert the other night. He takes a pack of Rizla and tobacco out of his apron pocket and begins to roll a cigarette.

I sit next to him. 'She's my boss.'

'She that bossy with you?'

'With everyone.'

'The best chefs always are.'

'She works hard and doesn't particularly like not doing anything as you can tell.' I nod towards the kitchen. 'This is the first time she's been away from the restaurant for more than a night for as long as I've known her. I think she's suffering withdrawal symptoms.'

'Well, she's welcome to it.' He licks the edge of the paper and sticks it neatly down. 'I'm going to enjoy the sunshine, my cigarette and have a nice cold beer.'

'That sounds like a plan.'

Despina's salad is a hit and Robert's burgers, sausages and chicken drumsticks are cooked perfectly. The barbeque attracts like a magnet, particularly now dusk has settled and the warmth of the sun has dispersed. Everyone's gathered around the glowing coals, clutching drinks and plates of food.

'I like your family,' Despina says.

'Family?' I say. 'You mean Mum?'

'Robert's like family, isn't he?'

'No. I don't know. I guess. To Mum maybe.'

She beckons me away from the crowd around the barbeque. 'Everyone's very welcoming,' she says.

'You sound surprised.'

She sits down at a picnic table at the furthest end of the garden and puts her plate of food down. 'I am. I always think of the English as being very cold. Not easy to get on with.'

'What, like me?'

She shakes her head. '*Ochi*. I know our relationship has been strained this last year or so and we've both said and done things that we regret. But I want you to know you're a part of our family and we're glad... I'm glad to have you in it.'

'It didn't sound like that to me this morning.'

'I'm only concerned about Alekos and his happiness. It's only natural for a mother to feel that way.'

'I think it's impossible for me to live up to your expectations.' I sip my lemonade and watch her carefully.

She frowns and looks away. 'Lena says I can't expect everyone to be like me and want the same things from life.' She taps her wedding ring with her red nails. 'I only ever wanted a husband, a house and children. And I got it all.'

'In the same order?'

She studies me for a moment before turning her attention to her chicken drumstick. 'In that order.'

'It's not because it was what was expected of you?'

She shoots me a stern look. 'No! I remember being fifteen and jealous of my older sister being married and pregnant. She was twenty-one. I was twenty when I had Lena.'

'Did you not want a career?'

'What do you think I have now? I've always worked but my family's come first. We're lucky. We have the restaurant, it's a family business, more than my parents ever had or could have offered me.'

'But what if Lena and Alekos don't want the family business?' I say each word carefully, slowly, ready to take it back.

Despina's lips purse white for a second. 'It's there for them in ten, fifteen years' time,' she says, just as carefully. 'Takis and I have worked all our lives to give them stability and opportunity. They'd be fools to turn their backs on it. Lena's different, she has a husband with a good job, they have an apartment, land to build on. It's Alekos I worry about.'

'Me too.'

She nods. 'I don't know where his heart is. Besides with you.'

Alekos is standing with Mum, deep in conversation, both with a pint in their hands.

'My mother was one of seven brothers and sisters,' Despina says. 'Seven. And they had nothing. Two bedrooms for all of them. Her Dad worked at Thessaloniki docks. Their place stank of fish. I went there when I was small. The smell made me sick. I would have taken the opportunity Lena and Alekos have without hesitation.'

'The restaurant?' I ask. She nods. 'What makes you think he doesn't want it?'

She looks across the picnic table at me. 'Don't mess him around, Sophie,' she says quietly. There's anger in her voice. 'If you don't want him then let him go. He deserves to have a wife that loves and respects him and wants what's best for him. I hope that can be you… But if not…'

I wonder how she'd react if I told her I was pregnant. Would she be more careful with her words, more reluctant to warn me off? 'Thanks for the advice.' I swing my legs over the bench and leave her sitting on her own.

Mum and Alekos are still chatting. I interrupt them. 'Can I talk to you?' I grab Alekos' arm and pull him away. 'What have you been telling your Mum?'

'What is wrong with you? Are you trying to start a fight?'

'What have you told her about us?'

He sighs. 'She asked awkward questions.'

'You do realise what she's trying to do? She's guilt-tripping us into staying at *O Kipos* forever.'

'Don't be so dramatic, Sophie,' he says. 'Just because I talk to my Mum, it doesn't mean that I can't make a decision for myself.'

'Despina doesn't need to know the details of our relationship.' I clench my hands into fists.

Despina and Mum are watching. I wonder if Ben is. Alekos runs his hands up the insides of my arm. He leans towards me until his forehead rests against mine. 'This hasn't been a great birthday for you, has it,' he says.

'I've had better.'

'The first one in Greece was good.'

'It'd be difficult to top that.'

'When we get home, why don't we sit down together with Mama and talk to her, tell her we need some time and space, make her see things from our point of view.'

'I'm not sure I'm ready to go home yet.'

He stares at me and loosens his hold on me. He shakes his head. 'I don't understand.'

'I love it at *O Kipos*, but at times I hate it. I've fallen in love with it here, I've found what I used to have in Greece, how I felt on Cephalonia,' I say, gesturing towards the clear dark sky pitted with stars and the trees behind us.

'But I'm not here.'

'Can I have everybody's attention?' Robert shouts from the other side of the garden. The lights circling the lawn have come on now it's dark. The barbeque is still glowing red and it throws a warm light on to Robert's face. 'Let's raise our glasses to the birthday girl. To Sophie!'

'To Sophie!' everyone repeats as glasses are raised.

'In the three weeks she's been here she's brought a breath of fresh air and Greek cuisine to *The Globe*, and, most importantly, she's been a great support to Leila.' He looks straight at me and raises his glass of red wine. 'I hope you can stay a while longer.'

Everyone claps. Alekos leaves my side and walks back towards the barbeque.

'Hello stranger.' Ben appears behind me. He pinches my side and his touch sends shivers wriggling through me. I glance at him and then at Alekos, safely in conversation with Mum, Robert and Despina. 'You've been avoiding me,' he says.

'Not really,' I say. 'You've not come and said hello.'

'Or happy birthday.'

'Indeed.'

'Well, happy birthday.' He leans forward and kisses me, brushing my cheek with his stubble.

I pull away.

'So what's the problem between you and him?' He nods towards Alekos, sandwiched between Mum and Despina. Alekos and I catch each other's eyes. I look away.

'Let's walk.' I don't wait for an answer. I can feel people watching us. I don't stop until we're outside the front of the pub. It's quiet and dark, with only the lanterns throwing light on to the lane in front. I sit down on the bench to the side of the front door.

'What was up with you the other day?' Ben asks. He sits next to me. Our thighs touch.

'What do you mean?'

'You having a dig at me. I know it was difficult with Fraser and Bella being here,' he says. 'But I thought you were interested, you know, before.'

'What? Because of our fumble in the sand dune? We were drunk.'

'That's never an excuse.'

'No. But things have changed since then.'

He leans closer to me and I feel his breath on my neck. For a moment I wonder if he's going to kiss me. 'What's changed? I enjoyed myself, I'm pretty sure you did too.' He pulls away from me and takes his cigarettes from his back pocket. 'Marcy's talking about us.'

'There is no *us*.'

'Try telling that to your boyfriend.'

'Leave Alekos out of this. What's happened is between you and me. Nobody else should be involved, not Marcy and certainly not Alekos. I saw how uncomfortable you were when your Dad introduced me to Mandy.'

He lights a cigarette and inhales deeply. He blows smoke into the darkness. He rests his elbows on his knees and I can see the strong contour of his back showing through his pale top.

'I'm not an easy replacement for your marriage, you know,' I say.

'Your relationship with your boyfriend hardly seems straightforward.' His gaze is fixed on the darkness and not on me. 'What is it with women and their mind games? It's exactly what Mandy was doing – emotionally blackmailing me.' He takes another drag. The cigarette glows and fizzles.

'Don't compare me with her,' I say quietly. 'You want to know what's changed? Last Sunday when we went on the boat trip and then to Stiffkey was the first time in a long time that I felt I was living life and that's mainly down to you. I loved seeing you with your kids but the way you talked about Mandy made me realise that what happened on Sunday was us escaping from the real world. I was fooling myself to think that spending time with you would enable me to forget about Alekos and having to make a decision about my life. And then on Thursday I found out that I'm pregnant.'

'Jesus.'

'Now you know why I had a dig at you on Friday. I've never had any intention of "emotionally blackmailing" you or Alekos. At the very most my behaviour has been out of confusion. I honestly like you and yes, I was drunk but at the time my feelings were real.'

Voices from the party travel across from the garden. The laughter sounds inviting. The darkness in front of us suffocates. I strain to make out the field on the other side of the lane. Ben taps ash on to the grass.

'That's complicated,' he finally says. 'What does he think?'

'Alekos? He doesn't know.'

'Shit. Things are bad.' We return to staring into nothingness. 'We all come with baggage, Sophie…'

I touch my stomach and shake my head. 'Baggage?' I say. 'Is that what Fraser and Bella are to you?'

'I didn't mean it like that,' he says, taking hold of my hand. 'These last couple of weeks with you have been the best time I've had since I moved here.'

'*Ti kanis,* Sophie?'

I pull my hand from Ben's and stand up.

'Is he the reason?' Alekos steps into the light cast from the lantern above. 'For "loving" being here, for not wanting to come home?'

'Ben's a friend.'

Ben chucks his cigarette stub on the ground and grinds it with his boot. 'We haven't properly met yet.' He stands up and holds out his hand.

'*Ilithea,*' Alekos mutters.

'What did he say?'

'Nothing,' I reply.

'I called you an idiot.'

'I'm the idiot?' Ben says. 'You have no idea what you're about to lose if you're not careful.'

They both look at me.

It's as if I'm looking down on myself. The three of us facing off. Alekos jumping to conclusions. Ben defiant. Me not knowing what to say or think. Ben's words leave a bitter aftertaste. He has the upper hand over Alekos. I've confided in him, told him a secret all the wrong people now know, and the one it affects is oblivious. Alekos tenses and clenches his fists. He punches Ben once, hard enough to send him reeling back into the bench we'd been sitting on. I come back to earth with a bump. 'Alekos!'

He walks away.

Chapter Twenty-Nine

Blood trickles from Ben's nose, dark against his skin. He's managed to sit himself upright on the bench, with his hand cupped beneath his chin.

'I'm pretty sure he thinks there's a problem between you,' Ben says. 'He's mental.'

I shake my head. 'I've never seen him behave like this.' I fight back tears. 'You're very calm.'

'What? You'd rather I went round there and hit him back?'

'No.'

'Well then…'

I find a tissue in my pocket and hand it to him. 'We need to get you sorted.'

'It's not broken if that's what you're worried about. I've broken it before, I'd know.' He puts the tissue to his nose and winces. 'Hurts like hell, though.' Spots of blood have dripped on to the front of his top. 'I have no idea what I did for my twenty-ninth birthday, but you won't forget yours,' he says.

'What the bloody hell's going on?' It's Mum's voice this time. 'Alekos looked upset.' She stops in the pool of light in front of us. 'Fuck me. Did he do this?' She leans on her crutches and glances between us.

'Apparently talking is a crime,' Ben says.

'You should get that seen to,' she says.

'No.' He stands up. Blood has oozed through the tissue and between his fingers. 'I'm going inside.'

247

We don't say anything until he's closed the front door of *The Globe* behind him.

Mum turns to me. 'You want to tell me what happened?'

'Where's Alekos?'

'Out back.'

'I should talk to him.'

'You need to talk to someone.'

'That someone being you?'

She leans heavily on her crutches. 'Yes, if it helps. It's obvious what's going on. Marcy's been full of it: Sophie and Ben. If you're trying to give Alekos an excuse to leave you, it's working a treat.'

'I'm not doing anything. I have no master plan. I wish I did. I wish I could see where I'll be in six months' time.'

'And who you'll be with?' she asks. She shuffles over. 'Don't be like me, always running away from the good things in your life.'

'Maybe you should go and talk to Robert then.'

She frowns, and her eyes flicker away from mine.

'Alekos…' I say. 'He's so… I don't know.'

'Nice. Handsome. Thoughtful. Do you want me to go on?'

'Predictable.'

'Punching Ben was predictable?'

'No, and I'm almost glad he did it. At least he's showing some kind of emotion. Anger is better than apathy.'

'So, there's nothing between you and Ben?' she asks. 'Sophie, tell me there isn't.'

I shrug. 'I don't know. There's something appealing about him. His energy and impulsiveness for life is how I wish Alekos was.'

She hooks her arm in mine. 'Ben's in the wrong place emotionally to be getting involved with,' she says, brushing a loose hair out of my eyes. 'And by the looks of things you are too. Don't turn into me. It doesn't make for a contented life. Go and talk to Alekos.'

'You didn't think Alekos and I would last.'

'I've said a lot of stupid, selfish things. It doesn't mean I was right.'

'What do you think of Despina?'

'She's a character.'

Headlights dazzle us as a car comes round the corner, and beeps as it passes. Mum waves.

'Alekos didn't invite her,' I say. 'She insisted and he couldn't say no. Don't you think that's odd?'

'I wouldn't want to say no to her either.'

'But you know what I mean. He's thirty.'

'It's a different culture, Sophie.'

'I know but you haven't seen the way she puts him down and destroys his confidence. He used to sing, play the guitar and write music, now he just works for his mother with very little thanks.'

'Tell him how you feel.'

'I have done.'

'Tell him again.' She grips her crutches and still with my arm linked with hers we start walking.

I can't see Alekos in the garden. People are standing in groups talking or sitting at the picnic tables nursing bottles of beer and glasses of wine. Despina and Robert are toasting marshmallows over the hot barbeque coals. I walk with Mum across the grass.

'I was wondering where everyone had got to,' Robert says. He holds up a pink toasted marshmallow on a skewer and waves it in front of me. 'Do you want one?'

I shake my head.

'No Alekos?' Despina asks.

'No,' I reply, before leaning towards Mum. 'I'm going to find him.'

I avoid everyone as I head back across the grass to the patio doors. From outside the conservatory looks dark and empty, but as I get to the door I see flickering candlelight. Alekos is alone at a corner table. I close the door quietly behind me. He doesn't look up. His hands are clasped around a half-finished pint. I sit opposite him. The knuckles of his right hand are red. He takes a sip of his lager and places it carefully back on the table. It's difficult to tell in the candlelight if he's been crying, but the rims of his eyes look red.

'I'm glad you hit him,' I say.

He snorts and shakes his head.

'At last you're showing some kind of emotion.'

'That makes you happy?'

'It's a start,' I say, leaning forward in my chair. 'We were only talking.'

'I see what's going on. Don't tell me about falling in love with here. Don't make me look stupid.' Where his cream T-shirt meets his skin it emphasises his tan. His dark eyes fail to meet mine. 'It's obvious you're in love with him,' he says.

'Obvious? I don't like myself much at the moment, let alone have the capacity to love someone else. If you're looking for an explanation for why things aren't right between us, then you've got it all wrong. I'm not in love with him. I don't know how I feel about anything any longer.'

My words hang heavy in the empty room. I reach my hand across the table. He looks sharply at me when I touch his arm. I'm the reason for the downward curl of his lips, for his glistening eyes. I want to undo time. Erase the sadness and the not knowing. His hand is solid and warm beneath my palm and I don't want to let him go.

The patio door creaks open. 'There you are.'

'Mama, leave us alone.'

There's a pause. I don't look behind me. And then the door scrapes closed again.

'I wish we could go back and recapture what we had,' I say slowly. 'If only it was that simple.'

He pulls his arm from beneath my hand and stands up. 'Can I have the house keys?'

'Aleko, talk to me.'

'What do you expect me to say?' he shouts. 'Give me the keys.'

I reach into my back pocket and pull out the keys Robert gave me just a couple of weeks ago. Alekos snatches them from me before slamming out through the patio doors.

I blow the candle out. The view outside becomes clearer in the dark. Mum and Despina are both staring after Alekos. I turn my back on them and go into the main part of the pub. I close the conservatory door shut and lean against it. The room is dark but the bar is lit up. Ben is perched on the worktop at the back of the bar holding a whisky glass filled with a golden-coloured liquid in his hand. His nose has stopped bleeding but there are still spots of fresh blood on his top. He rattles the ice against the glass. 'At this precise moment, I couldn't give a fuck who caught me.'

'Did I say anything?'

He downs what's left and pours himself another from the bottle of Bells next to him.

'Do you want one?'

My hands automatically reach for my stomach.

'Is it his? The baby?' Ben asks.

'Of course.'

'I didn't know if there was anyone else.'

'No. No one else.'

He jumps down from the counter. 'You can't not let Alekos be a part of your baby's life. Take it from someone who knows what it's like.' Still clutching the glass, he picks up the whisky bottle. 'I'm calling it a night. I'm sorry you've had a crap birthday.'

I stand in the middle of the pub until I hear the bar door close behind him. I'm truly alone. I weave my way in the dark between the tables to the ladies and lock myself in one of the cubicles. I stay there crying until Mum finds me.

Alekos is asleep when I creep into the living room. His gentle snoring provides no comfort. The room is as dark as my mood. I can't sleep. To think I might never see *O Kipos* again. I'll miss it: the view from our window, the smell of the grapes in the evening, the endless sun in summer and snow in winter. Even the cooking, I'll miss that. I'll miss my spot by the fence and the idea of thinking I was doing something great with my life. Tonight is my beginning, even if it doesn't feel like it at the moment. I pull the sleeping bag tighter around me, up under my chin. I need to make a doctor's appointment. I hope Ben can keep a secret. I close my eyes but I'm thinking too much to sleep. I don't want morning to come.

I wake up late. It takes me a moment to first of all realise where I am, and then realise I'm alone. Daylight streams through the blinds, spilling dusty light across the room. I shift on to my elbows. Alekos' bed is empty, the bedcovers pulled back and his T-shirt and boxer shorts discarded on top. Voices filter in from the kitchen, their words obscured. My head feels heavy, as if I'd been drinking, and the nausea is back. I struggle out of the sleeping bag and creep barefoot into the hallway. The kitchen door is ajar and sunlight streams through the crack. I can smell coffee, and lemon and chicken on the grill. I run up the stairs and just make it to the bathroom in time.

The smells from the kitchen have subsided by the time I've showered and dressed. My hand hovers momentarily on the kitchen door before I push it open.

'*Kalimera*!' Despina's voice is too cheerful, even for her. Her lips are strained into a smile.

She doesn't hug or kiss me good morning. Alekos leans against the doorframe of the open back door, playing with his evil-eye beads, a nervous habit he gets from Takis.

'We're all going for a picnic,' Mum says firmly. Her eyes are wide as if daring me to refuse.

'A picnic?'

'Despina's been busy making salads and *souvlaki*...'

'I teach Leila Greek,' Despina says in English.

'Great.'

252

'Breakfast?' Mum hands me a plate with a croissant and a dollop of apricot jam on it.

'It is very beautiful day,' Despina says. She joins Alekos in the doorway and hooks her arm in his.

It is a beautiful day and I'm glad we're not all stuck in the house together. Mum gives me directions to Holkham before we leave the house and whispers in my ear, 'Let's make the best of this.' The coast road is clear and the scenery we pass makes up for the lack of conversation in the car. We drive through Morston and Stiffkey and pass the pub I got drunk in with Ben. I can feel my cheeks flush at the memory. And then I'm driving into virgin territory.

'Turn right here,' Mum suddenly says as we arrive at Holkham. I swing sharply into a tree-lined drive, straight as a Roman road, leading to a forest of pine trees at the end. We pull up on the grass verge alongside a camper van. It looks like a long walk to the beach and I think Mum's mad to have suggested it, as she hobbles away from the car on her crutches. The four of us walk down the dirt track in a row, still silent, our attention taken by the cows in the field on either side, the looming pine forest ahead and the birds flitting in-between. We have no choice but to pair off when we reach the wooden walkway leading through the forest. Alekos and Despina lead the way and Mum and I follow slowly behind. Sun filters through the thick branches and casts patchy light on to the sandy path. I'm struck by how quiet it is beneath the canopy of trees. There's no breeze to disturb. The thud of Mum's crutches on the wooden walkway is amplified. Alekos and Despina have gone on ahead. I glimpse them before they disappear between trees.

'How are you coping?' Mum asks. Her voice disturbs the peace. I preferred the silence.

'I've messed things up. Alekos won't speak to me.'

'Not with all of us together. No.'

'I'm kind of glad about that. I'm glad you're here.'

She squeezes my arm. 'I'm on your side, Sophie. I always

have been, even if it hasn't seemed that way. Take as long as you like to think things through.' She leans towards me and kisses me on the cheek. 'Come on,' she says, pointing to Alekos and Despina standing on top of a sand dune at the end of the path, 'we're nearly there.'

As the forest opens on to the sand dunes and beach, the sound of the wind and sea envelops us. Mum struggles up the path until we join Alekos and Despina. The beach stretches endlessly before us, the sand rippled and dotted with shallow pools of water and snaking streams reaching towards the smudge of blue-grey sea on the horizon. This is the wilderness I was after. It's not desolate; there are people about, but not within hearing distance, just sparse dots of colour over on the far sand dunes.

'You have beautiful country,' Despina says in English.

Mum nods. 'We certainly do.'

We find shelter from the wind in the curve of a sand dune, only a short walk away from the pine forest path. Tall grasses serve as a protective wall against our backs and the dry sand is warm to touch. Mum settles herself on a canvas put-up chair while I help Despina lay out our picnic on a rug. Alekos wanders off along the ridge of the sand dune but returns at the sound of Despina yelling, 'Food!'

Mum is happy to talk, which is good because no one else seems to be. Alekos' face is permanently creased in a frown. I catch Despina's nervous glances between us. Alekos has obviously not talked to her for once.

'I always wanted Sophie to grow up with surroundings like this,' Mum says, 'where she had beaches to play on and forests to explore, rather than a tiny back garden in the middle of a city.'

I translate for Despina while the potato salad is passed between the four of us.

'Alekos and his sister were always lucky,' Despina replies in Greek. 'Takis and I had to travel from job to job when they were young, but we were always working by the sea. We spent many years working in hotels and restaurants in Halkidiki. We worked briefly in Athens, so at least they got a taste of city life. Alekos hated it there. He was always drawn to the countryside or coast, the quieter life.' She looks at Mum. 'Like you here. I never imagined there were places like this in England. I think of London and rain and rude people.' She laughs. 'I was mistaken. The only regret I have is that, growing up, they never had a real home.'

'Home was wherever I felt happy, Mama,' Alekos says. It's a relief to hear him join the conversation. He reaches for a line of skewered chicken, squeezes fresh lemon over it and stares towards the sea as he eats it. I translate for Mum the gist of what Despina's just said.

This is the beach where the final scene in *Shakespeare in Love* was filmed. The last shot is of Gwyneth Paltrow leaving footprints in the sand as she walks away from the sea. To what? The unknown? What's next for me? Alekos is running sand through his fingers. He hasn't smiled all day. Mum is tired and we have a long walk back. We pack up the remains of our picnic and head towards the pine forest. Mum walks ahead with Despina. Their conversation is stilted, Despina speaking Pidgin English and Mum answering with nods and hand signals. I don't know what to say to Alekos and so I let the silence between us grow and become more awkward.

'We're flying home tomorrow,' Alekos says. He stops suddenly on the path and leans against the wooden railing. Mum and Despina continue walking.

'I know.' I join him, half-perching on the railing. If I reach my hand out I can touch him but I don't. 'There's something I need to tell you, Aleko.'

'Nothing you're going to say will make this situation any better.' He kicks sand between the wooden planks. He pushes away from the side and strikes up a fast pace along the path.

'Are you sure about that?'

He shrugs.

'I can't put up with things the way they are!' I shout after him.

'I might surprise you,' he says, waving a hand at me as he continues walking. He's going home. I have no idea where home is. Bristol didn't seem quite right: a familiar place yet so much had changed. I don't know if here feels more like home than Greece and *O Kipos*. Home should be where I'm happiest. Alekos' own words. I link my fingers across my stomach. Where we will be happiest.

Chapter Thirty

The sun is shining. I'm sitting outside on the wall that borders the lawn, with a cup of camomile tea. It's early. I left Alekos sleeping; Despina hasn't appeared yet and Mum is in her study catching up on emails. The butterflies have gone. Over the last few days I've seen the odd one or two doing a silent dance on their own. And then all of a sudden they've disappeared – off chasing sunshine.

I hear footsteps and a shadow falls across me. 'Morning,' Mum says. She sits next to me on the wall.

It's peaceful. I could stay out here for hours and watch the horses grazing in the field. My sketchbook and pencil are next to me on the wall, opened to a new page. I've made a start, sketched the fence and the gnarled trunk of a tree.

Mum picks it up. 'When it's finished, can I put it on my study wall?'

I nod. 'Of course.'

She flicks to the page before and my rough sketch of the salt marshes after the boat ride with Ben. She runs her fingers over the pencil marks.

'I spoke to Robert this morning,' she says.

'About Ben?'

She nods. 'He wouldn't have said anything, but the bruised nose and the stench of alcohol on his breath gave him away. Robert's furious.'

'With Alekos?'

'No. With Ben. I told him what happened. Ben shouldn't have put you in that kind of position.'

'It was as much my fault as his. I've done nothing to stop his advances,' I say. 'He didn't deserve being punched.'

'Maybe not. But he asks for trouble. Robert was really upset your birthday was ruined. I told him it could've been worse. It could've been your thirtieth.'

'Is that meant to cheer me up?'

'You used to be so positive.'

'I used to be a lot of things. Funny how life works out.'

'How have things worked out?'

'For the best,' I say.

Mum reaches down and plucks a blade of grass. Dew still coats everything. 'Despina's up,' she says. 'I heard her in the bathroom.' She rips the grass in half and flicks the pieces into the air. 'What time are you leaving?'

I glance at my watch. 'In about an hour.'

Despina turning up might have been the best thing to happen. She's given me closure. The butterflies have moved on and now it's my turn.

The tension in the car on the way to Heathrow is unbearable. The pressure to start a conversation builds as the journey continues, but the further we get the harder it is to think of something to say. So we remain silent, even Despina who's never lost for words. The morning remains sunny, but it's depressing leaving behind the countryside for service stations and the suburbs backing on to the motorway. I glance in my rear-view mirror. Despina has her eyes closed. I can't tell if she's really asleep or just pretending in the hope that Alekos and I start talking. We don't. Instead we listen to the radio. All the conversations I've had over the past couple of days keep playing over and over again in my head. Signs for Heathrow don't come soon enough.

Despina pushes a trolley with her suitcase on towards departures while Alekos strides ahead with his hands shoved in his pockets. A memory of him on Cephalonia walking along the harbour with his guitar slung across his bare chest flits into my head. I shrug it off. I'm letting him go. My thoughts are quickly swallowed by the noise from the amount of people in the departures building. I leave Despina and Alekos in the check-in queue and go upstairs to the café where, only three days ago, I waited for Alekos to arrive. It's hot and packed and I wait in the queue to get us drinks. It's interesting to see the mix of people gathered in a place like this and wonder who they are, what they do, where they're from and where they're going. My artwork always used to feature people. I'd study and draw faces. I've always liked photos featuring people however beautiful the location. I took countless photos of Alekos on Cephalonia, on the boat, the beach, in restaurants, in bed… I sketched him too – impressions of him playing volleyball or of his arm muscles clenched as he pulled on a rope aboard *Artemis*. If it's not too late by the time I get back I'll go to Salthouse and sit in the fish restaurant or on the pebble beach and sketch the people around me.

The girl behind the counter takes my order and hands me two lattes and a hot chocolate. At least three plane loads of people have poured through the arrivals gate while I've been queuing. Clutching three large drinks I make my way back down the stairs and hand the lattes to Despina and Alekos who are near the front of the check-in queue. Alekos doesn't look at me. There are a lot of other Greeks waiting in the queue. I catch snippets of conversations, in Greek and English as the queue shuffles forward. Greek is now so familiar. I force back tears as I think of the excitement I felt arriving in Thessaloniki just over four years ago and seeing Alekos.

After check-in I trail after them to the departures gate. I should have just dropped them off in the car park and said goodbye there. A sharp pain. My hands clutch my stomach. I gasp and then it's gone.

'Are you okay?' Alekos asks. He moves towards me.

I reassure him with a nod.

Despina has wandered off and is browsing through magazines in a shop. Dressed in jeans and a jumper, Alekos looks more comfortable than when he arrived wearing trousers and a shirt. I reach for his hand. 'Give me some time, Aleko.'

'Don't call me,' he says while rubbing his thumbs up and down mine. He leans towards me until his forehead is touching mine. 'Unless it's to say you're coming home.' I can smell his cologne, a rich spicy scent. He gently kisses my forehead before pulling away. 'There's nothing to keep me at *O Kipos* without you.'

I shake my head. 'I was what was keeping you there? All this time I've been talking about and begging you to move out and you didn't want to and now...' My words are a muddle. I want to shake him, kiss him, hug him, hurt him.

'I don't belong anywhere without you.'

Despina taps her way towards us in her heels. 'We can go through,' she says to Alekos, and points towards the departures gate. 'Get your ticket and passport ready.' She turns to me and says firmly. 'I hope we see you soon, Sophie.' She squeezes my shoulders and kisses me on both cheeks before walking away.

'Aleko,' I say, taking a step towards him.

'I know,' he says with a nod.

All I can do is watch them walk through the departures gate. Despina waves. Alekos doesn't. They disappear from sight.

'You're out of your mind,' Mum says. 'If you're not going back what the hell are you going to do?'

'I don't know.'

That's the truth. I don't know. Mum looks at me from the other side of the kitchen, where she's leaning against the worktop, her crutches propped up next to her. She shakes her head at me. 'This is all very sudden, isn't it?'

'Not really,' I say. 'I haven't been happy for a long time.'

'But you're engaged?'

'We were, yes.'

'And the other morning, in this kitchen, you both said you loved each other.'

'Maybe that's not enough.'

'You're throwing everything away.'

'No more than you did when you got pregnant with me.'

'That's totally different.'

'No it's not.'

'I had no choice. I couldn't have any kind of life in a place I wasn't wanted. I wanted to keep you. I didn't kiss goodbye to everything because I wasn't happy.'

'Don't trivialise my situation.'

'You can't always have everything you want. You have to compromise.'

'I'm aware of that,' I say. 'Alekos needs to compromise too and he's never been willing to do that.'

Mum tucks a loose hair behind her ear. She flicks the kettle switch on. Her face is drawn into a frown. She folds her arms across her stomach. 'From what I've seen, Alekos is one hell of a decent guy. I even approve of him punching Ben...'

'You have it in for Ben.'

'Maybe. But how can you walk away from Alekos?'

'You've broken up with plenty of decent men.'

She doesn't reply straight away. Her eyes search the floor. I sit down at the kitchen table.

'This isn't about me,' she says after a while. 'I've messed up every relationship I've ever been in and I've learnt to deal with that. I thought you were different, particularly when you met Alekos. I thought you were crazy leaving everything and running away to Greece but I understood you were in love. I'd have done the same for Elliot, dropped everything for him. But I had no choice. I couldn't be with him, even though I desperately wanted to.'

Mum turns her back on me and puts a teabag in the

teapot. Her shoulders are hunched.

'Did you get pregnant on purpose?' I ask.

She pauses. 'No. But I wasn't shocked. We weren't careful. At least I wasn't. I didn't care. I was in love.'

The sun's nearly disappeared behind the hill. It's dark in the kitchen, with only a dull pinkish glow seeping through the window. Mum pours boiling water into the teapot. Steam rises into the dusky kitchen.

'Do you regret not being with anyone?'

'I'm always with someone,' she says dryly.

'You know what I mean. What about Robert?'

Her shoulders tense. 'What about him?'

'You get on well.'

'Nothing's worth risking our friendship for.'

'But it might work.'

She snorts. 'I've never made a relationship work.'

'Maybe you hadn't met the right person before.'

She looks at me sharply. 'Your father was the right person.'

Suddenly she's on the verge of tears. The honesty of what she's just said hits me. Of course she's never been able to move on if she's still in love with Elliot. I scrape my chair back and move towards her. She doesn't flinch as I put my arms around her.

'I didn't mean to upset you. I wasn't thinking.'

Her shoulders and back are fragile beneath my hands. I feel her struggle to control a sob.

'You haven't upset me. I'm just being stupid.' She pulls away from me and plucks a tissue from the box on the worktop and wipes her eyes. 'It's pathetic. Thirty bloody years later and I'm still crying over him. And the truth of it is, I'd rather have had you, than be with him,' she says firmly. 'He wouldn't have been happy if he'd left his wife, I'd have felt guilty.' She looks at me. 'Guiltier. And I wouldn't have the life I have now.'

I nod, unconvinced.

'I was with a married man who happened to be my father's best friend, either way it would have been a mistake.' She turns to the teapot and pours us both a mug of strong tea.

She's subdued for what's left of the evening. I never make it to the beach because it gets dark. We both sit and watch television for an hour before going to bed. Our conversation must have played on her mind during the night because she's waiting for me at the bottom of the stairs in the morning, and the first thing she says to me is: 'Pack a bag. We're going to see Elliot.'

Chapter Thirty-One

A month after Mum first told me about Elliot, I went to see him. It had taken me less than twenty-four hours to decide that was what I wanted to do. I spent the next three or four weeks trying to find out where he lived. It was pointless asking Mum. Firstly we didn't talk much after that night. Secondly, I didn't want her to try and stop me.

When Mum was out doing a Body Shop party one night, I phoned Grandma. I hadn't seen her or Grandad since I was a child. For years Christmas and birthday cards with a token fiver tucked inside was the only contact I had with them.

'Sophie, is that you?' Grandma said quietly.

'Hi. Where does Elliot live?'

Silence. I heard the sigh of an armchair as she sat down. 'Is your mother there?'

'No. She's working.'

'Does she know you're ringing me?'

'No.'

'She told you?'

'Yes.'

She cleared her throat. 'She wasn't going to tell you.'

It was dark in the hallway except for the orange glow of the streetlight filtering through the stained-glass panels in the front door. My grip on the phone tightened. 'So you were happy to deceive me too.'

'My interest has always been to protect Elliot.'

'How touching. Where does he live?'

'Sophie, you best leave well alone,' she said and put the phone down.

I lied to Mum. I said I was going to Cornwall for a couple of days with Candy, when really we drove to Sheffield. Candy was livid with Mum and with my Grandma.

'You have a right to know,' she said every time I attempted to justify Mum's or Grandma's actions. And I agreed with her. The fact they believed I would go charging into Elliot's life and destroy his family disappointed me. That wasn't my intention.

'What are you going to do if you find him?' Candy asked. We had stopped in a lay-by on our way towards Buxton and were leaning against Candy's Fiat, eating prawn cocktail flavoured crisps. We were on the edge of the Peak District. Stoke-on-Trent and the M6 were behind us and we faced a rolling landscape of fields heading towards a craggy outcrop of rocks. At that moment, I didn't know what I wanted to do or say if I found him. I was just thankful Candy was with me otherwise I would probably have turned round and headed home. But together we kept going north to my grandparent's house in Sheffield. Grandma, whether she liked it or not, was going to tell me where I could find Elliot, Candy was sure of that.

As far as I knew, Mum had only one photo of her parents that she kept on her dressing table in her bedroom. I hadn't seen Grandma since I was very young and my memory of her was vague. The woman in front of me had short silvery grey hair and wore very little make-up, and there, the resemblance to a fifty-something grandmother stopped. She was dressed in a bright red and gold Indian style tunic, loose over wide-legged black trousers. Her feet were bare. I expected a conservative, uptight woman, not an older version of Mum. The colour drained from her face. I wondered if it was true that I looked a lot like Elliot. We stared at each other for a moment. Behind me, Candy squeezed my arm.

'We need to talk,' I said.

She nodded and stepped back to let us in. She ushered us into the living room.

There was an old photo of Mum and me on the mantelpiece amongst lots of photos of people I didn't know. The windows were open and a welcome breeze filtered through along with the rumble of a lawn mower. It was peaceful suburbia on a weekday afternoon in August.

Grandma came back into the room carrying a tray with a pot of tea, cups and a fruitcake on it. 'Do you remember this house?' she asked, putting the tray down on the coffee table. She settled herself in the armchair by the open window.

I shook my head. 'I didn't think Mum ever brought me here.'

'She did once.' She leant forward and poured us each a cup of tea. 'You were only five. We all sat out in the garden. You were fascinated by the snails and were filthy by the time we went to the pub for Sunday lunch.'

Candy fidgeted with her bracelet. Grandma handed her tea and a slice of cake, I think she was glad of having something else to focus on.

I took a bite of the rich and moist fruitcake. Now I knew where Mum's love of cooking came from. It was ridiculous to think how little I knew about my own family. The woman staring intently at me, fiddling with the crease of her tunic, my grandmother, was a stranger. The man I wanted her to help me find, my father, no more than a name. I took a deep breath. 'Why wouldn't you tell me where he lived?'

'Sophie,' she said with a sigh. 'We all made a promise – your mother included – that the situation would never be discussed again. Leila promised she'd never contact him. The best way to protect him was for you not to know.'

I looked at her in disbelief. 'Was that your idea?'

'To begin with. But Leila saw sense.'

'I bet she had no choice.'

Candy put her cup and saucer on the coffee table in front

of us and stood up.

'I'll leave you two alone.'

I waited until Candy had closed the door behind her. 'I can't forgive Mum for not telling me. But I'm beginning to understand why she's not close to you.'

Grandma shuffled in her chair. 'It was in everyone's best interest.'

'Except mine.'

'Elliot's wife is my best friend. Your grandfather and Elliot play golf together every week. We're godparents to their eldest daughter. Leila was reckless and thoughtless. We didn't kick her out when she was pregnant. She chose to go. We weren't involved in your upbringing or what she decided to tell you about your father. As for why she's chosen to tell you now, I have no idea…'

'He sent her a letter. Mum opened it on the night we were celebrating my degree results. She was drunk. It took her by surprise. You tell him stuff, don't you?'

'When he asks,' she said quietly.

'Because he knew I was graduating. And Mum certainly hadn't spoken to him. Seems to me she kept her promise and he was the one to interfere. So, I'm giving you the choice. You either give me his address now so I can meet him, no nasty surprises, or somehow I'll find it by myself, and believe me I'll have no qualms about causing trouble then. All I want to do is meet him. I want to know who he is. That's it.'

Grandma stood up and went out into the hall. My hands were sweating and my back ached where I'd been so tense. The lawnmower had stopped and all I could hear was the tick, tick, tick of the clock on the mantelpiece. She walked back in with a scrap of paper clutched in her hand and passed it to me.

His house was sandwiched between the wild openness of the Peak District and the urban sprawl of Stockport and Manchester. Candy and I sat in the car on the grass verge a little way from the house. It was an impressive stone house, very different from Mum's terrace or my grandparents' relatively modern semi-detached. Its backdrop was a valley of trees and the nearest neighbour an equally impressive house a hundred yards or so away. Grandma had told me that Elliot's wife would be home but I couldn't see anyone. Candy and I sat in comfortable silence, with the windows wound down, letting the breeze flow through. We were parked in the shadow of a tree and I felt camouflaged enough in case someone came out of the house. We waited for over an hour before a silver Mercedes drove past and pulled into the driveway. I shuffled upright in my seat and pulled my sunglasses on from where they were wedged in my hair. A man climbed out of the driver's side. He was tall, with reddish-brown hair and wore grey suit trousers, a pale shirt and loose tie. I knew he was in his early sixties but he looked younger. There was an undeniable familiarity about him. If I walked past him in the street, I might have turned, wondering where I'd seen him before. But it was the woman who got out of the car with him that struck me. She was too young to be his wife but a good ten years older than me. She reached into the car and lifted out a sleeping toddler. Her hair was the same reddish colour as mine, the shape of her face recognisable. We were too far away to see the colour of her eyes or the shape of her lips but she looked unmistakably like me.

Chapter Thirty-Two

Mum isn't joking about going to visit Elliot. Her bag is packed and by the front door before I've even finished breakfast and we're on the road not long after. There's a quiet determination about her. She's decisive and calm and I go along with her wishes despite feeling it could be a big mistake. When I needed a father I didn't have one and now... now I'm going to be a parent myself. What can he teach me? What it's like to miss growing up with two parents? I think of Alekos and swallow back tears.

I get déjà vu as we reach the Peak District National Park, even though it's Mum in the car beside me, humming along to the radio, instead of Candy. The sun is still shining as the landscape opens up and we leave behind any hint of urbanisation for fast roads winding over high hills and moorland.

'I came up here to see him after you told me about him,' I say when we turn on to the Buxton road towards Stockport. The road is familiar now: the last part of the route Candy and I took from Sheffield to Elliot's over eight years ago.

Mum looks at me. 'You've met him?'

I shake my head. 'I bottled it. He was playing happy families with his daughter and grandchild. I was with Candy. We turned around and went straight home.'

Mum reaches into her bag on her lap and pulls out her mobile. 'Not this time.'

'Who are you phoning?' I ask.

She raises her hand to shush me and dials a number. I hear it ring and someone answers.

'It's Leila,' Mum says. 'We're on our way to see Elliot. You might want to warn him. We'll wait outside his house. If he's home he needs to make his excuses and then drive somewhere where we can talk. Yes,' Mum says, glancing at me. 'Sophie's with me. Tell him he's got fifteen minutes before we get there.' She ends the call. 'I always wondered if you'd try and find him.' She pulls the mirror down and slicks berry-coloured lipstick across her lips.

'I wasn't exactly successful. I was mad with you and Grandma, with him and his bloody daughter and grandchild for being there and stopping me from speaking to him. But I'm glad we're doing this now. It's long overdue.'

We stop talking as I turn on to the long winding road that leads to Elliot's house. Mum switches the radio off. My fingers clench the steering wheel. A minute later and I pull up on the grass verge beneath the tree Candy and I parked under all those years before. I switch off the ignition and the engine stills. It's peaceful here with only the occasional car shooting past to disturb the chatter of birds.

'He's lived in this same house for thirty-five years,' Mum says absently. 'He never liked change.'

'He was taking a risk trusting you not to come knocking.'

'If I'd wanted to I'd have found him even if they'd moved.'

'How long should we leave it?' I ask, looking towards the closed front door.

'As long as it takes.'

There are two cars in the drive but no sign of anyone in the house. They could be outside. I imagine a huge back garden with breathtaking views. Mum is quiet next to me, her fingers drumming on her leg cast. I'm not even sure if I really want to turn an impression of my father into reality. The first time it had been anger that had driven me to see him, mixed with intrigue and a desire to meet my father. It was uncertainty and the feeling of being emotionally out of my depth that had driven me away. No, it was the fear of not being wanted that had scared me off. Candy didn't understand how I could leave without actually meeting him. What I don't understand is how he could have carried on with his life without wanting to meet me. He looked so happy and relaxed with his daughter and grandchild. He's been described as a family man. He doesn't know the meaning of the word.

Mum's hand suddenly grips mine. I look up as Elliot closes the front door behind him. He's alone. He looks along the road and his eyes rest on Mum. He falters, smiling briefly before glancing back to the house. I start the engine and he gets into a silver Mercedes and backs out of the drive and on to the road. He slows as he passes us. My father looks at me for the first time.

Chapter Thirty-Three

We follow him back towards the open roads of the Peak District. He's not hanging about and he keeps glancing in his rear-view mirror. I slide the gear stick into fifth. Mum's hands are interlinked on her lap and her knuckles tensed white.

'Have you any idea where we're going?' I ask.

Mum shrugs. 'Somewhere he won't be spotted with us I presume.'

The beauty of our surroundings is lost on me as I concentrate on following Elliot. I catch glimpses of moorland stretching to the horizon, patchworked by sun and shadows from the high white clouds. After fifteen minutes he indicates and pulls into a lay-by hidden from the road by trees. I pull up behind him and switch off the engine. No one moves. A secret rendezvous in the middle of nowhere feels shifty, like I'm doing a dirty deal rather than meeting my father for the first time.

'Help me get out,' Mum says.

I open my door and the wind nearly knocks me off my feet. Elliot's not getting out because he's on his mobile. I wonder if he's making excuses to his wife. I pull the crutches off the back seat and help Mum out of the car and on to her feet.

'Bloody uncivilised,' she says. The wind loosens strands of hair from her ponytail. The colour in her cheeks has returned after her stay in hospital and her smooth and flawless skin defies her age.

A car door slams. I turn and Elliot's walking towards us. His hands are shoved in his jeans pocket and a dark grey jumper keeps out the wind. It looks as if his wife buys his clothes from M&S. He sees Mum's crutches and falters. 'What happened?'

'I was in an accident.'

'Anna never said.'

'I never told her.'

I'm sidelined. His attention is solely focused on her. I'm the stranger; I'm the reason they didn't remain together. I'm the result of an illicit love affair. His eyes are green – I was right about that. I must remind Mum of him every day because it's blatant that I'm his daughter. We have the same shaped faces, the same red hair, his is thinning on top and flecked with grey but it's identical in colour. Up close he's tall and despite now being in his late sixties, he has an athletic build.

'I'm Sophie.'

He looks at me. I'm not sure what I expected this moment to feel like. His handshake is warm and firm yet we keep the distance of strangers.

'Well,' Mum says. 'This is about as comfortable as I imagined it would be.'

Elliot looks between us both. 'I'm sorry. You took me by surprise, Leila. It's a shock seeing you... both.' He looks back at me. 'I've wanted to meet you since you were born.'

Mum's not buying it. Her cheeks flush red and I can sense her anger building.

'I've only known about you for eight years,' I say. 'I came up here when I was twenty-one, determined to meet you.'

'I know. Anna told me. I had no idea. She couldn't understand why you came all that way to meet me and then didn't.'

'You were with your family and I felt like a trespasser or a stalker or both.'

'Are you mad we came?' Mum asks him.

He shakes his head. 'God, no. I'd given up hope that you'd ever reply to my letters. I never expected you to come and visit.'

'Visit?' Mum laughs. 'That sounds like we were invited, and welcome.'

'You are,' he says quietly.

'Oh right, that's why we're standing out in the cold, miles from anywhere or anyone. You're ashamed. You were ashamed even when we were together. And you're sure as hell ashamed that Sophie looks like your daughter. That's why you can't let your family meet us. Because they'd know.'

I wish I didn't have to witness this. Mum has a history with him. I don't. He can barely look at Mum let alone me.

'So why did you come, then?' he asks.

'To tell you I don't ever want you contacting me again. No letters, no phone calls. My mother should never have given you my new address, but she'll seemingly do anything for you. I've stayed out of your life like you and my bloody family asked; I lied to Sophie for years about you because I thought that was the right thing to do. I was wrong. It's up to you and Sophie what happens to your relationship but you leave me out of it. We haven't been together or had anything to do with each other for nearly thirty years and that's the way it's going to stay.'

She struggles back to the car and leaves me standing alone with Elliot. He suddenly looks older, particularly now the earlier smile has been wiped from his face.

'For being pissed at you for thirty years, I think she controlled herself quite well.'

'Let's take a walk.'

We don't go far. Moorland stretches away from the lay-by, the grasses and plants buffeted by the wind. We walk far enough to put physical distance between the cars and us but we're still close enough for Mum to see us.

'This isn't how I imagined I'd meet you,' he says.

'You've had twenty-nine years. Surely there's been enough time for you to find the opportunity for us to meet?'

'It was too complicated.'

'You mean too risky.'

'Leila brought you to your grandparents once. You were five. I was desperate to meet you but Anna didn't think it was a good idea. My wife and our children would have come too. Anna stopped us from coming because it would have been obvious that you were my daughter.'

'I still am,' I say.

He shoves his hands back in his jeans pockets and stares out at the wild expanse of moorland in front of us.

'I've messed up,' he says after a while. 'I shouldn't have had an affair with Leila. She may have been the one to make advances but I didn't stop her. She's a beautiful, incredible woman and I was greedy. I love my wife very much, we have three children together and I didn't make a mistake in sticking by them. I'm only sorry that you had to grow up without a family.'

My fists clench. 'I did grow up with a family. Mum is my family. It certainly wasn't a conventional childhood but I wouldn't change it. Not for you anyway.'

He can't even look me straight in the face. 'I'd have had regrets whatever my decision was.'

'I would never choose to give up my child, however hard the situation might be.' I hadn't intended to come all this way just to argue with him but I can't help myself. I thought on meeting him I would recognise myself in him, understand what Mum saw in him or at least be comforted by his reasons for not being a part of my life.

'I had three other children to think about.' His voice rises, empty words carried by the wind.

'It must have been hard for you, lying to your family all these years.'

'I'm protecting them.'

'You're protecting yourself.'

He turns to me and raises his hands in mock helplessness. 'Fine. Think what you want. I've tried many times over the years to contact Leila. I sent her letters addressed to you but I know you never received them. I wanted to know how you were, what you were doing.'

'My grandmother could have told you that.'

'Leila barely tells Anna anything.'

'I don't blame her,' I say. 'What gets me is the fact you told Mum to never contact you again and you're the one sending letters and interfering with her life years later.'

He becomes very quiet and his eyes shift away from me and back to the view. 'I still love her. I always have done.'

'You need to stay out of her life. For her sake. You made that decision twenty-nine years ago, now honour it.'

This is my father. The man I've wanted to meet since Mum inadvertently told me about him that night in Hazel Road. I've wanted to know who he is for eight years but I realise I know enough. How can I ever be a part of his life when he's ashamed of me? I'm his dirty secret. His wife can't ever know about me, which means his children, my half-brother and half-sisters won't ever know either. I don't want to be a part of those lies.

'I was always sorry that Leila felt she had to move when she was pregnant with you,' he says. He's calmer now, trying to draw me back into a conversation rather than an argument. 'She was a true northern girl and I never thought she'd cope moving to a strange city with a baby.'

'She coped just fine.'

'I always thought she'd come back up North.'

'There's nothing for her up here.'

He points to the landscape in front of us. 'There's this.'

'She's got a version of this where she lives now. And the sea. It's one of the most beautiful places I've been to.'

'Better than Greece?'

I look at him sharply. 'You do know stuff.'

'I know your name, I know your date of birth, I know you

276

did a degree in Illustration and got a First and I know you moved to Greece to be with your boyfriend. That's all I know about you, what Leila's written in occasional Christmas cards to Anna.'

'That's more than I know about you.'

'We can change that.'

'How? How can we possibly put things right? Are you going to introduce me to your children? Or will it just be a case of us meeting somewhere neutral where there's no chance of anyone catching us. Because I don't want to be a part of your and my bloody grandparents' lies.' I start to walk back towards the car.

'Sophie, please.'

I falter and turn back to him. 'The person who really is the victim in all of this is Mum. She's put her life on hold for you; she's never been able to move on. And I thought it was her fault. I've treated her like shit and she hasn't deserved it. She took the blame just for protecting you and we've spent the last eight years barely talking to each other. Wasted bloody time.'

'So that's it.'

'You've got your family and I've got mine.' I walk towards the car and don't dare to look back. I'm shivering or shaking, I can't tell which. It feels like the longest walk of my life. I battle with the car door in the wind and shut it with a bang. Mum's eyes are puffy and red. She's got her elbow resting on the ledge of the door and her hand against her cheek. Elliot's still standing outside being pummelled by the wind. He walks slowly back to his car and glances at us before getting in. He doesn't drive off straight away and I begin to think he's not going to. Mum tenses. But his hesitation is momentary and with a quick look over his shoulder he pulls out from where he's parked and drives towards the main road. We watch him until his taillights disappear behind trees. I don't know whether to cry or breathe a sigh of relief.

'How did you leave it?' she asks.

'I left it. He gave me a load of bullshit about family. He's not family. I don't even consider Grandma and Grandad to be family – when do I ever see or speak to them? Calling them my grandparents doesn't mean anything. Takis and Despina, now they treat me as part of the family...' It's my turn to go quiet.

'He didn't live up to your expectations then?' Mum says.

'I don't know what my expectations were,' I say. 'But no, he's not the man I imagined to be my father for twenty-one years. And even seeing him with his family, after you told me the truth, I at least hoped we could have some kind of relationship. I was wrong. All I saw was a man scared of his wife finding out about a twenty-nine-year-old love child and an affair he wishes he was able to continue. I have no respect for him.'

'I'm sorry.' She wipes a tear from the corner of her eye.

'Don't be.' I say. 'This is closure for both of us.'

Once we've put enough distance between Elliot and us, we stop off at a pub on the Sheffield side of the Peak District. It's a pub Mum remembers going to on Sunday afternoons when she was a child. It's an old country inn, set in a secluded garden that backs on to a wood. We find a free table next to a window so we can look out on the garden. I get Mum settled and order two pints of lemonade at the bar.

'I'm starving,' Mum says when I rejoin her. We've had nothing since breakfast and we've clocked up a lot of miles and time since then. She flicks through the menu. 'Do you know, I've never wanted to leave anywhere and go home as badly as I did today? I feel so stupid for getting upset over him after all this time. He's not the man I remember.'

'Or who I imagined.'

'I'm so glad you came over from Greece.' She looks back at the menu. 'I think I'm going to have sausage and mash. What about you?'

'I might need to stay with you a bit longer.'

'You can stay for as long as you want. The steak pie

sounds good too.'

'I should have told you this as soon as I found out… but things were different then.' I wait until Mum looks up from the menu. 'I'm pregnant.'

She stares at me, showing no emotion for a moment until her face relaxes into a smile. She leans towards me and takes my hands in hers. 'I don't know what to say. Congratulations.' She pulls away and looks hard at me. 'Are you happy about this?'

'I wasn't to begin with but I am now.'

'How long have you known?'

'Just over a week.'

'Alekos kept it quiet.'

'He doesn't know.'

She leans back against the high-backed bench. 'Bloody hell, we're a right pair.'

'You must have been so scared being pregnant and on your own.'

'Is that what you're worried about?'

'Maybe. I don't know.' I look through the choice of main dishes.

'With me everything clicked into place one day. It was after you were born. I was renting a tatty flat, didn't have much money but had got to know a few people and didn't feel so much of a loner any longer. I suddenly felt happy. For some reason I knew I'd done the right thing.'

'Even though you weren't able to let Elliot go?'

She shrugs. 'You'll figure out what you want in good time. Now let's order and talk after.'

Chapter Thirty-Four

I haven't spoken to Alekos since he went back to Greece eight weeks ago. Despina's phoned a couple of times to organise shipping my belongings back, and when I've asked after Alekos she's curtly replied, 'He's away.' She doesn't elaborate and I don't question her further. It hasn't felt as long as two months. My time's been continually filled helping Mum with her business and organising the food for winter weddings – a bittersweet experience. Robert has me cooking at *The Globe* two nights a week. And my bump's beginning to show. Mum wasn't best pleased when she found out Robert knew before her that I was pregnant. I failed to mention that I'd told Ben too.

The biggest change besides my bump is seeing the tail end of summer merge into autumn and now, before I've even got used to darker evenings, we've been plunged into winter. The crunch of fallen leaves underfoot has turned into frosted ground. Icy pools have formed in the dips in the lane and they make a satisfying crack when I step on them. Frosted breath greets me when I go outside in the morning and the air is clear and cold and the wind stings my ears. There's been no snow but on very cold mornings the garden, fields and trees have been dusted with frost.

It's the third week in November and Mum's already dug out the Christmas decorations from the attic. We've reverted back to my childhood with both of us getting ridiculously excited about buying a Christmas tree – which is now in the window of the living room and permanently twinkles with silver lights. Christmas Day is planned. Mum's invited Robert over for Christmas dinner in the evening once he closes *The Globe* and he's staying with us for Boxing Day too.

'It'll be a proper family Christmas,' Mum keeps saying.

Robert, family and Christmas says more than just friendship to me but I'll wait and pass judgement on that at the time. Ben will be playing happy families too with Fraser and Bella in London for a few hours on Christmas Day.

I'm now fourteen weeks pregnant. Twenty-six weeks from now I'll have a son or daughter. My life is suddenly scarily meaningful, even more so because I'm sitting in the waiting room at Norwich hospital waiting for my first ultrasound. Mum's next to me, flicking through an old *Hello* magazine. She no longer needs the crutches and her bruises have disappeared. Even the scar on her arm has faded from an angry red to a healthy pink.

'I guess I'm old enough to be a grandma,' Mum says with a sigh. She's looking at a page of barely twenty-something models in bikinis and sarongs.

'Forty-eight is the perfect age to have a grandchild.'

'You think?'

'Some women your age have toddlers. At least you're young enough to enjoy having a kid around.'

She frowns, unconvinced.

'And you can hand them back to me when you've had enough.'

'I like that idea.' She closes the magazine and puts it on the empty chair next to her. 'I hate being in this place.'

'Well I appreciate it.'

There are pictures of pregnant women all over the waiting room walls – details of NHS help lines and clinics, and posters about giving up smoking. The woman opposite us is so pregnant she needed help from her husband just to sit down. Being here isn't helping to calm my nerves about what the next five months will bring. Whenever I think about the baby, I automatically think about Alekos not knowing. I've got company in Mum, but not a man with me like the majority of women in this room have. I keep waking in the night in cold sweats worrying about having not told Alekos and then worrying more about how and when I'm going to break the news to him. Mum's suggestion was to wait until the first trimester had passed and then tell him – it wouldn't be too late that way, he'd understand. That time has been and gone. I get guilt trips about this unborn child not knowing their father. I think about how proud Alekos would be all the time.

'Sophie Keech?'

I turn to Mum. 'Come in with me.'

We follow the nurse into a large, bright room and she motions me towards a bed while she sets up the ultrasound machine.

'Is it your first?' she asks as I lie down and prop my head upright on a pillow.

I nod.

'And my first grandchild,' Mum says.

'Nervous?' the nurse asks.

'Who? Me or Mum?'

She laughs. 'Sophie, I want you to roll your top up and then lie back and relax.'

I wriggle my jumper up over my stomach and leave it crumpled beneath my bra line. Mum's standing next to the bed and from this angle I'm face to face with the green and red butterfly embroidered on her black A-line skirt. It looks like it's smiling and when I glance up Mum's echoing that smile.

The gel the nurse spreads on my bump is cold. She turns the monitor towards me so I can see the screen. She smoothes the scanner up and down my stomach. Bu boom, bu boom, bu boom. My breath stills at the sound. I stare at the image on the monitor and it takes a moment for my eyes to adjust and register the arms and legs of a tiny baby floating in the grainy triangular image. I don't know who starts to cry first, me or Mum.

'Pass me my mobile,' I say. 'I need to talk to Alekos.'

Chapter Thirty-Five

Thea is asleep in my arms. Only her pink chubby face is visible through her Babygro. We're cruising at altitude somewhere over France. Trying not to wake her, I carefully shuffle closer to the window and rest my head against the cool glass. Below, through the glare of the sun and the occasional white cloud, a jagged mountain range stretches to the horizon.

'They'll be on their way round with food and drink soon,' Mum says.

'I thought you hated plane food?'

'I do. But it's always interesting to see just how bad it is.' She leans towards me and strokes Thea's soft cheek. 'She's better behaved than you ever were.'

She's an angel. I know I'm biased. But looking at her now with her eyes closed, blowing bubbles from her rosebud lips, I can't help but want to kiss and cuddle her and show her off to everyone on the plane. I don't though. More than anything I want her to stay asleep until we land.

It's been a huge undertaking shipping my few belongings from England ahead of us and then planning a trip that includes a coach ride, a three-and-a-half-hour flight followed by an hour's drive when we land. All of this with a six-week-old to think about.

'Thank you for coming,' I say.

'Are you kidding?' Mum says. 'I get to spend two weeks with Thea on a beach while you and Alekos bust a gut. I still

284

think you're mad taking on all this.'

'I'd say exactly the same thing to a pregnant nineteen-year-old going it alone in a strange city.'

'You got me there.'

'And it turned out all right for you, didn't it.'

She looks between Thea and me. 'More than all right.'

I hold Thea close and lean down and kiss her smooth cheek. What I thought would be the hardest conversation of my life ended up being the easiest. After weeks of keeping my pregnancy secret from Alekos my decision to speak to him was effortless. I knew it was the right one as soon as he answered his mobile.

'Sophie.' There was openness to his voice, not the bitterness I expected or felt sure I deserved.

'I'm so sorry, Aleko. I've been thoughtless. I've had so much to deal with and I've reacted in such a selfish way. I'm going to come home. I want us to be together. Nothing else matters.'

There was a pause and I thought I'd blown it. He didn't want me to come back. I couldn't blame him. My silence over the past three months must have been killing him. Mum looked at me intently; she reached towards me and clasped my hand and mouthed 'what's he saying'. I shook my head at her.

'I've got something to tell you,' he finally said.

'It's okay, Aleko, I've left it far too late to be changing my mind, I understand if...'

'Sophie,' he said with a hint of laughter in his voice. 'I've bought us a home.'

It was my turn to go silent.

'On Cephalonia. It needs a lot doing to it. It used to be a taverna and we can easily turn it into one again. I didn't want us to live in an apartment in Thessaloniki or a house across the road from O Kipos. I want to be by the sea again. When you said about being happy like we first were, I knew we had to come back here.'

Tears streamed down my face. I squeezed Mum's hand

and said to Alekos, 'I've got something to tell you too.'

Thea's still asleep when we land with a gentle bump. We left a fresh day behind at Heathrow, the sky smudged with high white clouds. I peer through the window and can see only blue sky beyond the tarmac. I'm impatient to get off the plane and out into the day, to start a new life where everything began five years ago. Mum takes her time getting up from her seat, waiting until the crush in the gangway has dispersed before allowing me out with Thea. The summer heat is welcome as we walk down the steps from the plane and are ushered towards arrivals. Thea wakes with my movement and the slight breeze wrapping around us. She gurgles and I feel a small patch dampen on my shoulder. There's a crowd around the luggage belt but no sign of any suitcases. I glance towards the arrivals doors.

'Go, go,' Mum says. 'I'll wait for our luggage. Go find him.'

I kiss Mum on the cheek, hoist Thea higher on to my shoulder and walk towards the arrivals gate. Thea is about to meet her father for the first time. Delays with connecting the water and electricity at the taverna kept Alekos in Cephalonia. Thea's blown kisses down the phone to him and he's seen the hundreds of photos Mum and I have taken of her, but this is something else. It's the longest walk of my life. I'm introducing my daughter to her father. I'm crying before I even walk through the gate. And then I see him. Alekos. Exactly as I remember him.

Thank You To...

Thank you Mum and Dad for your unwavering support and to my husband Nik for always believing in me. Thanks to Judith van Dijkhuizen, Tamsin Reeves, Paul Dale and Andy Warburton for your invaluable advice during those many lunches in Bath spent workshopping our novels. Thanks also to novelists Lucy English and Tricia Wastvedt for reading and commenting on those very first drafts of *The Butterfly Storm*.

My proof reader, Kate Haigh, was a joy to work with and her attention to detail helped me put the finishing touches to the book. The wonderful Jessica Bell revamped the original ebook cover and designed the paperback and I couldn't be happier with the finished result.

Lastly, thank you for taking the time to read *The Butterfly Storm*. If you enjoyed this book, please join my mailing list to be the first to find out about my future book releases. To sign up simply go to www.kate-frost.co.uk, click on 'Fiction Newsletter' and enter your email address. Subscribers not only receive a freebie on sign up, but occasional news about new books and special offers.

If you liked *The Butterfly Storm* please consider leaving a review on Amazon and/or Goodreads, or recommending it to friends. It will be much appreciated! Reader reviews are essential for authors to gain visibility and entice new readers.

You can find out more about me and my writing at www.kate-frost.co.uk, or follow me on Twitter @Kactus77, or on Facebook at www.facebook.com/katefrostauthor.

Printed in Great Britain
by Amazon